State of Fear

State of Fear

MARY NAPIER

HUTCHINSON
London Melbourne Sydney Auckland Johannesburg

01084168

Hutchinson & Co. (Publishers) Ltd

An imprint of the Hutchinson Publishing Group

17–21 Conway Street, London W1P 6JD

Hutchinson Group (Australia) Pty Ltd
30–32 Cremorne Street, Richmond South, Victoria 3121
PO Box 151, Broadway, New South Wales 2007

Hutchinson Group (NZ) Ltd
32–34 View Road, PO Box 40–086, Glenfield, Auckland 10

Hutchinson Group (SA) Pty Ltd
PO Box 337, Bergvlei 2012, South Africa

First published 1984
© Mary Napier 1984

Phototypeset by Wyvern Typesetting Ltd, Bristol

Printed in Great Britain by The Anchor Press Ltd
and bound by Wm Brendon & Son Ltd,
both of Tiptree, Essex

British Library Cataloguing in Publication Data
Napier, Mary
State of Fear
I. Title
823'.914[F]   PR6073.R54
ISBN 0 09 155450 0

18414345

FS
5/6t

1

Two days after my mother's funeral, I packed two suitcases and left home.

I stood a moment in the oak-panelled hallway, which smelled of late roses and polish, more than half-tempted not to tell anyone I was going. I wanted simply to walk away from everything I'd known in the twenty-seven years of my life, and leave only a letter to keep everyone quiet. I couldn't do it though; I felt no remorse at all for going, but didn't want the last action of my old life to be one of cowardice. The sitting-room door was open so I left my cases in the hall and went in to find my father there; he had his feet up and was reading the newspaper as usual, firelight flickering on panelling. In the valleys of Northumberland it is often cold in September and fires are welcome for nine months of the year.

'Goodbye,' I said. 'I'm away now.'

I thought my voice sounded odd, but father didn't notice anything unusual. 'Don't be late back. Your Aunt May is in to tea.' He went on reading the paper.

I took a deep breath. 'I won't be back. I'm away from here for good.'

'Don't be silly, girl,' he said irritably, reading still.

There didn't seem anything else to say. I had felt defiant and excited after having planned for years exactly how today

5

would be; now only an unexpected sadness remained.

My father caught up with me as I walked down the path. 'Where do you think you're going with suitcases, then?'

I didn't stop until I'd clicked the gate shut between us. 'I don't know. It'll be a while before I come back to Northumberland, though.' It would have sounded more dramatic to say I was never coming back, but I knew that some time in my life I would have to see the valleys and wilderness hills of the North Tyne again.

He grabbed at the gate. 'Don't talk nonsense. You can't leave here. Why . . . how would I manage if you did?'

I smiled, enjoyment born again. 'After thirty years of marriage you'll be discovering where your own kitchen is. Turn left by the stair and left again at the end of the passage.'

I'd seen how Mary Tyler watched him with those slanting eyes of hers at my mother's funeral; he wouldn't need to cook his own meals for long.

'Don't give me that, girl!' One of the many things which infuriated me about my father was his habit of calling me girl, as if I were one of a lurcher litter, instead of Faith Milburn, his only daughter. 'After all these years, you've got a nerve, haven't you? And how, may I ask, do you expect to live when you're away from here? Go on the streets, when you've no more than this week's housekeeping money in your pocket? There's many tramping the cities for work these days, you know.'

'The housekeeping money is in its place on the kitchen mantel,' I answered coldly, and I looked away at long grass rippling on the hills, at trees on the skyline bent by the wind and the valley unravelling beside the young Tyne river brawling over its rocks. Very little here showed the passage of the centuries, nor was there any sound except the wind. No sound, except our quarrelling voices; I expect men quarrelled from the very first day they came to the valley.

My life was woven into this place; I ached to go, and yet now my time had come at last, I could hardly bear to leave. Of course I felt regret, whatever I'd pretended to myself while I was packing. Not so much regret over leaving, but because I must sometimes have shown resentment at being tied down for so long when that was no one's fault. I wanted so much to be free, yet on the day of my freedom it was this bitter sadness which took me by the throat. I had loved my mother, and remembered now the times when my impatience had lain like scum over our affection. But earth on a coffin means you can't go back, only learn a little more about yourself.

'Goodbye, Father,' I said gently. I no longer wanted to walk away from him unreconciled, so leaned across the gate to kiss his cheek.

He drew back, annoyed. 'You can't sweeten me that way, my girl.'

I laughed, and went, hearing laughter hollow in my head. My father was still shouting as Willy Charlton drove up to give me the lift he'd promised into Newcastle, playing a tune on his horn and grinning.

He also drove like the devil, and I can't remember opening my eyes all the way from Blackwater Ford to Blaydon, which was probably as well, because when I did the streets of Newcastle were ahead and the valley only a memory.

Sadness vanished at once. I'd done it; I'd left, and the world lay ahead. An hour later I was sitting in a train, racing south through country which looked oddly tame when the only landscape I knew was the Border hills, and while I sat there I thought what an absurd melodrama I had made of something most people did as a matter of course long before they reached my age. But the truth is, to me it remained dramatic, extraordinary, splendid. Here was motion at last after all of my life in one place, and the roar of motion all around me. Once I remember laughing aloud, excitement like metal in my throat. The wheels echoed that I was away, away, away; from this moment, and whether I liked it or not, each day would be different from the one before.

I had never been farther than Newcastle in my life and although my parents allowed me to do a course at the polytechnic there, even then I'd had to race home every evening to cook dinner and help my mother into bed. She had a serious fall a few years after I was born and broke her back; the doctors said there was no reason why she should not have made a fuller recovery than she did, but she suffered a lot of pain and lost heart after a while. So I took my degree, but she became a complete invalid soon after, and I was forced to stay all the time at home. Of course I didn't just stay there, helping her. Everyone in the valley knew I was there, so I became a kind of odd-job person for them all. I drove tractors and combines when the regular drivers were sick, joined search parties for walkers lost on the fells, sat up shivering the night through with a shotgun on my knees when a fox kept raiding old Mrs Mackenzie's hens. 'Don't worry yourself, Faith Milburn's free,' they said, 'she'll come if ye're fashed.' And mostly, I did. It irritated me sometimes, but at least I learned a lot and wasn't sheltered by my confinement in one place. Also, I never had time to sit around feeling sorry for myself. I was used to accepting challenges; even during our childhood my brothers had never made allowances for girls: if I wanted to tag along with them, then I had to do what they were doing. I missed them very much when they left home, but I also enjoyed the times late at night when I wrote or read alone; I'd become very tired of just being sporting, helpful Faith Milburn by then.

I knew I had to get away, or rot; I also realized that I couldn't go anywhere so long as my mother lived. She wanted to die in her own house and we couldn't afford a nurse. I understood that, I would have felt the same myself, so it was a question of planning; because when eventually I was able to leave, I intended to go a long way. Working as someone else's secretary in London wasn't my idea of breaking away at all.

I decided I would need at least two thousand pounds, but since I couldn't leave the house long enough to earn more than pocket money, I sat down to write short stories for the sillier women's magazines. The standard plot didn't take much analysing, and on coloured cards I wrote out as many ways for true love to come to disaster as I could think of. Characters went on another colour, and happy endings on a third. Then I shuffled them and picked out half a dozen at random, no cheating allowed; whatever order I drew them out, that was the way I had to write the story. It was a challenge of another kind, and one whose absurdity I enjoyed.

Ambition had been born during those quiet evenings, too. The desire one day to write something I believed to be worthwhile, to shape words and imagination into something more than either, to know in myself that what I wrote was good.

But first I needed to know and touch and feel; to understand more than just the one place where I was born and rid myself of lonely claustrophobia.

Now, four years later, I had still written only marketable stereotypes, but the meagre two thousand pounds was safely banked. I also had an address in my purse which might well open up my breakaway to the sun. Because it was the sun I wanted, a wider world, and some of the reality I had read about so avidly, and which I believed was what my writing lacked.

I looked out of the train window, but flat fields were still reeling past; no sign of London yet.

The city stretched out towards me as it began to get dark. An ocean of buildings and clogged streets, lights coming on and lives snatching past before the train spewed me into a booming station full of scurrying people. I kept looking around for someone I knew; I had never been anywhere before where I couldn't expect to recognize friends, and it was a shock to discover the coldness of true anonymity.

I stayed the night in a hotel I'd picked out of a guide two years before, when I was considering this part of my journey. Whenever the monotony of sickroom routine and solitary household chores made me particularly desperate, I had thought through some specific problem to do with my eventual escape, which usually made me feel better. It took me a long time to sleep that night, though, partly because it was London outside the window instead of the Tyne valley, and partly because of Willy Charlton, who wanted to marry me.

9

I didn't want to marry him; fast cars and a great many acres are all very well, but not enough when that's about all there is that interests a man. I liked Willy sometimes but reckoned I came after the land and, if I was lucky and it was a good day, before the cars. Every girl from Hexham to Otterburn would have given her socks for Willy, which made me pretty unpopular when I could have had him, and refused. I suppose I'm an incurable romantic, and years of scribbling those saccharine stories hadn't helped to make me any harder-headed. I'd have been a fool if I hadn't realized that men liked my brown-gold hair, hazel eyes and fair skin, but I thought such looks conventional myself. I suppose being conventional was my trouble. Deep down, I believed in all the conventional things: that great writing comes from having scraped the world for emotion, and love is a glory waiting for those who search it out, never the inertia of marrying the boy next door.

But that night, I could not help thinking of Willy. He was good-looking and had not been as angry as I expected when I refused to sleep with him. Instead, he had asked me to marry him, which finally settled any doubts I might have had, because my first thought was how to refuse without hurting him too much. His offer was a compliment I treasured though, because everyone knew the Milburns didn't have much money. My father inherited Blackwater Farm but sold the land years ago, keeping only the house, because he practised as a solicitor in Hexham. He went on practising as a solicitor in exactly the same way for years, and consequently most of the business went elsewhere. We lived very frugally, and I don't suppose Willy's parents were at all pleased when they heard he was becoming serious over Faith Milburn. There isn't a farmer born who hasn't his eye on a marriage for his son that will bring in more land. If I'd asked his people, probably they would have subscribed to my fare to London. I slept on that happier thought and woke full of anticipation.

Prodam's offices in Fitzroy Square were unexpectedly impressive, when I had thought that a relief agency wouldn't waste much money on rent. Once I was inside though, it was exactly as I'd imagined it, and I was passed from one willing but amateurish hand to another. I had collected money for the British Programme for Development and Relief in Latin America, Prodam for short, and recognized a long time ago the part it might play in my plans, but even at four hundred miles' distance, I had not been bowled over by their staffwork. At closer sight it was even less inspiring, as I watched a great many people running around the Fitzroy Square office clutching papers and apparently speaking a foreign language to each other.

'Who would have thought that Uscaf would turn over Gutaid into Unifac?' said one earnest lady to another.

'Good gracious, Unifac isn't even into prod yet,' was the baffling reply.

Later I was to discover that aid agencies function exclusively on acronymic jargon, but at the time I began to wonder whether I had something missing between my ears and my brain. After a while someone brought round a tray of saucers, each filled with stuff like wallpaper paste which we were told to sample.

'It's a new variety of maize,' explained a girl who had her baby in a pen beside her. 'If it's edible you can grow it a thousand feet higher than maize has ever been grown before.' She plastered several different blobs on her child's arm: it sucked for a moment and then began to howl. I didn't blame it one bit.

'A thousand feet higher?' an elderly lady said doubtfully. 'Well . . .'

'It's good,' said the mother, popping a sweet into her child's open mouth. 'There now, ducky. That's better, isn't it? Of course Bobsy doesn't like it, but he isn't used to an Indian diet.'

I surreptitiously took a tissue and spat my mouthful into it; I might, probably would, have to eat unpleasant messes in the future but, like Bobsy, I didn't see any reason for starting in Fitzroy Square.

After half an hour's effort I had worked my way upstairs to

the director's office; I might never have left the Tyne before, but after all those years spent slotting my plans into place, persistence was one thing I really understood.

The director, Mr Fraser, was a large, fair-haired man with an expression like a very resigned nursing cow. 'I'm busy,' he said, over toppling piles of files.

'I won't waste your time.' I hoped he would recognize from my tone that I wouldn't waste it only if he agreed to what I wanted right away. 'I'm Faith Milburn, and I collect funds for Prodam in the upper Tyne.'

'We're always so grateful to our helpers.' Although he looked surprised that one of them should come to see him personally, he managed to sound genuinely enthusiastic, which I thought creditable under the circumstances.

'Yes, well, in your newsletter you often say how you need qualified volunteers willing to go to Central America at their own expense.'

For the first time he gave me his full attention. 'Does that mean you are qualified and willing to go?'

'Oh, yes! That is –' Be businesslike, I told myself. However ramshackle its organization might be, Prodam was unlikely to jump at the chance of sending to Latin America a girl who had done nothing except nurse an invalid mother. 'I have a business studies degree, and considerable savings from my own trading profits since I qualified. I also have nursing and housekeeping – domestic economy experience.'

He smiled sourly. 'I prefer to call it housekeeping, really. Do you speak Spanish?'

'*Sí, aunque estaba decidado a mejorar el conocimiento de la lengua.*' I spoke as fast as I could, slurring the words like a Madrileno born.

His eyes flickered and I knew my gamble had paid off. I had studied Spanish from radio and television courses but certainly could not sustain a conversation in the language; I was fairly sure now that Mr Fraser couldn't either. 'You realize that Central American Spanish is different?' he answered after a pause.

'My teacher was Peruvian. He always said that real

12

Spaniards covered their ears when he spoke.' I suddenly realized that I was beginning to enjoy my own capacity for deceit, which was dangerous. I must keep as strictly to the truth as possible.

'Hm.' He regarded me doubtfully; anyone in the aid business exists on a diet of more or less specious lies. Luckily for me, both telephones on his desk rang almost at the same moment; he gabbled more initials into one, while I answered the other.

'I'm able to pay my own fare and my keep while I'm out in Central America,' I said when he had finished. This had been the optimistic suggestion in Prodam's newsletter. The organization was one of those shoestring charities which hover on the fringe of respectability, but I wasn't interested in efficient set-ups like Oxfam, which might employ me to lick stamps in their London office if I was lucky.

The telephone rang again.

'Oh, hell,' said Mr Fraser. 'Look, go away and write me a letter, will you? Enclose references from your previous employers or business associates.'

Two hours later I emerged into Fitzroy Square with a letter appointing me to Prodam's Mexico City office as an unpaid clerk, which was where aid for the rest of Central America was coordinated in an atmosphere of reasonable political calm; as Mr Fraser said, you can't make the numbers come right if guerrillas are emptying guns into the roof.

Mexico City, I thought triumphantly. Mexico City – it's hot and different and a long, long way from the Tyne. Dear Mr Fraser with his alphabetical conversations and persistent telephones; I'd expected it to take a great deal longer than two hours to argue myself anywhere I wanted to go. Of course, he had nothing to lose since I was unpaid, and the one stipulation he made was that I should buy a return ticket. Prodam did not want to waste its own money if I proved useless and was shipped home.

In his way, Mr Fraser was a shrewd man who survived in the morass of aid politics by snapping up a bargain when he

13

saw one. Like the high-altitude maize, I had my drawbacks, but I was cheap and just might come in useful.

Now for the passport office, the Mexican Embassy, and a dismaying list of jabs and pills. By the time I reached the sun, I would already have learned a great deal more about managing for myself. I did a quick little tap dance of delight on the paving slabs of Fitzroy Square, and every one of the half-dozen passers-by turned to stare.

I felt exactly as I used to on the first spring morning after a long northern winter, when the skylarks were spiralling above Blackwater Hill: a violent pleasure in existence, each muscle tense, joy close enough to touch. This was what I had wanted and had struggled for; if today had been unexpectedly easy, then the years of waiting had been very hard.

I was reaching out into the world at last.

Goodness, how green I was.

2

My delight lasted through two weeks of delay; I couldn't help noticing how people smiled sometimes as I passed, my eagerness obvious even to strangers in a crowd. Nor did I waste a minute of those two weeks, since there was so much I had been longing to see. Somehow, I fitted in a week's course in Hispanic Spanish and so met others to whom London was as strange and exciting as it was to me; just for a week I enjoyed enormously being the carefree student I never had the chance to be in Newcastle. We skipped meals and spent lavishly on seats for the theatre, gawked at London sights, paid sixteen pounds for a bottle of nightclub champagne, and argued passionately about anything on which our ignorance was most profound.

A Cornish boy who had taken a job in the Peruvian mines sailed with me on a sightseeing trip down the Thames in a stinging autumn wind, and tried to persuade me to go out there with him. He was four years younger than I, and said my hair reminded him of excavated copper.

'I thought copper was green,' I said waving my hand at the many domes of old buildings on the banks of the Thames.

'That's verdigris,' he said, shocked. 'What people and their wastes do to copper. You're copper just cut by the drill, and it isn't only your hair. You'd have to come down a mine

15

to see such – such – ' He hesitated, groping for his meaning. 'Most of anything dug out of the ground looks dull and trashy enough, but just sometimes you hit the real thing, and it has a glow all of its own. Perhaps it's no more than a fleck in rock, but it's still unmistakable. Like you.'

The Cornish are Celts and have poetic minds, but I can't pretend I wasn't touched; he had already told me that mines were the most splendid and exciting places on earth.

He was too young and intense to tease, so next day I went alone to wander through the bookshops, dreaming that one day a work by Faith Milburn . . . well, not exactly that it would be on the best-seller table, but perhaps attract praise in some obscure review. No. That isn't true. I dreamed of my book everywhere, number one, the title people talked about; dreams are lovely sometimes, and cheap as well, providing they are kept safely locked away.

I also telephoned home twice. The conversation was stilted and became more so when I said I was going to Mexico, but anger was better than indifference. It didn't matter any longer that my father had always preferred my brothers and at present regarded me as a traitor; now I had broken away I had no desire to quarrel.

By the time everything was fixed, I was becoming alarmed by the way money drifted away in London. I didn't want to be forced to return within weeks because I had run out of cash, so I booked on a flight the day after my papers came through. The journey was long but uneventful, and when we landed at Mexico City I was disappointed to find the airport full of business-suited men, just like Heathrow. I don't know what I expected, but all I remember is a ridiculous sense of disappointment.

Security was more obtrusive than in London, voices louder, colours brighter, but the temperature was unexpectedly cold and the sun I had come so far to find was lost behind storm clouds.

The official at the immigration control desk took a long time studying my passport; I assumed this was because the visa allowed me to work as a volunteer, but when he looked up at last his face was unfriendly, as if it was my fault that he had to figure meaning into smudged stamps. '*Su formulario, señorita.*'

I produced the form issued by the Mexican Embassy in London, and eventually a great many other letters as well, signed by Mr Fraser on Prodam notepaper. The queue behind me was becoming restive and I could feel myself getting flustered; although my Spanish had improved during that hectic time in London I wasn't yet up to cogent, persuasive argument with the Mexican police.

'I ask your pardon, señorita, but did you say you were coming here to work for Prodam?' An elegantly dressed man had been scanning our line of passengers from the other side of the barrier, and now he called across to me in English.

I agreed that I was, and until a policeman snatched them out of my hand, held my letters so he could see. He immediately ducked under a rope and came over to talk to the police and passport officials, one of whom eventually turned back to me. 'Señor Calderon told us he was expecting a man.'

I laughed. 'I assure you I am the clerk Prodam is expecting, and I certainly am not a man.'

His eyes dropped lazily to my feet and back to my face, tongue flickering over his lips. 'As the señorita says. Señor Calderon suggests that you talk matters over with him in the transit lounge, which is irregular, but for you I will agree. Meanwhile, I must keep your papers.'

I hated to lose sight of my passport, but Calderon came through the barrier as if he ignored airport regulations every day of his life, and drew me aside. 'I will reclaim your papers whenever you wish, but there are reasons why I would prefer to discuss matters with you here. Let me find your luggage, and then we will talk together over coffee.' His English was excellent. 'We may be short of time, so perhaps you would follow me at once.'

I was pleased by his brisk manner, since I half expected Latin Americans to doze the day through, but also surprised by such apparent need for haste. 'Time for what, señor? I

17

haven't thanked you yet for coming to meet me,' I added hastily, because Fraser had described Calderon as field director for the whole of Prodam's effort in Central America.

'It was my honour, señorita, but also business since I believed the time for briefing was so short. Now, everything may be changed, but I am not sure. No, don't talk yet, please. Wait here while I find a porter for your baggage.'

He took my luggage checks and disappeared beyond the barrier again, while I remained in quarantine, nerves very much on edge. Now, everything may be changed, he had said. Could it be that Calderon had taken one look and had every intention of shipping me back to sampling maize in Fitzroy Square? He struck me as an altogether much tougher and slicker operator than Fraser.

He returned with remarkable speed, ordered a porter to put my suitcases where we could both watch them all the time, and sat down opposite me. 'Coffee, Miss Milburn?'

'Thank you.' I studied him carefully: he looked remarkably like old pictures of Clark Gable, but with an intellectual's skull formation.

He offered cigarettes. 'I have solved the problem of why we were expecting a man.' He flicked his fingers at the labels on my cases. 'Faith Milburn. Fidel in Spanish, which is masculine and a famous name in these parts.'

I must have looked as blank as I felt.

'Fidel, Fidelistras, Fideleros,' he said impatiently. 'Castro of Cuba, surely you have heard of him?'

I nodded.

'Someone in our office must have translated your name literally, and once translated it would stick. There is no better known name in the whole of Central America.'

'Does it matter?' I didn't see why I should be prevented from working in Prodam's Mexico office just because some office boy equated my name with a political slogan.

He stubbed out his cigarette and poured coffee with neat movements of well-manicured hands. 'Yes, it matters. I came to the airport myself, not because it is my habit to meet incoming employees but to re-route a replacement.'

'You will have to explain,' I said carefully. The coffee was excellent, fragrant and rich; which was certainly one change from Heathrow.

'Of course. You understand, I am sure, that although Prodam has its administrative offices in Mexico City, all our aid is channelled to the poorer Central American republics. Most of these are too unstable for financial or bulk transactions to be handled satisfactorily there. We do not want to tempt guerrillas into shooting our staff by making them seem rich. So we stockpile goods and keep our bank balances here, although naturally we maintain a few people at the distributing end.'

Fraser had told me much the same; field staff were quite exposed enough in places like El Salvador and Comayagua, without unnecessarily exciting local gun-happy greeds. 'You mean you came to the airport meaning to send me straight out as field staff?' My pulse changed beat, thumping blood in my ears. Mexico City was one thing, a Central American republic in the grip of civil war quite another.

'When I understood you to be Fidel Milburn, a Spanish-named, Spanish-speaking male, yes.'

'Why?' There was something here I didn't understand; male or female, why should an experienced man like Calderon think of sending a raw recruit from England straight out in the field?

The Clark Gable moustache exaggerated his smile, which did not reach his eyes. 'Because the vacancy occurred in Comayagua, which has a long-standing and very bitter quarrel with Mexico, so no one who has Mexican stamps in his passport is allowed to land there. I cannot send anyone from here, and unless I put a replacement back in our depot fast, Prodam will lose its entire Comayagua operation, which has taken us five years to establish.'

'And you've fixed it so I haven't any Mexican entry stamps in my passport yet,' I said slowly. He couldn't . . . surely he couldn't still be considering sending me to a place like Comayagua.

'Good, Miss Milburn. You are quick, and beauty is also of

19

great assistance among us impressionable Latins.' He patted my knee as if I were an obedient pet; in spite of his words it was not a sexual gesture.

'A disadvantage too, surely,' I answered drily, thinking of the immigration official's leer. If Calderon assessed my appearance on its business merits, then I wasn't going to muddy the argument by pointing out how hazel eyes and light English colouring left him completely cold. He was not in the least like Willy Charlton, or Barney Trehellion in London, and stared at me only to calculate his own advantage.

He stood up at once, in a flurry of apology. 'Of course, señorita. Naturally, you are right. I am afraid that in my anxiety for so many hungry people in Comayagua, I overlooked your very understandable fears.'

'Not only my fears,' I ignored this blatant and probably insincere appeal to sentiment. 'There is also the question of my inexperience, Señor Calderon. I do not think your aid project in Comayagua would be safe with me.'

'Perhaps, perhaps not.' He sat down again. Standing had only been a gesture, as I had suspected. 'Allow me to explain a little further. Our programme is centred not in San Bernardo, the capital, but in Quihuli, the up-country railroad terminal. Quihuli is a very quiet town which has belonged to the Mendoza family for four hundred years, and under their protection you would be safe wherever you chose to go, since a Mendoza is at present ruling the country. Also, now I have had the pleasure of meeting you, I am not sure that our programme, which depends entirely on tactful dealings with the authorities, would not be safer with you than with some so-called expert who wants to change everything in a hurry.'

'I might want to change things,' I said tightly; he might just as well have said straight out that an incompetent would suit the locals best.

'We all want to, but it can only be done with patience. Patience, and – perhaps – charm.' He smiled again, and again it was no more than a flicker of muscle.

20

I shook my head. I might be rash, but I wasn't a damned fool. This stank like a polecat, and perhaps precisely because he was so obviously intelligent, I distrusted Calderon for suggesting such a crazy scheme. 'When I have gained some experience I may be able to help in the field, but first there is a great deal I must learn. Including real fluency in the language. I should like to take up the position to which I was appointed in the office here.'

'You misunderstand me. There is no position in our Mexico office. It has already been filled by our late field officer from Comayagua when he returned here last week, sick.'

So there it was: stark choice.

Either I went to Comayagua or I returned to London at my own expense, having spent several years' savings in a couple of weeks without reaching farther into the world than Mexico City's airport.

'Why did your last officer leave Comayagua? Apart from being sick, I mean.' I was stalling for time, desperately trying to see some way out of such unexpected catastrophe, and also sceptical of glib patter about illnesses.

Calderon relaxed at once, flicking his fingers for more coffee. We might argue for a while longer, but as I hadn't immediately rejected his preposterous suggestion out of hand, he knew he had me. 'Shall we say that lack of tact contributed to his poor health?' He opened his dispatch case and brought out a file of papers. 'You will find the details of our Comayaguan operation here. Really, the more I think of it, the better suited I believe you will be to the task which awaits you there. It is not onerous, we simply need an employee to negotiate with the customs and to safeguard our consignments, since pilfering is so rife. The Spanish-bloods are chivalrous: so long as you encourage this chivalry and are under the protection of the Mendozas, you will be safer in Quihuli than a man might be. Never be tempted to behave like an emancipated Norteamericana there, because then the Comayaguans will treat you without the honour due either to a man or to a woman.'

21

This I recognized as the only unbiased advice I was likely to receive from Calderon. I stared at the fat pink file he offered me and thought about how I had been a damned fool, after all. Instinct shrieked that this was a racket, that I was totally unsuited to wrangling with officials of a state I could scarcely place on the map, yet I was going to Comayagua because the alternative was defeat. Over the years, I had laid and relaid my plans as carefully as I could, but had always realized how fragile they were bound to be. Circumstances might have made me self-reliant – some would say obstinate – but once I was away from the Tyne everyone would recognize my lack of sophistication and try to take advantage of it. But knowing this, I had still decided that only in the unprotected places of the world would I have a chance to find myself. I wanted to see bright colours under the sun and experience passion; face risks I wasn't sure I could survive. Beneath it all too, there was this certainty growing in me that I would never truly be content until I was able to write something I knew was good, whether it sold or not, and while I lived in security, so far I'd only written trash.

It was too late to turn back now.

Possibly I would die in Comayagua, as Calderon knew I might and did not care, so long as I suited his plans; but if I ran back to England now, then I should have lost a part of me which had come to seem as important as life itself. Perhaps only someone who has spent her whole existence in one valley and a sickroom, longing to get out, can understand how I felt. In the end, neither writing nor ambition had much to do with it. I went to Comayagua with my eyes open, understanding the risks so far as it was possible for someone as ignorant as I to understand them; elated, aware, and very much afraid, but not wanting it any other way.

I did not know then that the only people determined to face reality are those too simple-minded to duck when they see it coming.

I looked up and met Calderon's unrevealing stare. 'Tell me more about how to operate in Quihuli.'

3

Because of the quarrel between Mexico and Comayagua I couldn't fly direct, but had to travel via Jamaica. The connection left Mexico City just over an hour after Calderon bought me my first cup of coffee, and by the time I reached Kingston for an overnight stop I felt quite exhausted. I remember little of Jamaica beyond an impression of exotic strangeness.

When we took off again soon after dawn our twin-engined Fokker seemed very frail after the jumbo jet which had been my sole experience of flying so far, and I sank back into the apprehensive gloom which had replaced defiance as soon as Calderon bade me a suave farewell.

And that was how I met Pete Zeller.

I think he must have noticed my depression, and because he occupied the seat next to the windon he insisted on changing places so I could watch the sun coming up over the Caribbean. I needed to press my nose to the glass because we were flying nearly due west, but even glimpses of the tremendous sky behind us were sensational. The sea was glassy but not still, great swells pushing out of the south crinkling its turquoise surface; even as I watched, clouds were surging so rapidly over the horizon that they flamed golden, sultry yellow-brown and violet as they kept pace with the rising sun.

'Hurricane season,' observed my neighbour. 'We'll be racing the rain into Progreso.'

'Progreso?'

He grinned. 'Comayagua's international airport. They changed the name of the town too, but never got around to rebuilding it. I'm Pete Zeller, and I'll be in San Bernardo for a couple of days, so if you want any help just tell me.'

'Why, thank you, Mr Zeller – '

'Pete, please. Americans are goddam familiar, Faith.'

I glanced at the name on my hand baggage, and laughed. 'It saves a lot of bother. If Mexico is anything to go by, then some help past the airport barrier might be welcome.'

'You not being met?' he demanded incredulously.

I shook my head. Fright lodged again where I needed to swallow it down, hard. 'No, you see – ' I plunged into a confused account of Calderon's variety of blackmail; Prodam, the Quihuli operation and why I was drafted to go there.

Zeller listened in silence, frowning. He had thick shoulders and heavily muscled thighs; a tanned, sensual face. He looked a man whose help was likely to be valuable, but about as safe as flame in an oil refinery. 'Jesus Christ,' he said when I had finished. 'There's a few Limey banana growers left. I placed you as one of their daughters tiptoeing home to help smuggle out pesos while there's still time. Didn't you realize Comayagua's had three revolutions in four years?'

'No,' I said guiltily. 'At least, I've tried to read the file Calderon gave me, but it doesn't seem to make much sense. I suppose it's me.'

'You think so? Any guy who thought he understood the set-up in Comayagua went crazy long ago. The rest take what they can for themselves and keep a cellarful of guns.'

'I'm going to Quihuli though, not San Bernardo, and Calderon promised he'd telephone an introduction to the Mendoza family. Otherwise he said he wouldn't have sent me.' I thought about that, and added, 'I don't believe him,

24

but I suppose I might have had the sense to refuse to go. I thought that since one of the family is dictator at the moment – '

'General Miguel Mendoza, El Miragloso, the Miracle-Worker himself, sure. He's dictator, but like I said, revolutions come with the seasons here. And you won't like dictators, Central American style.'

I was quite sure I shouldn't, but didn't intend to start arguing all over again about whether I ought to turn back when I was only thirty minutes' flying time out of Progreso, a tropical coastline just hazing the horizon ahead. I stared, fascinated, as it thickened and darkened, mile after mile of jungle stretching in every direction. I had not expected it to look so limitless. In his brief rundown on Comayagua Calderon had dismissed its coastal province as insignificant; bananas, fever and primitives, he had said with one of those flicks of his fingers. Not political, not healthy, not rich. Bananas are finished. Yet there it was, wide rivers and uninterrupted green as far as the eye could see.

Pete Zeller dismissed it as unimportant, too. 'There's a quarter of the country down there, and the mountains in the west make up another half, but the middle quarter around San Bernardo is what counts. That's where the heads roll. Which is one reason why revolutions are so easy. Some ambitious guy bribes a few guards to make a suicide squad high on coca leaves so they'll storm the presidential palace for him, and if they succeed he's got it made. Until next time.'

'If I was a dictator, I'd put up steel shutters,' I said sceptically. Zeller's voice had a strange tone to it, as if he could imagine himself as one of those ambitious guys with a suicide squad, if only he thought a dump like Comayagua was worth the risk.

'Sure, and they keep out stray bullets just fine. But in a serious revolution, the biggest bribe of all goes inside the palace. The last two, three dictators have died in their beds as you might say.' He drew a finger across his throat and I tried not to stare at his hands. They were calloused like a

25

labourer's, even though his clothes suggested wealth. 'It's kind of interreactive. Purge your staff often and they're frightened enough to kill; treat 'em kindly and sooner or later they feel sufficiently safe to look around for the highest bidder.'

Below us, green jungle was shredding into yellow clearings and muddy pools; seat-belt signs came on as we dropped lower and the country opened out into chequered, empty plain.

I had a feeling that our pilot disliked the Comayagua run; he brought that Fokker down like a fighter, slammed it on the runway and kept the engines running while we disembarked, spraying grit all over the place.

'He's probably quarrelled with the cops here,' shouted Zeller, slipping his hand under my arm. 'Been refused clearance until he takes on fuel at three times the international price, perhaps. Keep your hands on everything you own, okay?'

I am quite tall for a woman but Zeller topped me by six inches, and when he turned to shout at a porter I felt the hard bulk of a gun under his coat. Still, from what he told me most Comayaguans went around armed as well.

The heat sat in wavy lines over the tarmac and gold scimitars of sunlight flashed in front of my eyes as we walked the short distance to the terminal, my spirits swooping upwards with each step. Because I still could not really believe it was me, here, in the tropic province of a Central American republic, my fears miraculously evaporated as I gazed about me.

Looking back now, my own rapid changes of mood are what strike me as most extraordinary about those first few hours I spent in Mexico and Comayagua, when, temperamentally, I am fairly equable. I was, I suppose, still in some kind of shock after Calderon's bombshell ultimatum, and events were to make sure that I had no time to catch my breath. The fact remains that for the moment even Zeller seemed insubstantial, and all I could think of was my own excitement.

Progreso Airport rioted with colourful weeds: pushing through the concrete runway, softening stark prefabricated outlines, bursting over soft-surface roads. Everyone was shouting at the top of his voice. A great many soldiers in bright green fatigues sat drinking on the terrace, a few of them using submachine guns to emphasize their gestures. Once, a burst of fire echoed from outside but no one took any notice. 'They don't believe in safety catches,' explained Zeller; he looked around, smiling slightly and crackling with energy, as if lawlessness made some vital connection in his circuitry. '*Buenas dias, teniente,*' he added unexpectedly, 'Colonel Mozon sent you?'

'*Sí, señor*. Welcome to the country of El Miragloso.' A slickly tailored young officer was standing by a board with Pete Zeller's name written on it. He saluted and opened a wire-mesh gate for us to bypass a swarm of other officials at the barrier, then kissed my hand very elegantly when Zeller introduced me, as if I, too, had a right to an official welcome. The lieutenant's name was Napoleon Abelardo Espinoza. I found it difficult to take my eyes off him, he was so exactly what a Central American officer should be. There were silver stripes on his sleeves and crossed machetes on his collar patches; his calf-length combat boots were glossily polished and a snouted automatic bulged out of a white patent-leather holster. A lanyard woven in yellow and green, the national colours of Comayagua, looped from its butt to both epaulettes and then around his neck. He took our passports and a clerk behind the immigration counter showered stamps on them without even bothering to look across to where we stood. Zeller's help was proving even more useful than I had expected, althought I was just beginning to feel uneasy about the payment he might expect.

'Seguridad – secret police,' he said now, nodding at Espinoza, but he need not have bothered to tell me. Espinoza might be difficult to take seriously, but the clerk's deference told its own story, even to me.

A green and white police car was blocking the steps outside, and we shot off with a screech of tyres before its doors were closed. Zeller took it for granted that I would accept a lift with the Seguridad, and since in the maelstrom of Progreso Airport I couldn't see any other means of reaching the capital, San Bernardo, I decided it would be absurd to refuse. In for a penny, in for a pound. Cliché comes in useful sometimes; in this case as an excuse, for even then I sensed how I was compounding one stupidity with another by accepting help from a man like Zeller, especially once I knew he was well-regarded by the secret police.

The road beyond the airport entry was crowded with people erratically riding bicycles and mopeds or trudging head down under burdens, but we drove as if on a motorway, horn blaring. How we didn't kill anyone I do not know.

Comayagua might have looked deserted from the air, its dirt roads and adobe houses blending into the vegetation, but once you were there it spilled over with life. The air was like warm oil, the colours brilliant; huge dusty leaves shaded the road, open-fronted shacks sold yellow gourds, red peppers and purple fly-spotted meat; deep pools from recent rain steamed eerily in sledgehammer heat. Clay-coloured, malarial-looking faces flowed past on either side, inscrutable under straw hats. The people on the road were mostly what I supposed to be Indians rather than the half-bloods or Spanish-bloods I had seen at the airport: they had thick-boned faces and short legs and talked to each other with their backs turned to us. Hatred was expressed by those backs, and if they had dared to, I believe they would have spat as we passed. I had dreamed for so long about how the world would look, but no amount of imagination could begin to paint from such a palette of primary colours as I found in Comayagua within minutes of my arrival, stroke in such contrasts, or suggest such elemental stenches.

I was mesmerized, entranced and repelled.

Progreso had bulldozed streets full of scummy ponds, presumably from old excavations when they thought they might rebuild the town in modern style. The few two-storey buildings were decaying, the rest not much more than shacks

28

painted in vermilion, cobalt blue and ochre. Daubed pictures showed what might be sold inside; a life-size bull charged from the wall of a butcher's shop, ten-foot bottles filled with technicolor liquids advertised the many cantinas. More Indians, many of them drunk, wandered the streets; enamelled sky stretched above vultures flopping on piled refuse; juke boxes roared out ancient hit tunes as we passed.

'The electricity is on,' said Zeller from the back of the car. 'It's off most of the time, which is the only relief you get from the juke boxes.'

'The electricity is always on now El Miragloso rules,' said Espinoza stiffly. There were pictures of El Miragloso staring at a sunlit future on every wall substantial enough to take them. He had a jaw like rock and a genial, well-fed smile.

'Christ, I hope not,' said Zeller. They began to talk Spanish again, Espinoza very fast and incomprehensibly in what must be the local accent, Zeller fluently but with a strange twist to his words which I later discovered to be Bolivian in origin. I was able to gather the gist of it though: Zeller had apparently come to obtain Comayaguan cooperation in tracking down some U S troublemaker believed to be in Central America.

'He was in the States two years ago, and I wasted one hell of a time running in circles after him there,' he observed once. I missed the next bit and then he said quite clearly, 'No, there isn't any reason to suppose he might be in Comayagua, but if he is then you should have heard of him. So unless your Colonel Mozon can turn up something for me, I've booked myself on to Costa Rica. El Salvador after that, I guess.'

'You must want him very badly, señor,' commented Espinoza.

I had pulled my sun visor down; there was a mirror set into it in which I had been covertly studying Zeller. Now, for a fleeting moment, I saw the expressive muscles of his face rope tightly into fury as he thought about this fugitive he had come to find, yet when he spoke his voice had not altered

29

pitch at all. The contrast between outward self-possession and such extreme personal animosity towards a man who Zeller presented as simply an enemy of the state he served was so disturbing that I came close to doubting the evidence of my eyes.

'There is enough trouble down here without having gringo political *asesinos* exported to you as well,' he said flatly, after a pause. 'Anyhow, I've been given the assignment, and my department doesn't take kindly to failure. Nor do I. I'll cross his trail soon, and then it's only a matter of time. If he is here, then you're welcome to keep him once he's caught. A Comayaguan jail will fix him quicker than some soft penitentiary in the States.'

I didn't catch Espinoza's reply, but they both laughed. *Asesino*. Murderer. An American mercenary who knew how to lead brutalized and hating Indians, if he did know, would be a dangerous man down here. Zeller wouldn't have any difficulty in obtaining whatever help he needed to track him down from precarious dictators fearing for their lives.

Once we passed Progreso the country opened into rolling prairie, patchily cultivated but much richer than the flatlands around the airport. A few cars and a great many trucks and buses belted past with a flurry of horns, all so ramshackle I wondered how they held together; even our police Ford was making the noise of a thousand imminent disconnections but the driver kept his foot flat on the floor and his hand on the horn, so the suspension screeched at every corner.

It became slightly cooler as the road climbed above the plain but a warm wind blew dust everywhere, through ill-fitting car doors and windows. Ahead I could just see a misty range of mountains recalling for a brief moment the Border hills; several times we crossed the familiarity of a single-track railway, once we passed a line of smart new tractors. No one was using them nor was there any sign anyone ever would; just a long red line of machinery rusting gently in the sun, but they, too, turned my thoughts back to the Tyne valley.

I calculated that there it would be evening, and if it was fine then the only sound would be cheery greetings as the men came down from the hills. The flowers on my mother's grave would have withered by now, and I wished I was able to go in the dusk and bring her some fresh, stand for a few minutes and feel close to her again, perhaps ask what she thought of me, jolting over the dirt roads of Comayagua. I could imagine the soft astonished smile with which she had always greeted my more outrageous scrapes; as if she was unable to believe she could have bred so turbulent a daughter. 'I expect you are doing what you enjoy, Faith dear,' she would have said, as usual, and then closed her eyes on folly. Resigned to pain and not complaining; wanting to die. That was what had always torn me apart with anguish for her, anguish and, even after all the years, a kind of incomprehension. I could not then believe that I should ever feel tempted simply to give up and die, no matter what my pain might be.

I had tried so hard to offer her some of my eagerness for life, sat through so many sleepless nights at her bedside, hoping to help a little by simply being there, but I never succeeded in doing more than deepen the affection between us. Because she had remained glad to die, I grieved both for her and for the gladness she had felt.

I wrenched my mind back to Comayagua; from now on straying wits could be perilous. 'How much farther to San Bernardo?' I asked Espinoza

'Eighty, ninety kilometres, señorita. Two hours.' He felt compelled to add an explanation for such a dramatic drop in speed. 'There is more traffic you understand, and sharper bends in the hills.'

'What he means is the road is just as narrow and has a much worse surface,' observed Zeller lazily.

'El Miragloso's roads are rebuilt and have excellent surfaces.' Espinoza even managed a ring of conviction in his voice.

I stared at Zeller in the mirror, beginning to wonder whether his knowledge of Comayagua didn't have a certain flavour of the well-digested briefing about it. 'When were you here before?'

I had not realized how his expression would soften when he was amused, although by now I was more than conscious of just how attractive such obtrusive virility could be. I had told myself he was dangerous; I *knew* he was dangerous, but when his eyes met mine softly in the mirror the bones weakened in my body. A completely physical sensation, and unmistakable even to the inexperienced, provided they want to recognize it. But at least I acknowledge my own foolishness when it is thrust under my nose.

'How did you guess?' he said now. 'Never, as it happens. But I'd bet a thousand dollars against Comayaguan pesos that I'm right.'

He was right, presumably because he knew the rest of Latin America well enough to place Comayagua in the corruption and poverty league by sight and smell alone. By the time we rattled over the surfaced streets of San Bernardo I had a throbbing headache and wanted nothing so much as a bath and to lie down in the dark.

San Bernardo was larger than I expected, crowded and insanitary on the outskirts, insanitary but less crowded in the centre. There was a modern section of glass and concrete flats, two or three attractive old squares and a church with people crawling up the steps on their knees; also a great many cantinas and cafés where most of the population seemed to be doing nothing very pleasantly. Gaudy American advertising and a tangle of draped wires gave the whole place a ramshackle hybrid air, except for a few narrow streets I longed to explore, where shuttered balconies almost met across the cobbles.

Our driver kept his hand on the horn even in the city, as did everyone else: the noise was indescribable and almost drowned the juke boxes. I twisted my head from side to side, trying not to miss anything, my headache forgotten: there were old Indian women in black felt bowler hats, a startling number of idling soldiers, and flowering bushes bursting over clay-tiled roofs. Slums down most turnings where nearly naked children stared at the traffic. Flowered shirts, market stalls humming with flies, a few very elegant shops. Contrast everywhere; no muted shades at all. We crossed a wide thoroughfare and Espinoza proudly pointed out the president's palace.

The president's palace. I goggled at it speechlessly; it was hard to believe that any serious president would live in such a building, but General Mendoza, El Miragloso, was a completely serious dictator dedicated to survival. The palace stood at the far end of the Avenida del Miragloso (lately the Avenue of Our Lady, Espinoza said) and looked like a child's fantasy castle, complete with turrets and battlements and drawbridges, all jumbled together and painted bright green. Incongruously, there was a tank parked outside and several bunkers full of guns dug into the side of the avenue.

'Have you an address to go to in San Bernardo?' asked Zeller. He made no comment about the palace, since he had come to ask favours from a colonel of secret police.

'Calderon said he would telephone a booking to the Hotel Miragloso, which was the best in San Bernardo.'

'Of course,' said Espinoza, shocked at the idea that any hotel could be better than one named after the dictator. In spite of his splendid uniform and formal manners he seemed unsophisticated even to me, but then each new dictator would surround himself with followers who, like him, would have jumped half a dozen ranks within six months.

Rather to my surprise, Calderon had telephoned: at least, I wasn't surprised he had done so, but completely astonished he had been able to impress the booking clerk sufficiently for the reservation to be waiting. 'Powerful guy, this Calderon,' observed Zeller, clearly as startled as I was. 'He might be worth a check.'

'Señor Calderon? Señor Alfonso Calderon? My friend, do not dream of such a thing! He is spoken of as a friend of Comayagua, of El Miragloso himself. An inquiry would be an insult!' exclaimed Espinoza.

'Sure, it's none of my business.' Zeller agreed peaceably

33

enough, but I had an idea that after he left Comayagua the inquiry would be forwarded to Washington all the same. 'They keep Spanish hours here, Faith. Would you feel like coming out for a meal if I called for you about ten tonight?'

I nodded, knowing I ought to refuse and also taken aback to discover it was still only the afternoon; our takeoff from Jamaica seemed another existence.

'*Bueno*. Have a siesta now like all good Comayaguans do. You've come a long way since Heathrow yesterday.' He waved a hand and followed Espinoza out into the sun again; he must have come a long way himself, but showed no sign of weariness at all.

My room was immense, colonial in style and decorated with moulded plaster. The water from the tap was only a tepid trickle but once patience had produced a hip bath full of it, I didn't care. Bath, bed and sleep were all that mattered.

When I woke, the room was lit by setting sunlight filtering through closed shutters, the air agreeably cool after the heat of the day. I lay trying to sort the tumbling impressions of the past few hours into some kind of order, conscious for the first time of how utterly, echoingly alone I now was. So much had happened so fast since I left London that it took a four-poster Spanish bed in the Hotel Miragloso, San Bernardo, to make me realize the full implications of what I'd done. From now on every decision, failure, success, uncertainty, was mine alone, unshared; there was no one to help at all.

When I remembered I was to dine with Zeller, I was glad. I neither understood nor trusted him, but I desperately needed the reassurance of a recognizable face among a population of strangers.

Tomorrow, I must take a train for Quihuli, another seventy miles into the foothills of the Picacho Mountains.

I had not slept as long as I expected to, but felt completely refreshed, my headache vanished; yet I was reluctant to leave the safety of that bed. This very special terror would suck my strength away if I allowed it any grip at all; nor could I afford to lie thinking about what I might be

34

getting into with Pete Zeller. I took a deep breath and threw back the bedclothes, and I don't think I had ever done anything so difficult in my life, though the next move was no easier, when I stood and went over to the window. Don't make a drama of it, I thought grimly. This is only the first of many battles I must fight in Comayagua.

Below my window the evening promenade was in progress: it appeared as if all the younger women of San Bernardo were dressed in flounced skirts and circulating slowly around the plaza outside. The men wore coloured shirts and were walking in the opposite direction; the two flows observed each other closely but seldom seemed to mix, and in their turn were watched by married couples chatting under the trees in the centre of the square.

I dressed and went out to join the women; all around me the shuffle of feet and whisper of conversation was like water in a brook. Everyone stared at me but no one spoke, the girls giggling as they discussed my English clothes, fair colouring and light eyes. Few tourists ventured into Comayagua any more, and I was the oddity that made their day. Although the evening promenade had so formal a structure, the underlying chaos was terrific, and that first evening I was still like a child on its first trip to the circus, my earlier terror forgotten. Little girls played together while their brothers sparred and picked quarrels; men pushing trolleys of fizzy drinks shouted, nut-sellers jostled for attention; some soldiers linked arms and barged straight through the strolling circles. They collected black looks, but no one dared openly to curse their boorishness. A fountain shot water high into sunset-tinted air, while drunkards lay sprawled against walls. As I progressed around the square for the second time I began to study the street signs: Prodam had an agent called Fernando Ulate who lived in San Bernardo, and when Calderon gave me his address he said it was close to the hotel.

The Calle de los Galones. That was it. I hesitated; a few figures sprawled in its shadows, either drunk or asleep, and away from the plaza the lighting was poor. But it was not yet dark, and I disliked the idea of returning to the Hotel Miragloso with only my own thoughts for company until Zeller came. Comayagua was still so strange to me that the risk of walking down a street with some drunken Indians in it seemed almost commonplace compared with what I had already done. I have no excuse for the chance I took, except that I suppose I was still disorientated by such a rapid transformation in my life.

So I left the plaza and the safety of its crowds, my footsteps echoing between the windowless walls of the Calle de los Galones. Barren stonework was broken only by massive doors through which a man could ride on horseback; few of these doors were numbered and I had to establish which was number four by a process of elimination, the bell when I pulled it pealing infinitely far away. Already I was regretting the impulse which had brought me here; my neck felt cold and I did not think I was imagining the shuffle of feet behind me.

'*Quien viene, por favor?*'

The door remained shut and the voice came from somewhere high in the timberwork. I realized I was faced by an electronic speaker of some kind; it seemed incongruous in a sidestreet in San Bernardo.

'Faith Milburn, from Prodam in Mexico City. I've come to see Señor Ulate. You should have received a message about me.' I wanted to beg whoever it was to open the door quickly; behind me, footsteps were quite definitely sidling closer.

He seemed to sense my urgency because the door clicked open immediately, and as I stepped through a guard appeared rubbing his eyes and holding a rifle. I bade him good evening but he stared back sulkily, annoyed perhaps at being woken.

Once through an archway in the thickness of wall, I came to a gravelled courtyard, softly lit by oil lamps. Plenty of windows here; all the rooms in the house must look out over this protected space. An open stair led up to a pillared first-floor terrace and at the foot of it a monkey-faced man in

36

a linen suit greeted me with a flurry of Spanish civilities.

But in spite of his welcome, I had the impression that Señor Ulate was disconcerted by my arrival, although he put it politely enough. 'Señorita, it is not safe for lovely English ladies to wander our streets at dusk. If you had sent a message from your hotel, I would have called tomorrow.'

I explained that I wanted to leave for Quihuli in the morning; he shook his head at such unseemly haste, and led me up to the terrace. It was floored with marble polished like an ice rink, and as I picked my way precariously across it I reflected that Ulate at least was exempt from the poverty which seemed to characterize Comayagua.

'You would enjoy refreshment?' Without waiting for my answer, he added, 'How do you like my country?'

'Very much,' I said feebly.

'Good. That is very good indeed.' He looked surprised, although his question was not of the kind which usually receives an honest answer. A buzzer sounded beside him; he frowned and spoke into the set. '*Quien viene?*'

'I must go,' I said hastily. 'I'm afraid I've come at an inconvenient time.'

'My house is yours,' he replied automatically, listening to a reply from the street. 'Nor would it be safe for you to leave without an escort. Just excuse me for a minute and I will return.' He walked with enviable confidence across the floor and ran down the stairs to intercept a uniformed man in the courtyard below. They stood talking for quite a long time. I was unable to hear what they were saying, but they seemed to be disagreeing about something, the officer offended by being forced into unaccustomed argument.

Eventually, they came up the stairs together.

'Señorita Milburn, may I present to you Colonel Mozon? He cannot stay, but was anxious to make the acquaintance of so beautiful a visitor.'

I was becoming embarrassed by Comayaguan-style compliments, especially since I had joined the plaza promenade and realized that this was a country where plump bodies were regarded as evidence of success. While

37

mingling with the San Bernardo beauties I had been left in little doubt that the males considered my slimness as cause for derision, my height as unfeminine and my fair colouring as unlucky. There was enough Indian blood even in the Spanish-speaking population for the average Comayaguan to be squat and dark, and I had seen how many covertly crossed themselves or exchanged mocking comments before looking at me directly.

When Mozon had finished with compliments, he regarded me with undisguised curiosity. 'I have just been in conference with Señor Zeller, and he told me about this enterprise of yours, señorita. Really, I cannot approve of Señor Calderon's action in allowing you to come here.'

'Sending me here. I wasn't given a choice, Colonel.'

He clicked his tongue but beneath his suave manner I could tell he was amused. Really, he thought Calderon had been very clever to send an *estúpida* woman to Quihuli. 'Well, señorita, I trust that your stay here will be agreeable. I am called to the presence of El Miragloso tomorrow and will take the opportunity of speaking to him about your need for his family's hospitality in Quihuli. It is a pleasant town, and under the protection of the Mendozas you should feel no anxiety there.'

'No, indeed,' echoed Ulate. 'It is always quiet in Quihuli.'

'I came here tonight so I could learn about Prodam's programme there,' I answered noncommittally. Lamplight touched greenery and old stone, the thick walls of the casa dulling sound from the street outside. Under the tropic sky such a setting was magically beautiful, and I wanted to enjoy it instead of thinking about the frauds I was now quite convinced I should find in Quihuli.

'The aid programme is running smoothly. The railway brings a consignment of food from the coast every three months and you will be responsible for accepting delivery of this from the customs in Quihuli freight yard. Then your anxieties will be over until the next time, since our army also works a relief programme and distributes Prodam's supplies with its own.' Ulate's tone was flat, definite.

38

'I'm sure I shall soon discover how everything is done.'
My worst fears were confirmed by the news that the
Comayaguan army distributed Prodam's relief.

'Yes, señorita,' said Mozon deliberately. 'I am sure you
will. Remember also that if you desire to accomplish
anything at all in an unfamiliar place, it is wise to pay very
careful regard to local customs and prejudices.'

I nodded, ashamed to find that even in these civilized
surroundings, I was afraid of Colonel Mozon. His uniform
was not flashily braided like Espinoza's and his face was
softened by good living, but the air was blighted where he
stood. This sounds fanciful when evil in material form is not
a modern concept and Mozon was the first colonel of secret
police I had met. But Comayagua is not a modern country,
and this was my reaction to Mozon after five minutes'
acquaintance; nor did I ever subsequently have reason to
believe that my instincts were at fault.

When he had gone, even Ulate relaxed. 'Now I will escort
you back to your hotel. Please, you must learn to behave
prudently while you are here; it is dangerous in our streets at
night.'

'I haven't behaved prudently by coming to Comayagua,' I
pointed out. 'But I certainly will try to be sensible. Tell me,
do the Indians around Quihuli benefit from Prodam's
programme at all?'

He hesitated. 'They are *primitivos*, you understand. Very
suspicious. Very grudging. We Spaniards have lived here for
over four hundred years, and still we do not know them.'

'But do they benefit, Señor Ulate?'

'A little, perhaps. See, I am honest with you. The land
around Quihuli has become exhausted, but the climate is
healthy. Many Comayaguans do not see why the Indians
should continue to destroy the little soil that remains, when
it is a place which could produce wealth. The Indians slash,
they burn, they grow a crop and then the rains come.' He
shrugged. 'Soon there will be nothing but rock left. So the
army moves the Indians into encampments where they may
be fed, and the land is sold to those who can farm it better.'

'The Indians are herded into camps, and there fed by Prodam?'

'*Sí, señorita*. The army . . . it is two parts of the same operation.'

'I don't think it is quite what Prodam's London office had in mind though, do you?'

'Things are so different here, señorita. And different again in Quihuli.' There was warning in his voice. We were still standing where Mozon left us, and involuntarily Ulate looked over his shoulder as if even in the protection of his casa, he, too, understood the meaning of fear.

'It is quiet in Quihuli,' I quoted maliciously.

He nodded, mournful monkey jowls flapping. '*Sí*, that is so. But there are many kinds of quietness. Many, many kinds. Listen to the street.'

Surprised, I listened. The thickness of stone about us was such that I could hear very little. There were only the stars swinging low in a velvet sky, and a few distant reports like firecrackers.

'We have perhaps thirty murders in San Bernardo during a bad night,' said Ulate quietly. 'So there is nothing except gunmen for you to hear once it is dark. Revenge. Hit squads. Criminals. Drunk or drugged Indians running crazed. Who knows which are the killers? And if the silence of our streets at night hides one kind of ruin, then the quietness of Quihuli hides another. I beg you to return to Progreso tomorrow and fly back to your London, where you may safely talk about how aid should best be spent.' He did not sound sarcastic, only sad.

I thought of Fitzroy Square with its ringing telephones and saucers full of glutinous maize, until a rapping crackle far out in the suburbs of San Bernardo interrupted thought. My own concerns and not pity had brought me here, but it wasn't only pride that made it unthinkable that I should scuttle home tomorrow because one day in Comayagua was enough. Food from Prodam apparently reached Quihuli; I ought to find out what happened to it next. When I had, then London might or might not be the right place from which to

40

start exerting pressure on corruption, but first I needed facts. I sighed. 'I can't do that. Not yet, anyway. And surely, if Colonel Mozon and Señor Calderon have both commended me to the family of General Mendoza, I must be safe in Quihuli.'

It couldn't be coincidence that the army had begun land clearances precisely in the area where El Miragloso's family stood to benefit most.

Ulate hesitated, rubbing his hands nervously together. 'Yes, of course. El Miragloso's softest whisper is heard in Quihuli.'

He had been intending to say something quite different, I was certain. 'I will be discreet, I promise.'

He shrugged. 'I am sure that Señor Mendoza, El Miragloso's uncle, will see that you are. Now, if you are ready, I will escort you back to your hotel. Tomorrow I will come with documents to show you, but I regret that I am engaged for the rest of this evening.' His eyes strayed to a dim loggia off the courtyard, and I was astonished to see a gaudily dressed woman lying on a couch there. She had not moved all the time we were talking and did not move now, but her eyes were open and regarded me with unwinking jealousy.

'I'm afraid I wasn't just imprudent, but also inconsiderate to come here this evening.' My tongue tripped over the formal Spanish, although I had been pleased to discover that I could follow a conversation when it wasn't gobbled by the local dialect.

He shrugged again, in complete agreement but too polite to say so. 'Come then, and I will call a guard.'

To my amazement, he thought it necessary to take two armed men with us for the fifty-yard walk back to the plaza. 'If you would order your men to accompany me, I could go with them and save you the trouble of coming too.'

He muttered something under his breath, and then drew me aside where his men could not hear. 'Señorita Milburn, you are in Comayagua. Possibly it would be safe to send you with Miguel and Domingo, but possibly not. What is to stop

41

them from raping you in the street and then cutting your throat with a machete? They would tell me they had delivered you to your hotel, and if your body was ever found, then the police would shrug and say you deserved to die for wandering the streets alone. I told you, we have thirty murders a night here; not many of them are ever solved. A few people may be garrotted, but they are men the police have swept off the street on the principle that some of them, sometimes, must be guilty. Ten years ago we had a little law here, but there is nothing now, not even the law of the strong. Nowadays they are often the first to be killed. Trust no one. Go nowhere alone. Watch what men do, and never allow yourself to be distracted by what they say.'

His words were chilling enough, but again I had the impression that he wanted to tell me more, that the really important warning went unspoken.

We left the house by a steel wicket which gave on to a narrow passage leading back to the calle along which I had come; the gate itself was loopholed and guarded, and when we came to the calle one of the guards went ahead holding an automatic rifle. The other brought up the rear, Ulate and I in single file between them.

It was an eerie sensation to be walking towards a lit plaza where the fountain still played merrily into a carved basin and hundreds of people had promenaded only an hour before, yet to be as alert as in a snake-infested jungle.

An occasional shot sounded some distance away. The same Indians were still sprawled on the cobbles; from behind blank walls the notes of a marimba sounded. Barricaded into splendid casas and miserable shacks alike, all that the population of San Bernardo could do was hope that tonight *los asesinos* would kill someone else.

The shot came from so close behind me that the roar of it was concussive, reflex alone throwing me flat on my face. Two, three, four, lighter whiplash shots followed, the flame and stink of them in my hair, cobbles jarring against my skull. I understood nothing of what was happening, and the speed of it outpaced fear. I lay against the wall, painstak-

42

ingly working out that the first shot must have come from our own guard and the lighter ones from Ulate: nothing else would fit – all of them were close enough to scorch. Yet still none of it made sense.

Silence. No sound in my ringing ears, no movement at all.

I lifted my head cautiously. The road surface and house walls were oddly elongated when viewed from the gutter. Inconsequential, disordered thoughts leaped through my brain; I was incapable of grasping the suddenness of disaster. The first guard, Domingo, who had been walking in front of me, now threshed in a pool of blood. Ulate had been immediately behind and lay hunched on one side, eyes open, blood dark on his chin. I reached out and touched him hesitantly, and he moved, choked on blood and lay still again.

I began to shake. Panic became a breaker piling out of incomprehension and horror. There was nothing I could do to stop Ulate dying. His clothes were soaked with blood and in the dark I couldn't see where it came from, only feel it flooding out each time I touched him.

'Trust no one,' he whispered, and smiled a sad monkey smile. 'I never thought . . . that Miguel might shoot me. My gun, it's . . . here somewhere. Take it. I killed Miguel . . . and Domingo . . . or they would have finished you, too. There's only one . . . bullet left. Don't wait. Run. Run very fast.'

I crawled to Miguel, too dazed to work out any answers now. He was dead. I inched back to where Ulate lay. Air bubbled through the blood in his mouth and I tilted his head to stop him suffocating, although anything I did was hopeless for no one came to help and I knew his lungs were drowning. There were shapes moving furtively in the shadows, looters probably, roused by the sounds of carnage.

The nearest of them sprinted from one doorway to the next; I stared numbly at where he was, quite close now, a vulture making sure his prey was helpless. The gun. Ulate had killed two men with his gun and it was still there somewhere. Breath was like iron in my throat as I groped

43

frantically for it; I would vomit if I thought about what I had to do. Comayagua – Christ have mercy, whatever had I imagined I might accomplish here? I found the gun at last, half hidden under Ulate and thick with blood.

'Go,' said Ulate, and choked.

I touched his face and then held his fingers as they cramped with pain, speaking English to him because my Spanish had vanished along with the other sensations I had lost. All I wanted was for his last minutes to be filled with a little human warmth instead of hate; because I knew that if I had not ventured down the Calle de los Galones tonight, he would be in bed with his jealous-eyed mistress now.

The nearest looter moved again, and another shadow too, farther up the calle. The one I could see looked quite prosperous in jeans and glossy shirt; most nights he probably found good pickings on the streets. I fired, and the recoil snapped my teeth shut on my lip. I intended to miss him and I did, but he jinked back into cover to think about it.

'Now. He's counting. He'll know . . . that kind always does. It was the last bullet.' Ulate had levered himself on his elbow, blood becoming a nightmare lake as it spread into a pool of refuse. 'Don't stay long in Quihuli.' He had almost reached his knees before his last defences broke and he fell face down in the filth. This time I did run: he had braved agony to make sure he died in time, and I owed it to him not to squander such a gift from a man I hardly knew.

The Plaza Real was only fifteen paces away and a patrol of soldiers stood chatting by the fountain.

4

I could never have visualized the squalid horror of the rest of that night. I wasn't unfamiliar with natural death, which probably had helped to control my panic when it mattered, but murder belongs to a different dimension of feeling altogether. Nor had I ever known the burden of guilt before, the fury provoked by bystanders who view tragedy with indifference.

The soldiers in the plaza whistled and laughed when they saw me, even though my clothes were drenched in blood. They could see I wasn't hurt, and would certainly have taken me behind the nearest wall if the hotel had not been so close.

I was not able even to tell them about Ulate's death.

The reservation clerk stared at me while I gabbled out what had happened. After the first couple of sentences I realized I was speaking English and had to start again. Then he shrugged. 'There are often deaths at night, señorita. One does not interfere.'

I remember behaving very badly, screaming at him and trying to reach the telephone myself, but the switchboard defeated me. One of the guests came to hold me by the arm, a woman with sad eyes who took me to the cloakroom and made me wash the blood off my face and hands. I told her all over again about how Ulate's body was being pillaged only yards away from where those soldiers laughed, and heard my own voice sharpen into hysteria.

She said simply. 'What is it you wish to do?'

'Tell –' Words died in my throat and I stared at her speechlessly.

She nodded. '*Sí, señorita*. That's how it is. There is no one to tell. This Ulate you say was killed by one of his own men – well, a man would not kill his employer unless he was paid more than his wage to do it. Who paid him? The police? The army? A business rival? No one will investigate for fear that if he should discover anything, he too will be killed. My husband and I own a coffee *finca* near Progreso and our eldest son was killed last year by *guerrilleros*. We went to the army, to the police, petitioned El Miragloso himself, but nothing happened. They came and executed some Indians in our village, that's all.'

The basin waste was blocked so the bloodied water would not run away, and I could smell the stink of the gutter on my clothes. 'I must go and change,' I said dully.

'That would be best, señorita. Tomorrow you will be calmer, and understand that it is not wise to become involved with officials.' She came with me to the stairs and then went. She was kind but understood the value of her own advice.

I toiled up those stairs like a crone, dragging on the banister. They led to a galleried passage and several guests were there because – incredibly – it wasn't yet time for the late Spanish dinner. They all turned to stare at my bloodied clothes; by now I was shivering violently.

There was a mutter of sympathy, or perhaps embarrassment, but no one moved. *Keep clear; danger*. That's what my appearance signalled. This woman has been raped or perhaps seen husband or lover killed, she is not rational so for the moment she will forget the rules of survival: see nothing, hear nothing, do not complain.

Trust no one, Ulate had said; which was a slightly more courageous reaction to the same precipice of barbarism.

I plunged past them, their faces and bodies reeling giddily

46

away from me on either side, reached my own door somehow and started wearily for the bed. I ought to . . . but nothing I did mattered any more.

I slumped across the bed, breathing hard.

The door snapped open. 'Where the hell have you been?' demanded Zeller.

I tried to explain, but could not explain again. His eyes narrowed at the sight of me and he came over in two swift strides. 'Where are you hurt?'

'Not me. Ulate. He's dead.' My teeth were chattering too much to speak clearly.

'Yeah? Who the fuck is Ulate? No, let's peel you out of that blood first, and make sure you're okay.'

I stood up like a dummy while he did just that; I felt his hands linger on my breasts and thighs and distantly understood that he wasn't thinking of Ulate, either. I did vomit then and, when the worst was over, realized that I was still stark naked while Zeller watched me with a tight half-smile on his face. The look in his eyes was a caress, his body tense.

'You're beautiful,' he said. 'Christ, am I tired of pork-bellied Latins.'

'I saw a man killed tonight. Three men, if you count his murderers.' Anger was a lifeline, I discovered. I no longer felt ill or confused, just bleakly furious, each thought stacked ready to be thrown. Let him look; I refused to amuse him by scrambling prudishly for a wrapper. Naive delight in Comayagua was no longer imaginable, and I was already changed by the reality I had come to find.

'So why the hell did you go out? You're liable to see people killed in this town if you wander around in the dark. Get killed yourself, too, probably.'

'It wasn't dark when I went out, and I could see the house I wanted from the Plaza Real.' The excuse which was not sufficiently an excuse to allow my guilt to rest.

'It just shows that you can't be too careful.' His eyes moved from my face to my body and he straightened. I could see the thrust of him against thin cloth and plunged instantly

47

to fresh humiliation, because instinctively I moved too, sensation uncoiling even across the abyss which now divided him from me. Violence triggers a great deal more than terror, and in its aftermath comes an overwhelming desire for comfort and release, but I was too ignorant to understand my own reactions. Bewilderment and shame engulfed me, Zeller's figure shimmering in unshed tears.

I turned away from him because I did not want him to see me cry; began sponging myself down, jerkily nervous now, and calculating, too. I knew he was still watching me with that same half-smile on his face, content to wait only because there would be more savour to it if he waited. Certainly Pete Zeller would be more than willing to help burn up my demons of hate and guilt.

As my senses steadied again, I knew at once how utterly unthinkable that was. How grotesquely horrible it would be to join the barbarians so soon, and for no better reason than the hope that sex with a stranger might prove more effective than a sleeping pill.

I did not want my cravings for illusory comfort to sweep me into a shoddy attempt to blot Ulate's death from my memory, and especially not with a man like Zeller.

I jerked at the shower curtain; it came away in a clatter of wicker rings and I wrapped it round me. 'Get out of my room.'

He grinned. 'Sweetheart, that's a goddam ugly drape and I don't think this is the right night for you to sleep alone.'

'I have seen a man killed tonight, and it was partly my fault. I don't intend to celebrate his death in bed with you.' It sounded disgustingly crude, but I felt too shocked and stupid to think of a better way of putting it.

'It would do you the hell of a lot of good,' he said roughly.

'I expect it would.' Agreement slipped out before I could stop it.

'Well, for Christ's sake –'

'You don't give a damn about a killing,' I interrupted, before he could move. 'Or that I'm sick and half-stupefied by what has happened. All that matters is to strip me naked,

48

and look.' On any other night I should have been stiff with fright, naked in my room with Pete Zeller looking.

'And a very nice look it was,' he said softly. 'Although I was also trying to help. Come here, honey.'

'No. Go and have dinner with Colonel Mozon instead, if he's the sort you understand.' A sudden thought struck me. 'I wouldn't be surprised if he'd told Miguel to shoot Ulate tonight.'

As soon as I'd said it, it did indeed seem quite possible. Mozon and Ulate had been disagreeing about something. It had not struck me as particularly odd at the time because I didn't meet Mozon until after they had finished talking. If I'd met him first then I would have known he wasn't the kind of man with whom any prudent Comayaguan openly disagreed.

Zeller seized my wrist. 'You bloody little fool. I don't give a shit about this Ulate, but you go around saying things like that about Mozon and you'll be a stiff in the street, too. Or screaming in the cellars of the *Directorio de Seguridad*.'

'You should know about that.'

'I guess I do,' he said softly. 'Don't be so fucking childish. You're out of your depth in a place like Comayagua, but tomorrow I'm flying to Costa Rica. Now that is a fine country for a few days in the sun. Have you ever seen the Pacific?'

'No.' I allowed my voice to hesitate.

'Then here's your chance. Come with me, Faith. Sure, I understand how you feel tonight – you've never seen blood before. But blood's cheap in Latin America. I've gotten used to it and it's too late to pretend I'm shocked when some guy gets wiped over the cobbles. Costa Rica's quieter than most other countries around here at the moment, you'd enjoy a few days down on the coast.'

'And I suppose you'd just leave me lying in the sun whenever you wanted to do a deal with the secret police,' I said. 'Since Mozon's too busy cleaning up San Bernardo to go chasing after Yanqui agitators for you.'

Zeller's face tightened. 'Yeah, I guess that's about it. After

49

the favours I offered him he'll be looking okay, but I shall be surprised if he finds anything. Comayagua's on the skids and not a place for any American to hole up alone. So I'm on my way in the morning and I'll be real happy to take you along.'

'Perhaps . . . I think . . . I might like that.' I wanted to scream at him, to scratch his face, then lie on the floor and weep. Instead, I hooked my fingers tighter into the curtain. I knew that if I moved, tried to reach my clothes, even looked away, he would have me on the bed and not wait until Costa Rica. And as he had said, if he chose to use the skills which he undoubtedly possessed, then probably I'd enjoy it. Until afterwards.

He looked at me consideringly. 'Okay. I'll have Mozon telephone Progreso in the morning to reserve another seat on the flight. Only the police telephones work around here. You should rate the compliment pretty high, you know. It isn't often I wait twenty-four hours for a woman.'

'Perhaps not every woman you've fancied spent her evening making a mistake that killed a man.' My voice jumped, control crumbling again.

He laughed. 'You'd be surprised! And not all of them were making mistakes, either.' He kissed me carelessly, and was gone.

I don't remember a great deal of what remained of the night, nor would it make anything better if I hauled memory out of oblivion. Tears helped, and exhaustion blurred some of the rest.

Eventually I slept, but very restlessly, and woke as soon as the first rays of the sun struck through the shutters. Awareness returned, bringing with it the petrified shapes of grief and horror, but the decisions about what I must next do were already formed. The only way was forward, and quickly too, before Zeller woke. He would be furious if I stayed long enough for him to discover that I had accepted his invitation only because I was desperate to get him out of my room; he was also quite capable of asking Mozon to deport me with him to Costa Rica. An enforced flight there in

Zeller's company would leave me isolated as well as nearly penniless, an easy victim.

I dressed swiftly, avoiding looking at last night's soiled clothes still tumbled on the floor, strapped my cases and went down to pay the bill. My watch said 5.30 but the streets were already busy, the few hours of cool daylight too precious to waste. There were taxis in the plaza and I had to risk taking one of them, firmly thrusting an echo from Ulate into the back of my mind: trust no one. On this occasion, fortunately, he was proved wrong. I was hurtled to the station in a vehicle which did not stop at a single intersection and looked as if it should have been shovelled into a scrapyard, but at least I arrived.

Once there, it became clear that this was the day my luck changed for the better. The train for Quihuli was due to leave in half an hour. Actually, I discovered it was yesterday's train delayed, but that was just part of my good fortune. Today's train would not leave until after siesta, if it left at all.

By the time the sun was fully up, we were pulling asthmatically out of San Bernardo past *barrios* fluttering with washing. The squalor of such slums was relieved only by the crude colours of the huts, but at last the urban straggle dissolved into wide plain interspersed with the remains of tropic vegetation. It was another brilliant day, puffed clouds stationary in a dramatic blue sky, steam rising from rich earth. Here and there a few Indians sat by the line as if they expected the train to stop, but without showing any change of expression when it gasped slowly past; stoop-shouldered *campesinos* hoed soil under the sun while others squatted on skinny buttocks plaiting straw. It became very hot, and the train went more and more slowly as the gradient steepened; the track was rough, and after several hours we began to cross a series of viaducts. They could not have been maintained since the day they were built and when the carriage leaned over the edge I could see dry rocks a very long distance below. Beyond the viaducts, the train began slowly shunting up a series of cuttings to gain height, and each time

51

we changed direction the points had to be driven open with a sledgehammer.

Most of my fellow passengers were Indian, some dressed in jeans and shirts, a few in traditional knee-length breeches and felt hats. The women were bundled into black and suckled their babies at drooping, underfilled breasts. All of them stared at the landscape with inscrutable, sad eyes; no one spoke and the children did not cry. Every time the train jolted there was a shower of their tattered belongings on the floor; these were meticulously put back where they came from, and fell again when we went over the next rough stretch of line. I had never seen countenances so void of animation.

Except when we were crossing the viaducts, I spent most of the time looking out of the window, my mind slammed shut on the night before. I would never forget Ulate's death, but could not, must not, think of it now. In the night, it had helped a little to realize that if Mozon had ordered his killing, then I had only helped to provide a convenient moment for execution; but that was only supposition, so today I tried to think instead of how I would do my very best for Prodam in Quihuli. I was under no illusion that it would be easy.

The countryside was becoming astonishingly beautiful as we climbed above the plain: mountains shaded to pale mauve against the sky, their lower slopes covered by bright yellow scrub. Close to the railway line the ground was broken by streams and dry ravines, the patches of cultivation small scale and interspersed by alpine-looking meadows. There were some splendid dark cypress trees, and unfamiliar scarlet-podded bushes. Only the humans spoiled the view: a series of bent backs and huddled huts all there was to show for centuries of labour. Occasionally, beside the track we saw troops in armoured carriers. Once, one of the soldiers levelled an automatic rifle at the train in mock hold-up; he pulled the trigger by mistake and sent a stream of bullets over the roof. I looked back and saw his fellows laughing and slapping him on the shoulders; a family of half-bloods in the next carriage shouted indignantly, the Indians stared at their feet and did not move.

On the map Comayagua is roughly triangular in shape, with its narrow apex on the Caribbean, where the country's only port of El Faro is built. San Bernardo is geographically quite close to the centre of the country and between it and El Faro the land is tropical, with bananas and a little coffee as the only products. The single-track railway has one terminus at El Faro and the other at Quihuli, passing through Progreso and San Bernardo on the way. There are virtually no other towns of significance. The wide end of the triangle is entirely taken up by the Picacho Mountains, and comprises nearly half the country; very few people live there and Quihuli is their only market, but though the town seems remote from the Caribbean, it is in fact nearer to El Faro than it is to the more distant mountain valleys. Roads are rudimentary and the railway system dangerously anti-quated. It is steamily hot in El Faro, where it rains eight months of the year; in San Bernardo it is nearly always hot but seldom unendurably so, while Quihuli is often filled by great cold winds gusting off the mountains and is disas-trously short of water.

I did not know any of this at the time and was simply glad when late afternoon brought us to Quihuli and it was cool. I refused the porters clamouring for my trade, and carried my own cases to the station entry; Zeller's advice to hold on to everything all the time was almost certainly valid here as well. Zeller – I'd tried all day not to think of him either, and thrust the shadow of him away again now. He was not the kind of man who accepted even trifling defeats willingly, and I was very much afraid that one day he might find time to come and search me out in Quihuli.

The first thing I noticed from the station steps was white dust everywhere; then streets like goat tracks leading from the single fine plaza of colonnaded Spanish houses. There weren't any taxis and the plaza was full of steel-helmeted soldiers assembling for whatever duties they carried out at night. Those nearest the station immediately began to stare, shoving each other joyously and shouting across at me.

53

A shoeshine boy was squatting on the steps and I sat beside him on my case. 'What's your name?'

'Rodrigo Teodor Cortinez, at your service.' The child was a *ladino*, or mixed blood, and not shy at all. His head went back proudly as he rolled out the syllables of his name.

Gravely, I responded with mine. 'Rodrigo, tell me, if you were me and carried two cases and wanted to pass all those soldiers to reach the Casa Mendoza, how would you do it? Perhaps you'd like to polish my shoes while you think.'

He took out his brushes and at once began cleaning enthusiastically.

'*Sí, señorita.* The soldiers are very bad, you understand.'

I nodded.

'The Mendozas . . . do you really wish to enter their casa?'

'Why shouldn't I?'

'Well,' he said cautiously, spitting on my shoe, 'they are great people. Very great. Unless you matter, it is not wise to disturb them.'

'And you think I might not matter enough to risk it?'

Rodrigo giggled and hid his face, polishing hard. Clearly he did, but was Spanish enough not to want to offend me.

'So we haven't solved my problem,' I said, eyeing the soldiers, who eyed me back. I had a feeling they wouldn't be satisfied with just watching for very much longer.

'I'm considering,' said Rodrigo with dignity. '*If* I was the señorita, and *if* I wanted to visit the Mendozas in their casa, then I would pay me to run there and ask for the jeep to be sent. Then I would go back into the station and keep away from the soldiers in the *oficina del Jefe* until the jeep came.'

I squeezed his shoulder, which felt like bird bones through thin cloth. 'What a marvellous idea, Rodrigo. I will write a note for Señora Mendoza, and give you two thousand pesos if you will run this errand for me.'

He gaped, chin jerked up on his shoulder. 'Two thousand pesos!'

Two thousand pesos were worth about a pound. 'You will be able to buy yourself a good meal.'

'A week of good meals,' he said reverently. 'Give me your writing, señorita.'

And so it worked out. I had planned to go directly to the Calle de Salvacion, where Prodam had its warehouse, but one look at those soldiers changed my mind. Prudence – I was learning it fast in Comayagua. If Calderon had not obtained hospitality for me from the Mendozas then I should not be able to operate in Quihuli, or even to walk its streets in safety.

The Jefe sweated the whole time I sat in his office, and bolted like a jack rabbit when he heard military boots outside. A patrol of six came in, flinging back the door and kicking at the furniture as soon as they entered the room.

Their leader had an armful of stripes but probably was only a corporal. He shouted something I couldn't understand, coming so close I felt spit on my face. Jesus Christ, I thought without blasphemy, and said aloud, 'I'm sorry, I don't understand.'

I had no defences at all against marauding soldiers looking for easy game. No defence and no hope after the shocks of last night, except somehow to hide craven fear. I don't know why it seemed important not to grovel, if grovelling might help. Except that I damned well refused to grovel. But I wanted to look anywhere except in that corporal's face and understood why, over centuries of domination, the Indians have learned to keep their eyes focused on their feet.

All six soldiers gathered around me, staring, while the corporal sat on the edge of the Jefe's desk. 'You have papers?' he asked, and then gabbled something unintelligible about San Bernardo; the peasant accents of Comayagua are tricky even for a native.

'Yes, I've come from San Bernardo with the permission of Colonel Mozon.' I guessed at his meaning and hoped that Mozon's name might frighten him, but he was too ignorant; his own captain was probably the only officer he would recognize.

He slung his submachine gun and snapped his fingers

55

under my nose, shouting, until I handed over my passport. All that decorous blue and gold on the cover looked singularly out of place in the station master's office in Quihuli, and I looked yearningly at the royal arms.

Of course none of the soldiers could read Her Britannic Majesty's Principal Secretary of State's measured request to all whom it concerned to speed me on my journey without let or hindrance, nor would it have made any difference if they could. Each of them in turn fingered the passport admiringly, then the corporal put it in his pocket and grabbed me by the arm, yelling questions I couldn't understand.

I yelled back at him, all the Northumberland imprecations I could rake out of the past. A scene seemed my only chance, or they might rape or beat me up even before they took me away. Besides, if I used all the air in my lungs for swearing at them, I might not have any left for the sheer screeching terror which had me in its grip.

The noise stopped abruptly, so I found myself shouting into silence. A very old man in a panama hat was standing in the doorway, leaning on a cane. 'Good evening, Miss Milburn,' he said in English.

I gulped. 'Good evening.'

'Ah, the English presence of mind. How scrummy to find it still exists.' His manner changed abruptly and he snapped something at the soldiers. They immediately fell over their weapons in an attempt to hide behind the corporal, who sulkily picked up my cases.

'He – he has my passport,' I said shakily.

'Jolly good of you to remember, Miss Milburn.' He had it back for me in a flash and then offered his arm, so I came out of Quihuli station keeping pace with an elderly Edwardian gentleman and exchanging pleasantries in the schoolboy English of seventy years before. I was beginning to reach a state beyond shock, where Comayagua became an insubstantial, illusionist's land, and nothing could surprise me any longer.

5

After that first violent introduction, I discovered there was a great deal I liked about Quihuli. The inhabitants were mostly *ladino*, vivacious and quickwitted, as if once it was adulterated then Indian blood changed its character entirely. The spectacular backdrop of mountains made up for some of the shortcomings of the town, the pace of life was easy, the Casa Mendoza a safe oasis away from the perilous streets.

It was an unusual household. Old Señor Mendoza must have been over eighty but never allowed the fact to interfere with his pleasures: he visited his mistress every day and no one was sure they simply drank wine together. He was El Miragloso's uncle and head of the family, Spanish-style. Señora Mendoza was his widowed sister-in-law, who until her son became dictator had lived in the comparative obscurity of a lesser Mendoza house; now she was suddenly presented with unbelievable opportunities for enrichment and her ambitions sprouted like jungle creepers. Innumerable cousins and nephews came and went, all wearing military uniforms and most of them busily conferring about fraudulent land deals. Señora Mendoza loved it all; she put fresh flowers by her son's portrait every day and sat knitting faster and faster, repeating aloud the enormous sums she heard discussed around her.

I suspected that old Mendoza was not above running a good racket if he saw one, but he did despise uncultured greed. Consequently he sat in the courtyard and read tooled-leather classics most of the day, where he could see who came and make biting comments on their activities. Everyone was terrified of him, partly because he always kept an ivory-handled pistol strapped under his waistcoat. Occasionally, he fired it at an idle servant or an impertinent nephew, the bullet ricocheting off stone an inch from head or leg. His hands shook with age but everyone assured me that so far he'd never done worse than blow some calf muscle off a gardener. Except in duels that is; I gathered that in his youth the male Spanish-speaking population of Comayagua had needed to watch its step very carefully indeed.

Once it was known that I was staying at the Casa Mendoza, I had nothing to fear in the street by day; the casa doors were barred at sundown anyway, when ordinary life vanished from the town. Then the streets belonged to the soldiers, to Indians who fought each other with machetes as soon as they became drunk, to wild dogs, and possibly, guerrillas. No one knew and no one ventured to find out, least of all the soldiers, who spent most of their time on patrol drinking aguadiente and firing occasional volleys into the dark.

The Comayaguan army was quite the most awful force of men it is possible to imagine. They were expensively paid in the hope that they might stay loyal; only intermittently disciplined and lavishly equipped with American automatic weaponry. Consequently, and entirely correctly, they regarded themselves as beyond the reach of such law as existed. They also loved the noise and power of the guns they carried, frequently fired them by mistake and even more frequently on purpose. I was certain they would run from any serious opposition, and so was Señor Mendoza.

'They are jolly poor scum,' he said to me, two or three days after I arrived. 'My nephew is a silly buffer to trust himself to such people and I have told Dolores so.'

'What did Señora Mendoza answer?'

He patted his gun. 'She said I was the silly buffer because El Miragloso always knew best, but we shall see. We shall see, indeed. The dictator before him lasted nine weeks so the boy has done well to stay in the palace behind his guns for six months, but until not so long ago we had one who lasted thirty-five years, so he still has the dickens of a way to go.'

I stared at a bush of Spanish broom blazing by the courtyard gate. 'Was it better in Comayagua when a dictator lasted for thirty-five years?'

'Oh, by Jove, yes, young lady! It was such a spiffing country to live in! No one could stay inside that jolly queer palace for thirty-five years, so a ruler had to be able to do what he enjoyed and go for a promenade when he wanted. My nephew never comes out without so many beezers with guns he can only see the sky.' Señor Mendoza was justifiably proud of his idiomatic grasp of the English language, which he had obtained in a preparatory school in Eastbourne before the First World War. He had never returned to England since, and conversing with him was like flicking through the yellowing pages of Rider Haggard or Beau Geste. I enjoyed talking to him very much.

'Do you think the beezers with guns will take over again one day?'

'Oh, yes,' he said enthusiastically. 'That will show Dolores how I am right. You need not feel cowardy-custard, Miss Milburn. Quihuli watches San Bernardo but does not join their jolly game. My nephew will run away to Switzerland and the soldiers will shout different slogans to make sure they are given a rise in pay, that's all. We Mendozas have lived four hundred years in Quihuli and, crikey, every revolution is the same.'

As I walked its streets though, I couldn't help wondering whether the rules of the revolution game hadn't been changed. The Casa Mendoza was so tranquil that the whole Mendoza clan, including El Miragloso himself, might not have noticed that the age of gentlemanly revolutions had ended. After all, they never had been particularly gentlemanly for the victims and now even the dictator had become

59

a victim, trapped in his palace behind trigger-happy hardware.

Meanwhile, life continued somehow, the sun shone through air like polished steel and pumas hunted in the foothills beyond the town. I ought to have felt alarmed by conditions in Quihuli; instead I was briefly happy. I had reached an utterly different world and found at least temporary security there, the streets so overflowing with life, colour and noise that I began to keep a notebook, where I could jot down and then try to polish descriptions of what I saw, although I was seldom pleased with the result. It was deeply satisfying all the same to sit by lamplight and look up from time to time, hesitating for a word, and at last be able to feel myself an apprentice at a craft in which I desired very much to excel.

Although spinning words on paper is a surprisingly companionable activity, I continued to feel very much alone. The Casa Mendoza was often bustling with visitors, and all the men paid me extravagant compliments, but I remained an onlooker, not yet part of what I saw. My determination to find out what was happening to Prodam's supplies seemed comic to them, my attempts to understand the layered politics of Comayagua unseemly in a woman. Still, I refused to brood; perhaps irrationally, but also very vividly, I felt I owed it to Ulate as well as the poverty-stricken inhabitants of the foothills to succeed in what I had so unwisely undertaken, if I could.

Prodam's warehouse in the Calle de Salvacion had not been difficult to find, but finding it was the least of my worries. The place was swept bare. A great many papers blew about in the draughts, but the padlock was off the gates and the inner doors had been wrenched from their hinges.

I thought about it for a couple of days, then refused an invitation to go hunting in jeeps with a selection of Mendoza cousins, and went back to see if the papers on the floor offered any clue to what had happened. Another consignment of food and fertilizer was due up from the coast soon and I needed to know how best to distribute it and, to put it crudely, which palms I should grease if I was to be allowed to distribute it at all.

'All of them!' said Señor Mendoza happily. 'Take my word for it, Miss Milburn. They will guzzle and swig everything if you miss out a single one.'

I hoped he was wrong, but without much confidence; yet surely Prodam would not have continued to operate in Quihuli unless at least some of their aid went where it was intended to go? I stood on the bare floor of the warehouse and looked about me, wondering where to start. After a morning's work I was no nearer to an answer. I had gathered up every paper and wrapper I could find but learned very little from them. Only some seemed to relate to food and many were not much more than hieroglyphs. All except three were in Spanish, although Calderon's pink file told me that Prodam's aid was mostly British or American in origin.

I smoothed out the exceptions carefully and studied them again. Two were grubby labels off sacks of beans from Wisconsin, the third a list of villages scribbled on the back of an agent's circular advertising a consignment of Second World War souvenirs. Medals, daggers, insignia, SS helmets. Semi-automatic Mausers, featuring detachable stock for easy carry and a thousand rounds each of authentic ammunition. Unrepeatable bargain, historic interest.

'The army came here, señorita,' said a voice from the door.

I jumped, but was relieved to see it was Rodrigo.

'When?'

'When the señor was shot.'

'What señor?'

'The *señor de secorro*. He who was here before.'

My blood chilled. *Secorro* meant aid, but Calderon had told me that my predecessor had returned sick to Mexico City. 'Who shot him? Was he badly hurt?'

'The army, of course, señorita. Naturally, he was killed. A squad with guns does not leave a man any chance. See, I will show you.'

He led me out of the warehouse and round a corner to the

61

back of the building. I stared at a blasted stretch of adobe wall, where the weather was already dissolving the exposed mud filling and completing the work of destruction. Rodrigo silently dug out an expended bullet and handed it to me. 'Until it rained last week you could still see his blood on the earth.'

'Why?' My lips framed the question but no sound came. 'Why did they do it?'

This was execution, no casual murder in the street.

Rodrigo shrugged, his face wiped of expression, suddenly all Indian. 'I do not know, señorita.'

I turned my back on the bullet-riddled wall and crouched to force him to meet my eyes. 'It may help me to stay alive if I know.'

'The Casa Mendoza is safe,' he muttered, bare toe digging in the dirt.

'I am not in the Casa Mendoza. I am here in the Calle de Salvacion, wanting to know what happened. I shall go on looking until I find out, and since I don't know where to look I'm bound to make mistakes. You could help me avoid some of those mistakes, Rodrigo.'

He looked up, his nostrils flaring as if danger were close enough to scent. 'Señorita, no! You must not look.'

'Then tell me what I want to know. No one is listening here.'

He dug furiously with his toe again. 'The *señor de secorro* is dead. There is no need to look, or ask. It is better to sit in the Casa Mendoza and talk to the old one.'

I thought about it, frowning. I had studied Calderon's file very carefully by now, but would have to look at it again and with different eyes. A thought struck me. 'Did the *señor de secorro* know why he died?'

The boy stared at the place where blood had so recently soaked into the earth. 'No, señorita. I do not think he did, so they shot him instead of . . . instead of the other things they do. He was lucky, I think.'

And I could have wept for a child who knew just how lucky a man sometimes was, only to be shot.

I sat that night in the high-raftered guest room of the Casa Mendoza with papers from Calderon's file stacked in approximate categories on the bed in front of me. I realized they had been put together with the intention of misleading anyone who read them, but some basis of truth must remain, if only I could separate it from the rest. Bills of lading; customs documents; lists of goods; a pitiful analysis of Indian diet, clipped together with soil studies for fertilizer programmes. Letters in official Spanish about delayed consignments. Expense slips for my predecessor: his name had been Bill Maynard. A letter from him complaining about the quality of shipped beans, which was cover for a carefully worded accusation of corruption. Apparently more than two thirds of that consignment had disappeared en route.

About four o'clock in the morning, I found what I was looking for.

A customs form originating from the previous March and stamped 'Seguridad del Faro' listed that quarter's total aid shipment as 2070 metric tonnes, comprising fertilizer, beans, dried maize and tools. Maynard had sensibly gone down to El Faro to escort the larger part of it up to Quihuli, and as a consequence lost nothing of value on the way. I stared at his figures for distribution, January to April, thoughtfully. All the food and fertilizer had gone immediately to only three villages: Agosto, Quelicatlan and Coetzal. Probably he was afraid to keep such stocks in Quihuli where theft was commonplace, but if so then he soon changed his mind. In June he had again gone down to El Faro, but then apparently not distributed anything for several weeks after its arrival in Quihuli. When I looked again at the list of villages on the back of the arms advertisement, Agosto, Quelicatlan and Coetzal were the only three scratched out. Three weeks ago Maynard had written to Calderon complaining, among other things, about a break-in:

'Luckily they only reached the tool section, and as I have not yet managed to interest the Indians in shovels and rakes they won't

63

find much of a market for the cases they took. This is only the second time I've had this particular trouble since the army put a guard on the place. The other time was in April, when they made exactly the same mistake of breaking into the tool store. Sometimes I can't help despairing of them, when even in crime the Indians never learn from their mistakes. . . .

He had written that only three weeks ago, and I couldn't believe letters took less than ten days to reach Mexico via Jamaica. I had arrived at Mexico City airport . . . I calculated carefully: nine days ago, I thought. *Heavens, only nine days.* By that time Calderon knew Maynard was dead, and had decided to send me to Quihuli instead. There is another consignment coming through, he had said, and we need someone from Prodam to sign for it.

I shuffled the papers together and stood up, feeling stiff and stale. Outside, the sun was rising over the plain, its rays just touching the mountaintops with fire. I leaned on the stone sill and gazed at pale sky and glowing peaks while gradually light strengthened and the glory of it dimmed. Comayagua was so very beautiful, and yet so sad I wanted to weep for the tragedy of such poverty and waste. I wondered whether Bill Maynard had believed that the little he had achieved here was worth dying for, and whether I should think so if I died too. I was almost certain he had died because of what he wrote in the letter I had found: someone had read it on the way to Calderon, and ordered Maynard executed before the next consignment came.

El Miragloso's army took most of Prodam's food, that was fairly clear. When Maynard prevented them from pilfering it en route, they distributed it to villages from which they had already evicted the Indians. When Maynard discovered this, he crossed them off his list and tried to distribute direct himself. I wasn't sure what had happened to the June consignment but I should have been surprised if the *campesinos* had kept much of it. Western-style tools were different. No one wanted those. Ten metric tonnes checked through El Faro in a year, ten tonnes checked out of the customs warehouse in Quihuli. Yet both times Maynard had gone to El Faro himself, a break-in had subsequently occurred in the Calle de Salvacion and only tools were taken. Maynard might have become so used to incompetent theft that he failed to query the coincidence, but someone else must have noticed what I had noticed, and realized how another organization besides the Comayaguan government was using Prodam for its purposes. Colonel Mozon would run a check on foreign mail and if illegal arms were reaching this area, then he would already have known enough to make the connection: Mauser semi-automatic rifles with detachable stocks were handy weapons for guerrillas in the hills.

Which brought me back to Ulate as well as Mozon, and possibly Calderon as well.

Just how had those Mausers passed the customs at El Faro and Quihuli, and where had they come from? Not from Brad C. Hoelingen of Charleston, SC, whose leaflet I had read, surely. And the people of Quihuli knew that this was where their means to fight back might come from, because someone had burgled the warehouse and even Rodrigo knew too much to talk.

Señor Mendoza would also know that a foreigner had been killed, yet he had never said a word to me. Keep off, stranger. Yet he was the dictator's uncle, patriarchal perhaps, but without a shred of sympathy for the guerrillas. Could . . . yes, of course. He would believe that Maynard had been killed for protesting too vigorously about misuse of Prodam's food.

I turned away from the window and stripped for a cold wash, to try to disperse the muddy feeling left by a sleepless night. Few of the Mendoza family ever appeared before midday, so I drank coffee and ate salty Quihuli tortillas alone, and then went out. Lost in thought, I walked most of the way to the station before I noticed how much quieter the streets were than usual. People went about their business but apprehensively, as if they too had only just realized that today they would have been wise to stay at home. When I

65

reached the main plaza it was completely empty, although usually filled with idling soldiers and their hardware. I stood under the pink-painted colonnade and stared at its emptiness, wondering. I had never seen Quihuli without soldiers before.

An old woman selling peppers and lottery tickets crossed herself. 'They went when the sun rose, señorita. How long a time we have prayed to Our Saviour for the soldiers to go, but now that they have, I am not sure.'

I knew what she meant. It was weird without them, a void which anything might fill. 'Where have they gone?'

She shrugged. 'With great noise and shouting in their jeeps, along the track to Agosto. All of them, except for a few guards left behind.'

Agosto. 'Isn't that one of the villages due for resettlement, whose *campesinos* have been driven off?'

Her eyes slid from mine. 'Men have been fighting over land since the time the earth was weaned.'

She refused to say another word, staring past me with masked eyes when I tried to question her, but once I reached the station the atmosphere seemed quite normal and the Jefe answered my questions with no more than his usual grudging surliness. 'The consignment for Prodam from El Faro? I do not know when it will arrive, señorita.'

'There must be some papers from the customs in El Faro. See, I have found a schedule which says our cargo was freighted on a ship due in last week.' This had come to light during my researches through Calderon's file and I was both suspicious that he had not warned me of it and annoyed with myself for wasting nearly two weeks in Quihuli when perhaps I should have gone down to the coast.

'Goods wait a long time in El Faro,' the Jefe answered gloomily.

'I expect they do, but not those of Prodam.' I had noticed this, initially with some surprise. Dilapidated rolling stock and dilatory customs seemed to function with admirable speed where Prodam's affairs were concerned. I had, of course, ceased to feel surprised as soon as I realized that

66

most of Prodam's goods went direct to El Miragloso's pampered army.

The Jefe muttered something and began flipping through clips of papers. He was ashamed of having left me alone with the soldiers in his office, and but for the fact that I was staying at the Casa Mendoza, he would have thrown me out as an affront to his pride. 'The train has left El Faro.'

'What!'

'Always Prodam's goods come up here on a special freight express. A train which must be ordered and made up from wagons normally kept in the sidings at El Faro. The wagons have been moved and a siding reserved at Progreso.'

It emerged that any train made up of more than four wagons had to wait at Progreso and then again at San Bernardo while the daily down train passed. There were no sidings between San Bernardo and Quihuli: once such a train left the capital it needed a clear line all the way to Quihuli freight yard.

This instructive information took a good deal of extracting, since I was ignorant about the workings of railways and the Jefe extremely reluctant to part with the secrets of his trade. Again, only the influence of the Mendozas tipped the balance in my favour. 'So you always have several hours' warning before this special freight arrives?' I said at last.

'*Naturalmente.* Since it arrives at night I must be on duty many hours earlier.'

'It always arrives at night?'

'*Sí, desde luego.* If the line must be open in both directions for twelve hours, of course it arrives at night.'

'And have you received notification that this particular train has left El Faro?'

'Señorita, the workings of the Ferrocarril Nacional de Comayagua are secret. You will be notified to collect your goods as soon as the *aduaneros* here have carried out their searches.' He stared at me coldly.

I bade him the prolonged farewell which etiquette demanded; I might have need of him again. I would have taken a handsome bet that the Jefe had already received instructions to open the line for a freight *espreso*, quite possibly tonight.

I decided that I needed Señor Mendoza's advice – how marvellous to have someone to whom I could turn for advice – and was about to return across the empty plaza when I remembered how Quihuli sidings ran alongside the road below the station. I did not trust the Jefe, and it was just possible that Prodam's consignment had arrived last night.

There were very few people about any longer, even though it was still early morning, nor were many trucks coming in from the country. Quihuli citizens must be as well attuned to political storms as they were to their mountain weather, and I began to feel very exposed in such emptiness.

There was a corrugated-iron fence topped with barbed wire around the freight yard; I couldn't see in and had to walk farther than I wanted to find somewhere to look over the top. Quihuli soon straggled away into a series of *barrancas*, or refuse-filled ravines, and the railway ran along a fenced ridge almost until it was out of town. A few women sat on their doorsteps and watched me pass; there didn't seem to be any men around at all. I felt that if I had been Comayaguan, I should have been able to tell what was happening from the signs in Quihuli's streets; as it was I could only guess, and also hope that enough time remained for me to return to the safety of the Casa Mendoza as soon as I had discovered whether that freight train had, in fact, arrived.

Once the central streets were left behind, I was soon forced to scramble over rough ground in order to keep close to the railway. A *barranca* sloped away steeply between it and the nearest roadway, the smell overpowering, flies rising in swarms as I passed. I nearly turned back then, but decided to go on to where the rails entered the freight yard, which was usually guarded. I hoped that today those soldiers, too, would have vanished. It was worth a try; from there I should be able to see in an instant whether there were any loaded wagons standing in the sidings.

The silence was uncanny, the sun hot on my face and

nothing except scavenging vultures and a great many rats for company. Haze shimmered where the rails curved away towards the plain: not far to go now. I tried very hard to believe that there wouldn't be any soldiers left in that freight-yard guard post; if there were, they would be nerve-tight in the strangeness of today and might no longer care about my being under the protection of the Mendozas. I could feel the muscles cramping nervously across my back, but there were more *campesino* refugees coming into Quihuli every day as the army scoured them off the land, and unless I could secure Prodam's food before it vanished, then they would starve when the winter came.

'Don't go any farther,' said an American voice, quite close.

I whirled around, sight darkened and blood drumming in my ears. I had shovelled recollection of that terrible night in San Bernardo so far into the corners of my mind that though I continued to worry intermittently about Pete Zeller, I had not realized quite how much I loathed the idea of ever meeting him again until I believed I heard his voice.

As soon as my sight cleared, I saw it wasn't him.

The man standing behind some rusting iron was much more lightly built; narrow hips; brown, slightly thinning hair; a blade-thin face.

'Who are you?' I said.

'Let's leave the introductions until later. Now would you like to get the hell off that bank and join me among the trash?'

I looked distastefully at foul heaps, heaving with flies. 'No, I wouldn't.'

He grinned. 'There isn't too much consumer choice at the moment. If you're wondering whether there are still any military in the watchtower, the answer is yes. Six of them – half-drunk, frightened, and very lonely. They'll just love you.'

I joined him among the trash.

6

We had to work our way quite a long distance back towards the town before we could cross the *barranca* without plunging into filth, and I was soon taking deep careful breaths to keep nausea at bay.

As soon as we regained the track, the American gripped my elbow and forced me to sprint with him to a hut where I had seen a woman knitting as I passed. She was still sitting on the step and did not miss a stitch when we arrived beside her.

'Go inside, will you?' the American said briefly. 'I should be back in about five minutes.'

I hesitated and then went in; apparently he knew what was happening in the freight yard, so the easiest way for me to find out was to ask him when he returned. I was also extremely curious about an unknown Yanqui who had appeared out of nowhere, and who seemed to be intent on something mysterious.

Once inside the hut, I stopped dead. I expected to find it empty and instead it was very crowded. Eight men, I realized after a moment, although there appeared to be more because the space was so cramped. Eight, and a woman serving something out of a pot.

'*Por favor, señores,*' I said awkwardly. '*El Americano—*' It was absurd not even to know his name.

No one moved, all staring at me with hostile eyes. They were Indian, but not the kind who humbly watched their feet.

I tried again. '*Nacsa man ayhuas ma.*' Rodrigo had taught me this Indian phrase of greeting.

One of the men swore and jumped to his feet, the gesture of menace cutting through all uncertainties of language; another answered with apparent courtesy, although I couldn't understand him. Muttering spread as the choice between threat and hospitality gaped in front of them. The hut had no windows and was lit only by a dip sputtering in some kind of animal fat. The waiting bronze faces were touched by red as they looked at me, and judged, and found me undesirable.

Instinctively, I turned to go, but the woman stood in my way. The man sitting closest to the door did not move except to heft a machete from his lap and look from it to me; people who seldom use words rely on other methods of making their meaning clear. I saw then that all the men carried machetes, broad-bladed cutlass-type knives capable of chopping a body apart from shoulder to thigh. The men would not lose dignity by scrambling to stop a woman from leaving, but simply kill me if I tried.

The woman grunted and offered a clay pot of the gruel she was sharing out; it was tepid and sour but I forced a little down somehow. Hospitality offered and accepted brings some protection in any language.

Since there was nowhere else to sit, I sat on the earth floor to wait for the American to return, cursing him for sending me into such a place; I cursed him steadily, fluently, silently, with words I had last flung at soldiers in the Jefe's office. Although no one was actually threatening me, I had become very easily alarmed since I came to Comayagua.

The stale air was almost impossible to breathe. After a while I tried standing, then squatting like the Indians. Each position was worse than the last, and I felt sweat glazing my skin, the silence beginning to numb my brain.

Five minutes, that damned American had said.

I'll wait another five, I thought, then I shall walk out of here, and they can do what they like. I stared at my watch. Two minutes passed. Three. Suddenly, I wanted to hold back the hands because when they reached five I wasn't sure whether I would have the nerve to walk out past those machetes. Yet it must be hours since I had first become anxious that Quihuli's calm might shatter before I could return to the Casa Mendoza, and the tension here meant that I had been right to worry.

There were footsteps outside, and the American came in. He spoke in dialect to the Indians and one of them, the oldest, replied.

'Sorry,' he said, turning to me. 'They aren't at their best with strangers, which includes me. Let's go out in the air.'

I nodded wordlessly, and followed him into the shadows behind the hut; from there we could see a sweep of grassland as far as the mountains, and also anyone approaching.

'I guess I owe you,' he said after a pause. 'So I'll start first. I'm Bruce Shryver, and I've been living for the past twenty months in the Picachero Valley.'

'The Picachero Valley?'

'It's behind the mountains. This is a split range with the valley lying between; it runs two, three hundred miles, walled in by peaks. In Aztec times it supported several thousand people and sent food as far away as Mexico, but only a few Picacho Indians live there nowadays. Usually, that is.'

I told him quickly about myself, although gossip had already given him my name and he was only interested to discover why Prodam had sent a woman to Quihuli. My first impression of Bruce Shryver had been confused, because his voice had sounded like Zeller's; now, his impact was immediate. His skin was burned dark by wind and sun, his face was sharp and fine-boned. Add to that slanting eyebrows; grey eyes, cold and steady; a humorous mouth set tight. A face with which one would be unwise to take chances, full of tension, not at all at ease with itself; a body made up of straight lines and angles. Another contradiction

72

was the odd diffidence in the way he spoke, and eventually I realized that he could not have used English during his stay in the mountains, and since he lived there among a sparse population of Indians, probably had seldom spoken in any language.

'Do you enjoy living in the Picachero Valley?' I asked him curiously: he seemed neither the modern type of hermit, nor to possess the plodding patience of those who would try to change the habits of primitive tribes. His movements were quick and definite, and in spite of living alone in the mountains, he was carefully shaved.

'No, and twenty months is a hell of a time to live anywhere with little more than a view of rock. But I've survived it, and I guess that soon I shall be back to survive some more.' His tone was flat. 'What were you doing along that fence this morning?'

'Looking for Prodam's freight train.'

'Why?'

Somehow, it didn't occur to me to tell him to mind his own business. 'Because I want to check it before the *aduaneros* fiddle the freight sheets. I had thought that most of the pilfering took place on the way up from El Faro, but now I have discovered that nearly all of the food ends up with the army, I'm guessing it goes direct from the customs shed here. So what were you doing, watching that same freight yard?' He must have come down from the mountains especially to watch it too, I realized.

His eyes met mine for an instant before he looked away again. There was a distance in him I did not understand, some fundamental tension so harshly held in check that he was having difficulty in sitting beside me in the dust. He ought to have been delighted to meet anyone he could talk to easily, and instead was impatient to be finished with explanations. 'I'm afraid I want Prodam's supplies too.'

'You can't have them,' I said instantly.

'I intend to take them tonight or tomorrow night.' He came to his feet and stood back, one hand on the adobe wall. 'You should be grateful. This way your organization's food

73

will at least reach the people it is meant to reach, and you perhaps will gain sufficient time to leave Quihuli with your life.'

I stood too. 'A great many refugees will come here this winter to beg for food; they will die if I haven't anything to offer them. I think you had better go back into your mountains, Bruce.'

He smiled faintly, the planes of his face for an instant more softly shaped. 'How will you stop me from taking what I want?'

'The train is already in the sidings?'

He nodded.

'Then it won't be difficult to stop you. I tell the Jefe I have heard rumours that the *campesinos* intend to raid the train, and suggest he puts an extra guard on it. A machine gun on the roof should be enough.' I thought of eight Indians with machetes; a single machine gun ought certainly to be enough.

He was silent for quite a long time, staring out over the dry grass hills.

'Yes, you could stop us,' he said at last.

'I wouldn't have any choice.' I resented the defensiveness of my tone.

He sighed. 'Listen, then. When the army returns, with or without a new master in San Bernardo, your supplies will be transferred to the customs shed and then into military stores. If by some miracle you were able to get them away and delivered to your warehouse, then they would simply impound them there instead.'

'With or without a new master,' I repeated. 'If you know what's going on, then I wish you would tell me.'

'Oh, Christ,' he said violently. 'There's the usual shootout going on in the government. And revolution in the campo, as those who have been turned off their land begin to starve. There are whispers of house-to-house fighting in San Bernardo yesterday. God knows who will win out of the dozens of would-be dictators there. The army will return as soon as they know who their next paymaster is: it's safer for them to wait out uncertainty in Agosto, and be free to toast the winner when it's over. You ought to be anywhere but Quihuli then.'

'Everyone says I'll be safe in the Casa Mendoza, no matter what happens.'

'Do you believe that?'

I shook my head. 'No, not really.'

Only a single-track railway ran out of here, and if Shryver was right, then nowhere in Comayagua was any safer than Quihuli. Also, I had a job to do before I went.

A nerve jumped under his eye. 'Then don't make things worse than they are by trying to cheat the army out of their food.'

'Prodam's food.'

'Their food. They've lived two years off that food. Sure, they reckon it's theirs.'

'And the guns?' I said softly. 'What about the Mausers with detachable stocks which come up here disguised as tools? I would think the army has too many modern weapons to be very interested in those.'

'*What?*'

I enjoyed being the one with information for a change, and explained what I had discovered. 'I thought perhaps you'd come to take them off the train,' I added.

'All those CIA scare stories have one hell of a lot to answer for,' he said absently, his mind elsewhere. Already he was easier with words. 'I've simply been trying to show the Picachos how they might live more richly in their valley, but when El Miragloso swept the *campesinos* off their land, those who didn't fancy military internment came over the mountains and some became guerrillas toting Mausers, among other weapons. I've been wondering where they came from, although I guess Prodam's only half the answer.'

'I saw their agent killed the night I was in San Bernardo, and I'm beginning to wonder whether gun-running was the reason why.'

'Could be. But my immediate problem is that instead of fifty families carrying on subsistence agriculture, our end of

75

the valley now has around two thousand refugees, and most of the men are armed. They mean to go against the government in the spring but they'll kill to survive meanwhile, if they have to. So unless I can get hold of that food of yours, the Picachos will starve this winter.'

'But even if you managed to take it, guerrillas with guns will steal it off you.'

'Perhaps. But, like you, I think most of that shipment is still in those wagons, which means there might be enough to see us all through until the next crop, when you add in what we already grow. One thing is for sure, we'll have something to bargain with. Yono – he's the guerrilla leader – is quite sharp enough to understand that wiping out the mountain Indians isn't a good way to start a *campesino* revolution. But he's a realist, too. If he has to choose, he'll save his strongest men and let the rest die.'

'All right,' I said slowly. 'I suppose I wouldn't have had the courage to run to the Jefe asking for machine guns anyway.'

Laughter lines I had not noticed before deepened around his eyes and then were gone again. 'I'll take you back to the Casa Mendoza now.'

We avoided the centre of the town and instead circled behind uneven huddles of houses. There was a great deal Bruce Shryver had not told me: from his account he lived harmlessly among the Picachos yet apparently he did not want to be seen by anyone in authority; nor had I heard anyone speak of an American in the mountains, although Quihuli was a place which lived on gossip.

'I'll go alone from here,' I said when we reached the alley behind the Casa Mendoza. The town was still dead, dust blowing in the side streets, nothing else moving at all.

Bruce stood staring down the shadowed length of passage which ran along one side of the defensively tall casa wall. 'Mendoza owns a smaller casa in the campo. Tell him . . . beg the old man to go there at once, before the army returns. You would at least be out of sight while the winners get drunk.'

76

I nodded, but did not think that Señor Mendoza took the Comayaguan army seriously enough to allow it to disturb his habits. 'I'll try. Good luck with Prodam's food.'

And only then did it hit me. I had given away my justification for being in Quihuli, though perhaps I merely acknowledged something I must have known ever since I came to Comayagua: how it was no more than dangerous fantasy to believe that an inexperienced woman could achieve anything worthwhile in such a corrupt and violent place. I felt no relief now I had faced this at last, no despair or disappointment. Only compassion for a people who needed help so desperately, and whom I no longer knew how to help. My own concerns were quite simply irrelevant beside such a great and incurable need as theirs.

I sensed Bruce watching me, as if he wanted to say something more. If so, he changed his mind and went without once looking back, the economical sharpness of his movements as recognizable as his features.

The timber gates of the casa were closed and barred, but after a shouted exchange a wicket was unlocked for me; when I clambered through I came face to face with Señor Mendoza's pistol.

'Ah,' he said, lowering it regretfully. 'By Jiminy, Miss Milburn, I was worried about you. On the day a revolution happens it is always best to stay at home, but you had vanished before I understood today was another of those times. You are all tickety-boo, though?'

I assured him that I was, and then asked what he thought would happen next.

He tapped his cane thoughtfully on the courtyard flags. 'There is no need to worry. Those blue funkers in uniform will stay in Agosto until everything is over, then they will come back firing their guns as if they had stormed the palace themselves. Afterwards they will drink too much aguadiente, and tomorrow they will be stinkers with sore heads. We keep the casa gates locked until the day after, I think.'

'Might it not be wiser to stay in the country for a few days?

77

Just until things have blown over.' He was so unperturbed that I felt shamefaced suggesting it.

'Oh, certainly not! Now I am too old to leave Quihuli, revolutions are just the ticket for passing some time.' He rubbed his hands in anticipation.

'Is there any news from your nephew – from El Miragloso?'

'The wireless is phut. He has scampered away or he is dead.' Señor Mendoza smiled a papery, valedictory smile. 'He was tired of that palace, I expect. Dolores is weeping, but I tell her another of her boys may try next year.'

The wheeze of his laughter followed me when I went to bathe and change; he had not commented on the *barranca* stink I brought with me, but I couldn't think properly until I was rid of it.

The shutters in my room were closed and a heavy bar had been placed across them; revolution drill seemed well rehearsed in the Casa Mendoza. I lay in the galvanized tub a long time, thinking over the events of the day. Although some questions were answered, a great many others had taken their place. Bruce Shryver had certainly told me as little as he thought he could get away with, and was himself an enigma; nor could I imagine how he proposed to break into the freight yard and then disappear into nearly trackless mountains with several tons of stores without being caught.

Even after a single meeting, I couldn't believe that I should never know any more of him than fleeting acquaintance. The impression he made was too great, the resilient spring of his personality too immediate, the contrast between obvious competence and inner reservations too intriguing for me not to lie there speculating on my chances of seeing him again. And, like Bruce with his Picachos, I, too, was stranded in a backwater, with not much more than a view of rock.

My thoughts switched abruptly. My most urgent concern was not Bruce Shryver, but what would happen when the army returned to Quihuli. Apprehension grew as the water cooled about me.

When I reluctantly left the tub, for the first time I ignored Calderon's advice and dressed in jeans and shirt, instinct whispering that swift uncluttered movement might soon be more important than appearance. I looked almost unfamiliar when I caught a glimpse of myself in the old-fashioned pier glass propped in a corner of the room. I paused a moment and stared, considering how much I had changed during the weeks since I had left home. My hair had lightened in colour from brown-gold to gold-brown, and glinted as if with trapped warmth from the Comayaguan sun; my skin was softly tanned. These physical changes were nothing though, even if the Mendoza cousins were now used to my English colouring and had become embarrassingly fulsome with their compliments. The real changes lay elsewhere.

I shrugged and turned away: there was something lost, although I could not place it at a glance. Then I remembered how Willy Charlton, with the devastating candour found only in childhood friends, had once said that, whatever compliments were paid to me, I was not beautiful. I agreed with him as it happened, but was annoyed at the time to hear him say it. Now, I knew what he meant.

It isn't looks, he had said, although I love those too. It's how you are.

And now I was different. Horror and suffering and fear had made me wary, and too often also made a light heart seem contemptible. My mouth no longer curved into laughter, and I tried to keep my expression guarded. It would, perhaps, become easier with time, if life in Comayagua continued in its present pattern.

I knelt to lace lightweight boots which I nearly had not brought from England, expecting sophistication in Mexico City. Señor Mendoza was about to be saddened by signs of imminent English funk.

7

Nothing much happened for the rest of the time daylight lasted. Quihuli slumbered as if through a lengthened siesta, doors tightly barred and only a few dogs on the streets, sunning themselves in traffic-free silence. Towards sundown people began to venture out, in search of aguadiente or to hawk from door to door those foodstuffs which, if left unsold, would be rotten by tomorrow. I could hear motor scooters in the back streets and a truck of chickens came in from the campo.

I began to feel remarkably foolish when Señora Mendoza covered her eyes each time she glimpsed my trousers, and the old señor drowsed peacefully in the courtyard.

Everything changed as darkness fell.

Without warning a heavy automatic rattle of shots streaked over the roof, followed by a hollow clatter not too far away where tiles must have been blown into the street. I leaped off my bed where I had been trying to concentrate on reading Spanish, and went to peer through a split in the shutter. A few children stood in the street, and they shouted gleefully as orange flashes lit the sky, then scuttled for cover as deeper thudding followed. Nothing heavier than bullets landed on the town so far as I could tell; presumably the gunners were only firing to overawe the population. If so, they certainly succeeded. Quite soon I was able to hear engines revving, followed by shouts; impossible to tell whether they were commands or simply signified exhilaration.

Within minutes the street below my window was filled with trucks and jeeps, swerving and hooting at each other, while soldiers standing in the back laughed and waved their weapons in the air. Noise boomed across narrow stone spaces, headlights slashed walls and cobbles, two personnel carriers locked tracks and crunched a truck. Then the column vanished, the street deserted again except for a single figure lying on the cobbles where he had been thrown off a truck and run over in the mêlée.

I grabbed up a few things, crammed them in a bag, and ran downstairs. Everyone gathered in the courtyard: three Mendoza cousins wearing civilian clothes for the first time since I'd met them; some servants either weeping or wide-eyed with excitement; Señor Mendoza checking the magazine of his pistol; and the señora praying at a little shrine behind the retama bush.

'Ah, news, Miss Milburn,' Señor Mendoza greeted me. 'The wireless says a Colonel Mozon is our new master in San Bernardo. He promises a great many things if we are good, and bullets if we are not. I told you all revolutions are the same.'

I glanced at the señora. 'And El Miragloso?'

'I think that for him it may be *el ley de fuga*.' For the first time he looked uncertain, nor could Edwardian English provide any substitute for the deadly modern phrase: shot while attempting to escape.

Colonel Mozon. I shivered, remembering his soft-fleshed face and emotionless eyes; this time a killer inhabited the gingerbread palace of San Bernardo.

We all heard the snarl of more engines coming, tearing past like devils, one stopping with a screech outside the casa gates. Blows resounded on the gate and bells jangled madly as someone swung his whole weight on the chain. 'Open the gate! Traitors and spawn of traitors!'

'*Ayudamé!*' gasped the señora. 'In the name of God, what are we to do?'

81

One of the servants moved hesitantly towards the unlocking handle, but leaped back with a squeal when a bullet smacked into stone by his hand. 'Who gave you an order to move?' demanded Señor Mendoza. 'Stay away from the gate, all of you.'

The Casa Mendoza had been built to keep out mobs with machetes, not high-velocity bullets. Without bothering to demand entry a second time, the troops outside sent a volley straight through the six-inch timbers and then drove at the weakened gate. It collapsed with a crash, leaving the truck wedged in the entry.

It was all so quick. The change from speculation about what might be happening to the imminent peril of death was so stunning that we all stared at the intrusive radiator of that truck as if what we saw was only mildly interesting.

These were heartbeats stolen from time while the soldiers scrambled past the obstruction. Señor Mendoza shifted slightly in his chair, but only to cross one knee higher over the other to provide support for his pistol wrist. 'Go out through the *comedor* window,' he said crisply. 'You have a better chance in the street than here. Lie up in daylight and go with God at night.'

He had taken less than thirty seconds to bundle seventy years of political experience aside and grasp that nowadays revolutions did not hesitate to kill the families of deposed dictators.

But violence had exploded too quickly for the rest of us. Caught between flight and protest, we continued to stand as if paralysed while the first soldier climbed past the truck and yelled at us, levelling his rifle.

Señor Mendoza's shot spilled him sideways, his expression ludicrously surprised. Two more soldiers squeezed through the archway, their teeth clenched in a mad killing grimace which I had never seen before, but which was to become horribly familiar. One of them fired at once, spraying bullets all over the place in a blast of sound; the other may have been stupider or simply crazed with excitement, but he came at us holding his weapon above his head like a club. Señor Mendoza dropped them both with single shots; he himself utterly relaxed in his chair, a smile of enjoyment on his lips. He was genuinely happy to die as a true *caballero* should, killing his enemies, the infirmity of age forgotten.

They took no more chances with him then. Several soldiers opened fire out of the darkness beyond the archway, blasting him to shreds against the wall, exploding his chair, hurtling chippings of stone all over the place.

I had been standing where the stairs curved down to the courtyard, so was protected when bullets flailed across its bushes and gravel squares; I was also the width of that killing ground from the dining room, which Señor Mendoza recommended as an escape route. One of the Mendoza cousins was kneeling to fire back before he too was killed, everyone else had already vanished: servants, Señora Mendoza, the other cousins, all disappeared into rambling kitchen and dining-room passages. I never discovered whether any of them survived, although I understood why the dining room offered the likeliest escape: the drop from there was directly into loose masonry stacked behind the church.

But escape through *comedor* and church was barred to me. It didn't seem to matter where I ran, so long as it was away from that blood-stained courtyard, and it was instinct alone which took me through polished parquet salons, down a stone-flagged passage and into Señor Mendoza's study. There was no way out of this part of the casa, except from this study by private stairs to the master bedroom, which would delay capture for only a matter of minutes. I lost vital seconds while I fumbled with the shutters in the study; when I had them open at last, I discovered that the drop to the street must be twenty feet and the tiny square outside was full of soldiers. Several were carrying makeshift flags flaunting Mozon's name, and all were eddying around shouting slogans and close to hysteria. The sight of a victim would send them wild.

I was shaking and shivering violently, my heart thundering in my ears; the desire to curl up behind the nearest chair and believe that no one would see me was almost overwhelming. The kind of self-reliance taught by the Northumberland hills offered no conditioning for this at all.

The sound of voices and splintering furniture in the flagged passage just behind me made me dive for the stair which led directly to Señor Mendoza's dressing room. And up again from there, bolting mindlessly now, because I could already hear more noise, this time of men looting the bedrooms. When I reached the top landing I expected to find servants' rooms, but they must have slept nearer the kitchen. As soon as the edge of panic cleared, I discovered that I was in a large attic full of junk. It was very dark except for moonlight showing through chinks in the tiles, and I made a fearful noise falling over things I couldn't see. If the soldiers downstairs stopped smashing furniture for long enough to listen, they could fire straight through the ceiling to where I was.

I simply had to stop and force myself under some kind of control before it was too late. I stood with one hand on massive timbers above my head, and almost at once perceived that my only chance was to break out through the roof, because soon the soldiers would come here, too. And once I had forced my body through the tiles, I must climb along the ridge until I was above the place where Bruce had left me that afternoon: from there I might be able to slither down to the guttering, and then reach the top of the adobe wall which edged the alley. It was horrifyingly risky of course, but there was nothing else I could do. Peasant soldiers would never resist the temptation to poke into every corner of the Casa Mendoza.

Moving very cautiously, I went over to a ragged line of pale sky where some tiles had slipped. The trouble was, I had to work so fast. Given time, I could have taken out enough tiles to enable me to wriggle through without making much sound – they were only curled over each other, with one in every dozen or so roughly pegged to wafer-thin battens. But I didn't dare take long about it, and working perched as high as I could reach among the rafters made everything more difficult. I kept thinking of Señor Mendoza, turned into splintered bone while I watched. But I knew I could not afford to exercise undue caution, and tore recklessly at the tiles. The wind on my face became something I desired more than life itself.

I suppose it took only minutes to clear a hole large enough to climb through, although it seemed a great deal longer, and before I hauled myself up I groped around until I found some ancient cloth. Once I was through, I turned and stuffed it into the hole in the tiles: in daylight it would show up at once, but until then might prevent moonlight from signalling to the searchers that a fugitive had taken this way of escape.

I found I was straddling the roof ridge on the far side of the courtyard from where I wanted to go. It was the kind of ill luck which is only to be expected on such a night, but a calamity all the same. Fortunately, only two oil lamps were still burning in the courtyard, and no one was bothering with the bloody wreckage there. A guard would be posted somewhere, though, standing under cover in the entry perhaps. If a single tile slid into that emptiness it would betray me instantly. Also, anyone glancing out of a window while they searched the casa would see me against the sky.

The longer I thought about it the worse it seemed, so very slowly I began to move, edging my hands along the ridge while I sat astride it, a leg trailing on either side. The tiles were old and no matter how careful I was, powdery chippings spilled away down the slope each time I moved; even grit could rouse a sentry's suspicions if he was alert enough. And after savage killing those soldiers would be strung up and wide awake.

Each shift of weight needed care, each curled tile meant danger, but I had nearly reached the first corner of the roof before I heard voices in the courtyard below. I froze, then realized what a splendid target I must make against a rising moon and lay nearly flat along the ridge, balance kept by knees and fingers alone. An officer wearing Seguridad green

85

instead of army fatigues strolled into sight, accompanied by a soldier. They stood looking at Señor Mendoza's body, talking and laughing together before going across to where the cousin lay. The soldier bent down and fumbled messily for a while, trying to find papers or valuables I supposed, and prove death, but after a time they gave up, cheerfully unconcerned, and disappeared inside the casa. This had been no casual killing but ordered from San Bernardo, where the authorities expected evidence that orders had been carried out. Comayagua might be more efficiently governed while Colonel Mozon lasted, but then efficiency isn't everything.

Two more security police tramped across the courtyard and disappeared into the house; it was alarming to know that the Seguridad, too, intended to search the building. As if in answer to my thoughts, the noise drifting out of the windows immediately diminished and my best protection was gone; the Seguridad despised mere troops and would stop them from looting, even though later they would steal for themselves.

I lay with my face pressed against the tiles and felt waves of fright wash over me. It was infinitely more difficult to start moving again once I had stopped. Then I became angry, angry at the way those men had laughed at carnage, angry with myself because I had not been able to do anything except stand gaping when crisis came, and now lay wasting time. Anger is a valuable antidote to fear, but it needs watching or it precipitates disaster.

I went on again but too quickly, and a tile slid from under my thigh. I gripped it frantically with my leg, stopped it, felt it tilt and slide again. I had to lean over and grab it with both hands, only the muscles of my other leg stopping me from falling. When I had it secure I didn't know what to do with a piece of curved clay twenty-four inches square. I wriggled awkwardly past the gap where it had come from, still holding it in both hands. Then I had to turn and bend down far enough to wedge it back, point down between battens in the gap.

By the time I had finished, every muscle in my body was burning. The last section of roof stretched ahead like a snowfield in bright moonlight, no cover, and twenty yards long. The first I would know of discovery would be a bullet smashing me into the street, and suddenly I couldn't worry about it any more. Moving automatically now, I reached out and took fresh hold on that infernal roof. Weight on my hands, shuffle forward, feel for loose tiles, weight on my hands. . . . Don't hurry. Don't hurry when you're nearly there. I heard myself whispering the words aloud, and then I was there, straddling the angle of ridge above the alley. Sloping roof swooped away below me, and beyond it was a clear drop to the adobe wall. A very long clear drop, with nothing to stop me when I reached the guttering.

Yet the rest of my life lay there, down beyond that perilous stretch of roof and leg-breaking fall into darkness. I couldn't give up now.

I leaned over as far as I could, feeling for loose tiles. When I found one I had to push it up and then lift, so it disengaged from the batten and left a handhold below. Then I must leave what now seemed the safety of my ridge and slither down, holding the exposed batten with cut and bleeding fingers.

And that was as far as I could go by stealth.

My next move would make a great deal of noise, and so I must move fast. I hesitated, my arms trembling with strain; I wasn't sure whether I could move fast any longer, nor where I would go if I managed to reach the alley below in safety.

I braced myself to kick my next foothold straight through brittle tiles; if there was any other way to climb down the slope, I couldn't see it.

Then I heard a whisper of movement below, saw a shadow move against the adobe wall I wanted so much to reach.

'Faith? Hold there a couple of minutes and I'll take your weight.' It was Bruce.

'Hurry,' I said stupidly. I felt dizzy, and had been telling myself not to hurry for what seemed a very long time. 'I don't think I can hold on much longer.'

'Keep it quiet, okay? Two minutes, like I said.'

Dimly, I heard more definite noises from below, then felt hands on my ankles. 'Let go, but gently. Slip down as slow as you can.' The relief of it came not a moment too soon.

I slid, and felt my feet guided into some kind of rest. I suppose I partly blacked out, though I retained enough sense to keep my weight stretched across the edge of the roof while deep sweet breaths unknotted my muscles.

Soon, I roused sufficiently to follow his voice, to realize my weight was on his shoulders and we were both perilously spreadeagled across wall, guttering and roof, but because I was no longer alone the last part seemed oddly easy. The ground swung up in my face when I reached it, then away and almost out of reach as Bruce forced me into moving, to run and crouch and walk beside him; to hide while a squad of soldiers crunched past. None of it was real any more. All around us church bells were clanging as Quihuli citizens decided they ought to show enthusiasm for the change of power, and yellow light reflected off the sky where a thatched roof burned. Children were scampering dangerously in the shadows, daring each other to watch the fun. We were forced to hide more often, to dodge another patrol and then climb several walls.

'Not much farther now,' Bruce said quietly.

I nodded, words stuck in my throat, feet dragging in the dust. I had been sweating and now was clammily cold, the strong night wind in my face an enemy to be fought. All that mattered was to place one foot in front of the other, one foot in front of the other.

I did not notice when we broke out of the town at last, only grasped that it had become darker and the ground rougher underfoot. Then Bruce said something and pulled me down behind some bushes: I had come alive from the butcher's shambles in the Casa Mendoza.

Unfortunately, as soon as the edge of my exhaustion dulled, it was the shambles which came back to haunt me. I had refused to think about Ulate after that first night passed, but my senses baulked at discarding two such murders without a struggle. And I was too tired to struggle any longer, also bitterly cold.

'Would you sooner go on slowly?' Bruce asked. 'I thought you ought to rest for a while, but –'

'I can't rest,' I said, and heard the shudder in my voice. The trouble was, I didn't think I could go much farther, either. How feeble I must have seemed when all I'd done was scramble across a roof.

'Let's go on, then. Slowly, and tell me when you want to stop.'

I felt absurdly resentful because he remained no more than a voice in darkness, a shape which seldom touched me. Soon, I was fairly simmering with rage, because what I really needed was some sense of humanity, of warmth to set death in its place; rage stiffened me and I felt better. Strange, but better. 'Where are we going?' I asked him next time we hesitated for direction in the dark.

'Back to pick up the Indians you saw in the hut this morning. Then drive out to hide in the campo during the day.'

'Drive?'

'We've just stolen four trucks to carry Prodam's food. I hope that the Comayaguan army may take a few days to sober up sufficiently to count the vehicles in its park and then realize what's missing.'

'Since you Americans gave a pack of louts so much hardware to play around with, perhaps they may,' I said acidly.

'Sure, the lucky old US taxpayer again. Wait here, will you? I'll go back and pick up the Picachos, while you stay hidden until we come. Two flashes of the lamps bring you out of the ditch, but nothing else. If we don't come by dawn, then you are on your own again.'

Flat, insistent voice, no softness in him. No hesitation though, and somehow his vitality fed a precarious energy back into my system.

When he had gone I sat and looked at darkness which might have been the edge of the world. The moon and stars had vanished, and on the wind came the loneliest sound anyone can hear, the faraway wail of a coyote mourning what was lost and gone.

The double flash of light and roar of engines was enormously welcome when they came. The trucks looked colossal in the dark, and when I scrambled into the first, the cab was full of grinning Indians, very far from inexpressive now.

'They're big,' I said, having had difficulty in climbing up.

Bruce translated my comment to the Indians, who rolled around laughing and punching each other in the ribs.

'When you have spent the past four hundred and fifty years being robbed, then you feel pretty good on the night the balance shifts,' observed Bruce. 'They haven't only stolen four trucks, but taken a sliver of revenge for Montezuma.'

I warmed to Indians drunk on delight that they were victors once again. 'Who is driving the other three?'

He laughed, relaxed for once. 'Three goddam maniacs. Two did a spell in the army and the third once drove a vegetable truck. Which is why I'm going first.'

I saw what he meant. He kept in gear all the way, and drove at something under fifteen miles an hour, while the Indians behind him nearly went beserk with frustration, wanting to race each other down the corrugated track in trucks twice the size of anything they had ever driven. We didn't go very far either, under five miles, I guessed. Then we turned off down a dry river bed, and pulled up.

I had been right about the jeans, I reflected wrily, climbing down from the high cab. 'What now?'

Bruce stretched, watching the sky where dawn was not now far away. 'We lie up here for today, and providing the Prodam freight stays loaded in those wagons and the San Bernardo passenger locomotive comes up in the evening, then we help ourselves to what we want tomorrow night. I hope.'

Some of the Picachos were cutting greenery with their machetes and piling it on the trucks, others walked back

90

flicking branches over the dust so no one might think it odd that tyre tracks came down here. I was certain this was Bruce's organization, but he left authority to the same old man he had spoken to in the hut. This was something for the Picachos to savour, without remembering that a gringo had set it up.

'How did you come to be in that alley just when I needed help?' I asked eventually. If Bruce didn't intend to tell me how he planned to lift four truckloads of freight from under the noses of the Comayaguan army, then there was no point asking.

'We took the trucks out of the compound quite easily, while everyone was firing at the sky. Then I didn't fancy what I saw of the town, so once we were out I came back to take a look at the Casa Mendoza.'

'And?'

'And what?'

'Did you plan to come in shooting from the hip?' I ought to thank him, and instead remembered only how terrified and alone I had felt. I was being bitchily unreasonable and was unable to help myself, when I wanted comfort and was infuriated by detachment.

He looked away, the flare of cheekbone all I could see. 'No.'

'I'm glad to hear it,' I said, goaded afresh. So he would have walked away again, would he, if he hadn't happened to see me stuck to the roof? 'Of course, I'm just a damned nuisance, and the Picachos wouldn't get far in this enterprise without you, so naturally you were right.'

He swung round, eyes narrowed. 'Has it never occurred to you that it's our goddam busyness the rest of the world can't abide? How it's only Westerners who insist on doing something all the time, refuse to accept that life and death are part of the same, so bust a gut trying to grab the one and avoid the other so long as they can? The Picachos are enjoying themselves tonight, but tomorrow they would be just as happy if they had to make a bonfire of the trucks and forget about food. So long as all Quihuli could see, and

91

marvel at what they had done. Dying of starvation wouldn't matter to them then, because they would have shown their world how splendidly stolen trucks burned. It is only us who think death matters so damned much.'

And he left me abruptly, striding so fast down the dry *arroyo* that only instinct stopped him from falling.

I stared after him, utterly astonished and attempting to work out exactly what he had been trying to say. And had he really seen me on the roof by chance, or had he been searching carefully and at considerable risk, to find me? At least Zeller's passions had been straightforward. He would have seized this time when I was almost overwhelmed by shock and horror to offer the refuge my many frailties craved, the refuge of someone stronger than myself.

Although I sensed from the first that there was something unexpected in Bruce Shryver, it was his magnetism I remembered. His drive and certainty too, which made me more than just relieved to find him waiting for me in the alley below the casa roof. Now, I was not sure about him; nor which of us might in the end prove to be the stronger.

8

It was full daylight before Bruce came to look for me again, and three or four hours must have passed. I had lost my watch during the night, and so began a long period of guessing at the time.

I had found a pleasant spot to rest where the *arroyo* curled between some trees before tumbling white stones down the side of a miniature valley. In winter a good deal of water must come this way but at the moment everything was paper dry, and I could see as far as the curve of railway line across the landscape, black stains marking where sparks had ignited the grass. I had slept for a while, but uneasily; dreams drizzled blood across my consciousness and hunger griped at my stomach. I supposed the Picachos must have fed, but if so then no one came to offer me a share.

The sun was hot, and I lay thinking that tortillas for breakfast yesterday morning was the last thing I had eaten.

It was then I heard footsteps on shale and recognized them as Bruce's; none of the Indians walked like that.

He sat hugging his knees, a good four yards between us. 'I'm going back to Quihuli now.'

I blinked. 'Why?'

'You came up from San Bernardo by the railroad?'

I nodded.

'What happened exactly when you reached Quihuli? To

the locomotive, I mean.' I could only see the outline of cheekbone and jaw against the dazzle of sun as he studied a stone held in his hands.

I thought back carefully. 'I wasn't really – yes, I remember. I sat in the Jefe's office while I waited for the Mendoza jeep, and everyone was very busy with sledge-hammers on the points. They uncoupled the engine and shunted it up the other end of the train ready for the next day's run down to San Bernardo.'

'Yes, that's what I've heard and it makes everything a great deal easier. There wasn't a passenger train up yesterday because of the fighting in San Bernardo, but today should be okay. We mean to stoke up the boiler fire again before it dies and use that locomotive to pull the freight trucks out of the yard and up past the end of this valley. There's flat ploughland alongside the railroad there and we can unload directly into the trucks. Be up in the mountains by dawn.'

I laughed involuntarily. 'I've never heard anything quite so brazen in my life. Do you think it will work?'

He grinned, taken by surprise. 'Do you?'

I remembered the disorganization of Quihuli station. 'As a plan it has more holes than an old lag's alibi, but yes, just possibly it might. If you can get past the watchtower in the freight yard.'

'That is the flashpoint,' he admitted. 'But if we're quick and shunt around quite normally I hope they may be too thick-witted to react in time.'

'But the Jefe – the moment he hears steam on that engine he's going to come running.

'Yeah. How long do you reckon for a fat Jefe to run five hundred yards from his office to the sharp end of the freight yard?'

I thought of the Jefe's tallowed bulk. 'Three or four minutes unless he has a fit on the way.'

'So we just have to be quick, that's all.'

'Bruce – '

'No,' he said quickly. 'You're staying here.'

94

'But don't you think – '

He stood up. 'No, I goddam don't. And once we've gotten those stores into the mountains I'll think how to get you back to Mexico.'

I came much more slowly to my feet. I was stiff and hungrier than ever. 'Have you anything to eat?'

Without answering, he climbed to where the Indians were sleeping and came back with a plate-sized tortilla rolled round cold maize gruel. 'I'm afraid they've eaten the rest. We've been hiding down here three days longer than we planned because of the coup in San Bernardo.'

I took it, thinking of Fitzroy Square. I would have eaten even those samples now. 'It's yours, isn't it? The Indians wouldn't have left just one unless it was someone's share, and I doubt whether an unwanted woman counts. So thank you, but we'll split it.' I tore half off the leathery mess and gave the rest back to him; he was already skeletally thin and had enough risks to run without being distracted by a cramped stomach. Until you've experienced it, you don't realize how crippling real hunger is; I'd never believed those clichés about tongues hanging out at the sight of food, but mine literally was. And over maize mush, too.

It wasn't much, but that tortilla made an enormous difference. I licked my fingers greedily when I'd finished, and looked up to find Bruce watching me, the trace of a smile on his face. 'Is this Northumberland place of yours full of women as obstinate as you?'

Stupidly, I felt myself blushing. 'At least you've looked close enough so you might recognize me next time around.'

The smile vanished but he did not look away. 'Faith, I'm going to tell you just this once. Stay out of my way.'

I watched him go, not immediately to Quihuli but back to the drowsing Indians, where he squatted beside their leader, talking earnestly. This must be a hellishly difficult operation to plan with only eight Indians to help, none of whom would have the slightest comprehension of split-second timing.

Bruce chose three men to accompany him; one bandy-legged from malnutrition, the other two very young and grinning with pride at being chosen. They fingered their machetes and threw out their chests until those who were staying behind began to scowl and mutter.

I waited tactfully out of earshot, but when Bruce came over to pack up some tools he'd found in one of the trucks, I asked him why he took the two youngest, when the resentment of their elders was so obvious. The boys looked brave, but so inexperienced I couldn't imagine them being of much use.

'I haven't any choice. Out of those who offered to come here with me, these eight alone have had some experience of life beyond their valley, so won't gape at a locomotive as if it is a god. Only three have ever driven a truck, so they must stay here, and also Atuli, their leader who takes charge of them. Which leaves four remaining, and the one I left out is the brightest. I've been giving him a dry run in the cab and he's willing to try driving the fourth truck down to the railroad as soon as they see the train go by.' He nodded to where we could see the railway. 'If we get those boxcars, we won't have long to transfer loads. They need to be down there with the trucks as soon as we get the doors open.'

It was on the tip of my tongue to tell him about the farm machinery I had driven at home; I was certain I could drive an army truck a few hundred yards down a track in low gear. But then I had a better idea. 'You do have a different kind of choice, though, don't you? You turned me down when you ought to have leaped at the chance of help from anyone who wouldn't think a steam engine might be a god. Particularly when I know the layout of Quihuli station and don't need to be shown how points work with bits of twig.' He'd been rehearsing the Indians, but for men who knew next to nothing about machinery, anything technical was bewildering.

'No,' he repeated.

I lifted my eyebrows. 'Tell me, do you have the slightest hope of success? Or is this whole enterprise not much more than a deathwish? Perhaps, like Señor Mendoza, you prefer to go out fighting.'

I intended to disconcert him, but for a moment he looked as if I had kicked him in the stomach. 'You gave the answer earlier, when you said it could work,' he answered after a pause.

'I still think it could, but not if some crazy kind of chivalry prevents you from accepting assistance you badly need. And talking of chivalry, I don't think I should care to be left alone among your Picachos if you fail. I have a feeling they dislike busy Western women even more than busy Western men.'

'Oh, God,' he said wearily. 'You do believe in having it both ways, don't you? Emancipated logic and female helplessness all in one mouthful. Okay, you win. You will be telling me you can drive a locomotive next.'

'No, I can't.' My victory felt oddly flat, which did not alter the fact that it had been necessary.

Quite unexpectedly, he laughed. 'Nor can I.'

We set off soon after, not along the road to Quihuli but keeping to such undergrowth as there was along the railway. Occasionally we saw *campesinos* in the distance and one or two saw us, but mostly the country was empty until we came quite close to the town. The sun shone and the track shimmered in still air; only one passenger train came up from San Bernardo each day, and if it did not run today, then all Bruce's plans were in ruins.

We walked in silence in single file, the going rough: Bruce in front, then me, then the three Indians. Once we had to lie up in jungly undergrowth while an armoured car drove down the track in a flurry of ballast. We could see the sleepers shift under its wheels and I wondered how often trains were derailed up here. 'How will you manage if you've never driven a steam engine?' I asked Bruce while we waited for the armoured car to disappear in the distance.

'The same as Techuac with the truck; I've had a dry run. The hut where you waited for me yesterday belongs to a retired loco driver. It was his wife serving food. He has described the layout and been through the drill with me. It isn't complicated provided we can take over the locomotive before the steam pressure drops too far. His only condition

97

was that I make sure no one from Quihuli is blamed. We don't want reprisals here, and once we reach the mountains, then we're safe until the spring.'

'How can you make sure the Seguridad knows it is the Picachos?'

He shrugged. 'I'll leave a boasting message as if from Yono's guerrillas – they'll enjoy accepting unearned glory. And I've brought a Picacho woven collar as a sign from illiterates. They're rare and much valued nowadays, not the kind of thing that Quihulañeros would get hold of.'

In some ways his preparations were meticulous, in others ludicrous, but this whole business was so enormously risky that preparations were meaningless. Yet I judged him as a man who did not normally take unnecessary risks. Closer perhaps to a perfectionist who was incapable of doing any job badly, whether it was stealing trucks or eating folded tortilla without dripping maize down his chin.

When we reached the outskirts of Quihuli we had to use the railway embankment for cover, and when that flattened out we crawled along the edge of the same *barranca* where I had met Bruce the day before. Impossible to grasp that it had been only yesterday, and twenty-four hours ago . . . I shut my eyes, thinking painfully about the Casa Mendoza and its inhabitants. This time yesterday I had been soaking in warm water, speculating idly about this man in whose company I was now about to risk my life hijacking, of all things, a steam engine.

'Wait here,' said Bruce at last. 'This time I mean it, Faith. I want to make sure the freight is still there and loaded, and I shall be safer alone.'

We waited for him a long time.

I didn't worry exactly, because that kind of reconnaissance was bound to be a laborious business, but we were all on edge. The Indian boys, Aztlin and Juan, jabbered together softly; the older man, who was called Timcal, rubbed work-battered hands endlessly on his thighs.

Quihuli was completely quiet, the military presumably sleeping off their exuberance of the night before and the

98

population trying to avoid attention. Today they would be using the side streets, talking in undertones, keeping the juke boxes switched off. There was some traffic because Quihuli was the only market in the foothills; mostly open pick-ups and old American sedans, but occasionally green-painted modern cars went past, flying the flags of Mozon's revolution. It was disturbing to find official activity already intensifying. The last thing we needed was a rash of efficiency breaking out in Quihuli.

Timcal stirred and grunted; I couldn't see anything, but a few minutes later Bruce whistled and then slithered down the bank towards us. 'It is still there,' he said in Spanish, which I as well as the Indians understood although not all of them spoke it. 'The watchtower is manned and awake, five men I think. There is also some activity in the station – I hope the passenger train doesn't come up too early.'

'The earlier the better,' said Juan, fingering his machete. He was so scrawny he looked about twelve years old, but probably was nearer twenty.

'Not so, blood-eater. We want that freight, not cut throats. If the passenger train arrives in daylight then its fires will be too low to stoke up easily by the time it is safe for us to move.'

I glanced at the sky; it must be several hours until dark.

We were too close to the refuse-filled ravine for comfort, but it was probably a safe place to wait unless someone came searching for us. The time passed very slowly, the Indians dozing once Bruce finished drilling each of us in the precise sequence of what we had to do. Timcal had the vital job of switching the points so that once we had the locomotive under way, Bruce could bring it out and then shunt it back into the freight yard without any waste of time. The points mechanism was simple but, as I had seen on the way up, almost certainly very stiff. Timcal had never operated points in his life and if he fumbled the job then we would be stalled immediately below the watchtower, with only the alternatives of surrender or sprinting for safety under fire.

'I think the beast comes,' said Aztlin.

We all froze, listening.

99

Bruce crawled up the bank and laid a hand on the rail. 'Are you sure?'

'No, señor. But the air quivers.'

The sun was still warm. It would be a long time yet before it set. 'The passenger *espreso* never comes through as early as this.'

'Sometimes,' I said reluctantly. 'If it is yesterday's train. When I travelled up here, it left San Bernardo very early and was here about this time, I suppose.'

No one answered while we all crouched there willing Aztlin to be wrong; but he wasn't, and within minutes we could all hear it: a gasping beat as the engine toiled up the steep gradient which separated Quihuli from the last of the viaducts.

'It might take as much as half an hour to reach here,' I said. 'And then they've got to shunt the engine round to the front of the train ready for tomorrow. It's still quite a while before they damp the fire.'

'Not long enough,' answered Bruce. He was squinting into the glare towards Quihuli station, perhaps a mile down the track from where we stood. 'I'd hoped not to tackle the last stretch into the station before dark.'

'All is finished?' asked Aztlin, crestfallen. Juan looked disappointed too, while Timcal showed no reaction at all.

Bruce looked at the two boys measuringly. 'Could you run alongside the train when it reaches here, and then jump on board? It will be travelling quite slowly.'

'Of course,' said Aztlin proudly. 'I have jumped trucks that way.'

Juan was silent; he had once gone all the way to San Bernardo by train and had been boasting of how much he knew about *la maquinaria*, but tackling a live engine like a bullfighter was a different matter.

'Well, Juan?'

'I do not know, señor. I will try.'

Bruce touched the boy on the shoulder, and smiled. 'It is all any of us can do. We all try then, except Timcal, who crawls slowly, slowly towards the points and then hides until

100

he hears us come. If one of us fails to jump the train, then that person stays to help Timcal with what he has to do, and feels no shame. Without the points we are all lost.'

Timcal gave the boys a venomous stare and nodded. 'Without my points, we lose.'

The train was much nearer, the beat of its wheels clearly audible. We all except Timcal scrambled up the bank and hunkered by the line, as Indians do to watch the trains go by. Bruce was wearing Timcal's straw hat, and crouching concealed his height; he was not a tall man but easily topped the Indians. 'Give me your cape,' he said to Juan. The boy wore some old print material on his shoulders, and when he handed it over Bruce hastily knotted it round my waist. It would be in the way when I tried to board the moving train, but Indian women did not wear jeans.

The train's noise deepened to a roar as it passed the last masking fold of hill and suddenly it seemed to hurtle down on us, screeching against badly set rails. It wasn't travelling fast after such a climb and with Quihuli in sight the driver was already applying his brakes, but the impression of weight and noise seemed overwhelming. The ground was rough and the cloth flapped about my knees; I just didn't seem able to run fast enough as peeling wooden carriages rattled past. I missed the first and the second of them, brass handrails whipping past before I could jump for the step.

Breath was stiffening in my lungs, heart hammering, not so much with exertion as panic that after insisting on coming, I would be the one left behind with Timcal. There were only three carriages altogether on the San Bernardo train, so I set my teeth and ran on, head back to judge grip and distance, not caring about rough ground any longer. If I tripped, I tripped. As if anticipating aguadiente at his journey's end the driver seemed to increase speed, and desperately I jumped, scrabbling for grip, feet trailing for one terrifying moment before I was up.

'Good girl,' said Bruce and smiled, hand on my waist. He had jumped up just behind and now held me against the side of the carriage. He groped for a moment and then swung open a door so we both landed in a heap on the floor inside. Crammed ranks of faces stared at us as everyone stopped in the act of picking up their belongings ready for Quihuli, but not one of them asked the obvious question of what we thought we were doing, jumping a train a few hundred yards short of the station. Of course, they recognized us as gringos, but at least this wasn't a time when stowage-class passengers wanted to draw attention to themselves by running to authority. The story would spread, but with luck not reach official ears until tomorrow.

Before we had even caught our breath the train drew up in the station and everyone poured off, revealing Juan gasping on his face farther up the carriage.

'Aztlin?' asked Bruce.

Juan shook his head. 'He tripped, señor. He will be very unhappy, I think.'

'I hope to God he doesn't try anything stupid.' Bruce had helped me to my feet and was still holding me, forgetful of how, until then, he had kept so much distance between us.

'There's nothing we can do about it,' I observed, although I, too, was afraid that Aztlin's pride would prevent him from accepting the humble role of Timcal's assistant.

The train had emptied completely and instantly, and we opened a door away from the platform side so as to lie out of sight on one of the boarding planks. Quihuli has only one platform with rails either side, so we faced a brick wall and were well hidden unless someone leaned over to look through a carriage window; and on this blank side there seemed no particular reason why they should.

In the end, it had proved easier to enter Quihuli station by daylight than if we'd crawled there in the dark.

That smut-covered plank was very hard and we lay there a long time while guards leisurely uncoupled the engine and, with a great deal of shouting, shunted it back up the opposite side of the platform.

'Stand by for a jolt,' said Bruce quietly. 'When they shunt it on the front, I'll be surprised if they do it gently.'

We all lay there gripping plank, but when the impact

came, it nearly had us off. Juan gave a screech, since he hadn't been able to visualize what would happen, but fortunately there was so much clanking no one heard.

Light was dulling but it was very far from dark when the sound of steam finally diminished, and we heard the driver and his fireman talking as they walked past. 'What now?' I whispered when they had gone.

'We wait a few minutes and then we go up to the footplate. I hope we'll be able to uncouple now; if anyone should come to check again they'll only think the crew forgot to link up properly. Then we start stoking again, but very carefully. We can't let that fire damp down too much, but mustn't risk blowing off steam either. Once we reach a working pressure we'll have to go, whether it's full dark or not. So we just have to juggle it right I guess.'

'The watchtower?'

'God knows. I don't suppose they've laid a direct line to the Jefe's office, though, so perhaps they'll waste time wondering what's happening until we reach the points. After that, we just have to hope that engine steel will give us two minutes' worth of cover.'

It wasn't as simple as that, of course. We would have to couple up to the freight train and also stop somewhere long enough to block the line against pursuing armoured cars; the best place was at the first viaduct where a curve of hill would cover us from automatic fire.

Carefully, we dropped down on the line between carriage and wall, and began to move slowly towards the engine. There was rubbish as well as clinker underfoot, and however carefully we moved, the noise we made seemed disconcertingly loud in the deserted station.

'Señor!' hissed Juan.

Then we all heard it; cautious footsteps on the platform, a carriage width away. At first I thought of Aztlin, but realized that even if he had come on his own, he would scarcely have walked the platform openly. Those footsteps were wary, but moving without concealment. Slowly, the sound of them drew away and vanished while we stood undecided. It

103

wasn't a patrol and it wasn't the Jefe, but anyone here could raise the alarm against us.

I looked at Bruce inquiringly and he made a slight gesture. Go on.

Steam pressure would be dropping all the time, we couldn't afford to wait.

All the same, those footsteps had shaken us all. There ought not to be anyone here now, with the station closed and guarded for the night.

We reached the engine without any further scares, and were able to see that the tender was filled with a mixture of wood and coal. Before we climbed up, Bruce edged himself between the tender and the last carriage to begin easing the coupling loose, while I squeezed in behind him and held the links out of his way. They were heavy, and clattered against steel bolts, the hook where they engaged closed by a rusted clip. One blow with a hammer was all that clip needed; fingers were not enough. Bruce whipped off his shirt and wrapped it round the metal to gain greater purchase, but still it refused to move. Very gingerly, I dropped the loose end of chain and added my strength to his, but the space was so confined that no matter how we struggled, we could not force the clip to move.

'I hope something comes easy, just once, tonight,' I said softly, while we stood looking at it.

'We've done the easy part.' He was wedged between me and the wagon, bare skin white against weathered face and forearms. And like his face, his body seemed all bone, muscles skeined so clearly I might have been studying an anatomical drawing. They must be nearly starving already in the mountains, with winter still to come. He looked up and caught my eyes on him, and annoyingly I felt myself redden, even though I had been thinking only of shunting clips and food.

'I shall have to slam it up with the truck spanner. Go and stand by Juan.' His voice was drained of expression and he was also back to not looking at me again.

He wrapped the spanner in a piece of cloth and twisted his

104

shirt around the clip, but even so it needed to be hit with all his strength, and when it gave way, it went back with a crack which rattled every link in the coupling.

Some fuel in the tender slipped too, and Juan and I exchanged startled glances; surely there had not been enough vibration to cause a cascade there.

We both ran round to climb up on the footplate, too late to begin wondering now whether Mozon's revolution put armed guards on locomotives in Quihuli station. I barked shins and knuckles scrambling up, almost convinced there couldn't be anyone there, then some woodblocks slipped and I grabbed at a slight and dirty figure as it scampered to escape. It was as elusive as freshly caught mackerel, and I needed to grab again.

I was on my knees in the coal before I saw his face. 'Rodrigo!'

He gaped, tongue sharply pink in a coal-seamed face. 'Señorita! Holy Mary, Mother of God, I thought you were dead. I even prayed for your soul,' he added accusingly. 'The padre was angry and said you were probably a heretic.'

I swallowed a laugh. We had made an appalling amount of noise, but must not unnecessarily make any more. '*Gracias*, Rodrigo. What are you doing here?'

Hesitantly, he opened his shoeblack's bag: inside was coal filched from the tender. 'There is a place by the station steps where I conceal *los combustibiles*, and when there is no trade tomorrow, I will take these a few pieces at a time to sell. Please, señorita – '

'Of course I won't tell anyone, and I want you to promise the same for me. Go home now, and forget you saw me here.'

He rubbed his face thoughtfully, eyes sliding from me to Bruce and Juan watching us from the footplate. 'What is the señorita doing here?'

I hesitated; I had become fond of Rodrigo, but could not estimate his discretion. 'Hiding from the army. Tomorrow, I hope to ride down to San Bernardo. No one connected with the Mendozas is safe in Quihuli.'

'But – ' His eyes narrowed. Rodrigo was sharp on a detail

and older than he looked. He pointed at Juan. 'That one with you is a Picacho.'

I wondered how he knew. 'Yes, and he has helped me.'

'And the other one is gringo, the one perhaps who is whispered about as living with the Picachos in the mountains. I do not think you are going to San Bernardo, señorita.' He watched me limpidly.

'I am.' I felt ashamed of lying to him.

'Then, I should like the señorita to take me with her. I am strong and will act as guard, also I am tired of shining shoes in Quihuli.'

I was taken aback by the aggressive determination in his voice, and for the first time began to suspect that Rodrigo sometimes used his childish appearance deliberately for gain. 'I don't need a guard.'

'Certainly you do, señorita. I should be worried if you went alone, worried enough to feel I ought perhaps to run to someone in authority who has the power to stop you.'

I stared at him, nonplussed. He should be in primary school, not threatening blackmail like a professional.

'Let him come if he wants to,' said Bruce. 'You're right, Rodrigo, we are going to the mountains and mean to take food from the freight yard with us. But if you come, you could die tonight.'

'And if I decide not to come?' asked Rodrigo coolly.

'Then I tie you up until we start, which leaves you with the task of explaining to the army tomorrow all about what we did. They will be very angry, and consequently not particular about whom they beat up in revenge, but you should have thought of that before you tried to get your way by force.'

Rodrigo smiled angelically. 'You could only catch me if I let you, Señor Americano.'

As soon as I recognized Rodrigo, I had felt more like hugging him in reassurance than holding him; he pulled away from my slack grip in a single fluid twist, grabbed his shoeshine bag and disappeared over the edge of the tender before I could move. Too late, I started up the slope of coal after him, and too slowly to throw anything heavy enough to stun.

He was gone.

At least, I thought he had, but Bruce vanished from the footplate and a few moments later reappeared carrying an inert Rodrigo. I had heard no sound at all.

'He is dead, señor,' said Juan with respect.

'No. He will have a sore throat when he wakes up.' By the time I had scrambled down from the tender, Bruce had gagged Rodrigo and tied him to a bracket.

'He'd helped me ever since I came to Quihuli,' I said ruefully. 'I never dreamed he would run off like that. How do you manage to keep in training, by sliding down the banisters?' If I had not been there, I would never have believed that a man could move as quickly as Bruce had done to catch that wretched brat.

He gave a gasp of laughter. 'Strictly ranch-type accommodation in the Picachero Valley, but I have spent one hell of a time learning what it takes to be a survivor up here. Rodrigo's a survivor, I guess, and he understands what we might be worth to him.'

It was a jolt to realize that a child I had regarded as a friend would have sold us to the army for the little credit we might gain him; but then who was I to judge how harsh life had been for Rodrigo, shining shoes on the steps of Quihuli station for most of his undernourished existence?

All this seemed to take a great time and cause enough noise to rouse a drunken regiment, but I suppose that not much more than a quarter of an hour could have elapsed since we first began to struggle with that coupling link: the station was still apparently deserted, and night did not seem any closer.

Under Bruce's direction, Juan and I began handing down coal and wood while he stoked up the fire and tried to make sense of an alarming array of levers and cranked wheels. It was impossible to close the firedoor properly without slamming it, and since we dared not slam it and had to stoke by the handful instead of with a shovel, raising steam was an agonizingly slow process. It would have been infinitely safer to wait for darkness before we moved off, but each minute we waited strung nerves tighter, until I at least was longing to build up sufficient steam so we could go if we had to.

Although the pressure gauges took an age to move, the engine was soon hissing steam from dozens of leaks, and however careful we were, some noise was unavoidable. Bruce had to rake out damped-down cinders and keep increasing the draught before the pressure needles would move at all.

'We may not make much speed.' Bruce looked unruffled as he said it, his dirty wrung-out shirt clinging to his ribs, but what he really meant was that lack of speed might kill us all. 'Even if we could stoke hard enough, I daren't reach the normal starting pressure because I don't suppose the valves are properly set. We'd blow off steam for sure.'

'We already are.' It was floating in clouds past the footplate, and I heard my own voice jump. I was afraid, yet at the same time exhilarated by the enormity of what I was mixed up in.

'Sure, but no one could miss a main valve blow. Don't worry too much though, because we have an omen. If fate means anything at all, then we are going to get safe out of here tonight.'

He took me over to a plate set in the side of the cab, which read: *L.N.E.R. Locomotive Workshops, Doncaster & Newcastle-upon-Tyne. No. 16206 July 1936.* Like me, the Quihuli passenger express was a long way from home, and as soon as I read those words it seemed to me as if the English north country had lined up behind my back. Though 16206 was nearly fifty years old, it ceased to be hostile metal and became my ally. Superstition is a strange thing, but the coincidence seemed too great for disbelief.

'You see?' Bruce said, smiling at the delight I must have shown. Flame from the firedoor reflected from the uncompromising bones of his face, so what I should have seen was the same harsh confidence as before. The confidence he intended me to feel – he, the professional encouraging a nervous amateur during the difficult waiting time before precipitous action. Instead, when I turned to laugh in response, and make some light reply, it was his smile I saw, and how it altered those planes and underlit patterns into something very different.

'Yes,' I said, very much at random. 'Though it is a pity that Tyneside boilers seem to have an even more insatiable thirst than its beer-drinkers.'

The labour and strain of stoking by hand was intense. We were soon filthy and our chipped knuckles bled over the fuel we handled, my back aching long before we had finished. Slowly, slowly, the gauges were beginning to swing, hesitating, falling back again as, without shovels, we could not work fast enough to keep pace with so many leaks.

'Okay,' Bruce said at last. 'We are going to make one hell of a noise anyway when we pull out of here. We shall just have to make it a couple of minutes earlier and stoke by shovel when we're ready to move. Everyone must have gone home, or they would have noticed something happening up here by now.'

I glanced to where Rodrigo was wriggling ineffectually on the steel floor. 'Are we going to take him with us?'

'Not all the way, the Picacho Valley is no place for a kid. I'd like to dump him on the platform for someone to find, but then we would have to leave him tied up, and the Seguridad beats up anyone they question, even cooperative witnesses. It's the way their minds work. He's safer with us for the moment, and we'll let him go when the trucks are loaded. He's quite smart enough to keep his mouth shut once we've gone.'

I didn't argue; Bruce clearly knew much more about Latin America than just the Picacho Mountains. He was also apparently used to leading dangerous enterprises under unfavourable circumstances, cracking jokes and offering his certainty for both Juan and me to lean on during those last, nerve-twisting moments before we went.

I wondered just how certain or confident he really was,

109

but his manner offered no clue at all, nor any suggestion that the next few minutes might be our last.

Whenever I had had time to think, I had been disconcerted by the mixture of cool tactics and outrageous gambling in his plans, especially when there was this shadowy contradiction in him somewhere, a weakness hidden among so many confident skills. Now I saw only how well he blended physical agility with an outsize capacity for withstanding stress. But weakness may be locked out of sight for a while, yet it remains there, waiting. I found myself comparing him to Zeller, whose toughness certainly extended all the way through, no weakness anywhere. My mind teased for an instant at something I had missed, then it was gone, swallowed up in the urgency of the situation.

We hand-stoked for another interminable stretch of time, snatching seconds to keep a lookout because we could not stay undetected much longer; dusk was falling at last, and Juan was on his knees with exhaustion. I felt the same but until yesterday had always eaten well, which was the only difference between my state and his.

Bruce picked up a shovel. 'I'll stoke now. Faith, you set her going, okay?' He led me across to a small brass wheel. 'Slam over the regulator the moment I say, and take off the brakes. Then wind open the valve.'

I had not faced the fact that because he could stoke quicker than I, then of course I should have to set 16206 on her way. This was the kind of emergency which baffled Juan, and why I had insisted on accompanying Bruce. I wanted to refuse. I knew nothing about a steam engine, whose size and weight seemed truly monstrous, which once released would romp away down the line beyond any control of mine. I wanted to, but went instead to stare dumbly at steel levers.

Come on, you Tyneside hinny, I thought. You Tyneside steaming hinny, we'll get out of this together. I grasped the regulator with both hands, then looked round at Bruce, groping for words to reassure him that I wouldn't panic however unreliable I must have looked. To reassure myself that I damned well refused to panic, when panic was

110

something I could feel. 'Sorry I forgot to bring any champagne for the launching.'

It was a dreadfully feeble joke, but for the first time he came over and held me to him, face and lips fleetingly against my skin, his body touching mine. Then he was back by the firedoor. 'Wait for it, then.'

After we had spent so long trying to be quiet, the rattle of shovelled coal and the uninhibited clang of the firedoor sounded like the Third World War. Juan crouched close to Rodrigo as if even a tied-up prisoner offered comfort, his lips moving in prayer. But he did not run, which needed more courage than standing at some levers.

I stood rigid at those levers, feeling sweat chill and watching the pressure needles creep round their dials.

'Juan!' yelled Bruce. 'Look to see if anyone is coming. Get your head back in the moment we move.'

The boy hesitated, then crawled to the side of the cab, said something I could not hear above the din.

'*Qué?*' Bruce was hurling fuel into the boiler.

'Someone by the barrier, Señor Broos,' Juan screamed.

Someone watching, or someone levelling a gun?

At that moment the main valve blew off pressure with the most appalling screech, rocketing steam into the air. I saw the needles quiver and stop rising, so without waiting for Bruce, I slammed over the regulating lever and wound at the brass wheel which should start us moving.

Nothing happened.

I had been braced for a lurch, turned to shout at Bruce because I must have done something disastrously wrong, then was nearly thrown off my feet as pistons snatched the wheels into motion. The pitch of escaping steam changed as we pulled out of the station, the dull redness where the sun had vanished looking oddly like another firedoor. The impression of speed was ridiculous yet overwhelming, within three hundred yards we needed to stop and wait for Timcal to throw over the points behind us, and then reverse into the freight yard. Metal shrieked on metal as a fog of steam blew in our eyes, fighting the inertia of God knows how many tons. Bruce must have been insane, we all must have been insane to believe that such a suicidal plan as this could ever succeed.

We passed the watchtower and I glimpsed soldiers gaping down at us, one caught in the act of urinating over the edge of packed sandbags.

Then we were past, 16206 enjoying the freedom of not drawing any load and picking up speed rapidly. We need not have worried about reaching minimum steam pressure after all, I thought stupidly.

'Close the valve,' said Bruce; he must have been as worried as hell, but looked impressively calm. 'The regulator first, that's right. Then that.' He threw his weight on the brakes which immediately squealed like elephants in rut. 'Stay there, and turn the wheel for reverse when I say.'

He climbed down on the footplate while I stood staring at recalcitrant metal, trying to work out the sequence which must be necessary for reverse. Pressure was leaking away even while Bruce stood straining his eyes into the dusk, trying to see whether Timcal and Aztlin had flipped the points. They should have run across and done it the moment we passed, and until they did we were stuck here spewing steam, waiting for the soldiers to grasp that this could not possibly be routine, for it tore routine apart.

'Juan,' I said, trying for the same calm with which Bruce had steadied me. 'You saw how Señor Bruce stoked with the shovel. Pick it up and do exactly as he did.'

Juan stared back at me out of shadow. The flick of boot sole which opened the fire door, the scrape and pitch of fuel, flick again to clang the door shut, scrape fuel . . . the integrated flow of such movements was beyond him, his reactions crushed by unfamiliarity.

'They're coming,' Bruce said.

'Timcal?'

'Three soldiers climbing down from the watchtower. Now we've stopped they don't know what to think.'

'Timcal?' I said again.

'No . . . Christ, they're levering the points over with a

112

crowbar.' He half climbed down then swung back in. 'Yes! Reverse now, Faith.'

I whirled the wheel frantically, forgetting whether the regulator should come over first, but slowly 16206 began to reverse, the wheels giving a harsh thump as we rode over incompletely closed points. We'd have to go dead slow over those coming out.

'Two hundred yards,' said Bruce, hauling Timcal up on the footplate beside him as we passed. 'Keep as you are.'

I couldn't do anything else, but the pressure gauge was swinging back very rapidly now. 'The steam! We'll never have enough to take the freight out! You'll have to let me go back to couple up while you stoke.'

He did not answer, leaning out to try to judge the distance in the dark: when we reached the freight he intended to run back and snap the coupling on. That would be the crucial moment now the soldiers were roused, because if only we were able to pull away again, then they would be lucky to hit us in the darkness and confusion, through half an inch of Tyneside steel.

Even above the sound of steam and slithering metal I heard the first shot, the clang of its strike somewhere on the tender.

Bruce was crouched, ready to jump, and I yelled at him, furious at heroics which would kill us all. If pressure dropped much more we would never leave the freight yard once we were coupled up to those loaded wagons, and I lacked the strength to stoke at the speed which would be necessary during the next few seconds.

Only minutes of manoeuvring, and all our reserves of steam were gone, every needle falling back across their dials.

Bruce shouted back at me from where he crouched. 'Swing over the regulator! Take off reverse!'

I wound frantically at the wheel – surely they could have thought out a better way to shut off steam. The double lever at my side kicked savagely and Bruce sprang back off the step to jam his boot against the shaft. We needed to use every ounce of leverage we both possessed before somehow it

113

engaged the brakes. The howl of locked wheels must have been heard all over Quihuli, and we slid into the first freight wagon so hard I heard the clash of couplings even above the seethe of the steam which enveloped us as soon as the valves were closed.

I was on the step before Bruce hauled me back. 'I'll do it!' I shouted. 'Bruce, I have to do it! Listen to that steam!'

I think a burst of bullets hit somewhere then, because the noise of vented pressure increased to a scream, but I was more than half-crazy at the time, and only remembered it later.

'Aztlin,' said Bruce, and shook me hard. 'Get back to those valves and I'll look after the stoking. Aztlin has gone back to do it.'

Selfish relief swept over me and he released my arm as soon as he felt me accept that neither of us had to go. God bless Aztlin, and keep him safe. Aztlin, ashamed of missing his footing and determined to salve his pride. He must have run alongside all the way from the points, keeping the engine between himself and the soldiers.

A distant squeak was all I heard when he yelled that the coupling was hooked up, sounding so childlike it was unbelievable that he should be risking death, as the smack of bullets and howl of ricochets sliced through the sound of escaping steam.

Bruce had hurled on only a few shovelfuls of fuel, but now moved to the step again, body tense and head turned like a runner waiting for the relay baton. 'Start off, Faith! He's coming.'

For a dreadful moment I stared at brass and steel and could not remember anything, all I had already done wiped off my mind by a mixture of triumph, terror and confusion. Then awareness snapped into place again and everything was flash-focused, including some soldiers racing down the line towards us. Through the driver's porthole I could see them less than fifty yards away. My hands moved more positively than I was thinking by that time: lever, valve, heavy brake-release grips. The wheels moved so sluggishly I turned to begin frantic stoking: probably I had everything set wrong, but 16206 would now drive herself out of here, providing too much pressure did not leak away.

I caught a glimpse of Aztlin running alongside, boyish face set into a fierce victorious grin, his hand in Bruce's, one foot on the step. In rapid succession there came a chatter of automatic fire and repeating, single shots. Aztlin stumbled, his expression changing to astonishment, his weight already dragging Bruce to his knees, head and shoulders curving downward to the line. Bruce threw himself back, his and Aztlin's weight depending on his remaining hand clamped to a slippery rail. I leaped forward as everything overlapped in a kind of madness, and then somehow the three of us were tangled with a yelling Juan on the floor.

Soldiers' faces by the firestep, guns levelled; a stream of shots whipping diagonally across the cab and hurtling into darkness. Everyone gasping and struggling for balance, lives saved because we were flat on our noses and no one had spare breath or a steady hand for aiming. Bruce swung a shovel horizontally at a soldier who grasped a handhold as we steamed slowly past, and he fell back on top of others with a howl, bullets spraying everywhere as he fell. And all the while 16206 continued to pull away, gaining speed very slowly but keeping moving, throwing the soldiers into more confusion as they tried to run and fire and climb up and shout all at the same time.

Aztlin moaned in pain when I scrambled out from beneath him and grabbed another shovel; steam, we had to have more steam. A single aimed burst of automatic fire or an explosive shell in the boiler, and we were finished.

I flung myself at the heaped coal, not thinking of bullets any more. It wasn't courage or even fear which discarded everything except shovels of fuel into the red eye of that furnace, but the fact that steam alone would get us out of here. The noise of it escaping through ruptured pipes was enormous.

Swing, clang, heave, throw; swing, clang, heave, throw; breath scalding in my lungs. A shocking, evil yowl behind my ear as a ricochet hurtled round the cab; a single snatched glimpse of Bruce again using his shovel as a weapon, this time throwing it with all the force he possessed at a swarthy face behind a machine gun, high on the watchtower. It struck a steel stanchion just by the gunner's head in a shower of sparks and I saw no more because we were past and the tender shielded us from his fire. Timcal was crouched by the step on the other side of the cab, light from the furnace burnishing his machete. No, blood. The blade and his hand were covered with it.

Then I realized track was flicking past faster, the noise of bullets striking the tender more noticeable as the sounds of battle dulled. Clouds of steam were blowing in our faces and boiling around our feet; wordlessly Bruce came over and raked ash from the firebox before taking over stoking. I rubbed steam off the dials and saw the needles dropping back, but now 16206 had gained some speed it did not seem to make much difference.

Another needle I had not noticed before was climbing upward into red etched on steel. 'Water,' Bruce said, between one shovel and the next. 'Some of those bullets hit where it mattered.'

I nodded, wondering whether that meant the boiler might blow up, but for the moment it was enough that the tender shielded us from bullets and we were pounding away into the dark. Cold wind seemed to blow through my brain, tumbling thought end over end. My splendid Tyneside hinny had taken us out of Quihuli, with only a handful of miles to go until we reached the trucks. Dear God, we mustn't overshoot.

Bruce heaved in another dozen shovels of fuel and then went to peer into the night, before coming back to stand by the controls. I felt us slow and could not think what he was doing, surely we hadn't reached the trucks yet. Relief vanished abruptly as I realized we still had to block the line.

We stopped with a shudder and instantly Bruce was gone, running back down the line with a firing bar in his hands. On our way into Quihuli we had loosened the precarious track on the first viaduct: Bruce intended to crash one of the wagons if he could. I stood on the step, feeling my own pulse beat hollow in my ears, and straining my eyes into the night: if I was able to see Bruce signal, then precious time would be saved.

Because of the glare from the firedoor I could see very little, but he saw me and distantly I heard him shout. Hoping to God that this meant what I thought it meant, I went back to the controls and unwound the valve one turn at a time, terrified I'd be unable to stop once I put steam in the works again. As I knew only too well, the line to San Bernardo sloped downhill all the way. If that engine had not been made on Tyneside, I don't believe I would ever have had the courage to open those valves while Bruce was away in the dark outside. If we did gather speed, then I knew I lacked the strength to put the brakes back on; but we were all a little crazy by then, and I still possessed a blind belief that that particular engine would not let me down.

The moment I felt the wheels turn I closed the valve, and even so we juddered forward a good fifty yards or so, with my weight thrown against the brake handles every click of the way.

I heard the crash from behind quite clearly, and a short time after Bruce was climbing back on the footplate, nodding some kind of reassurance at the look on my face. The line was blocked. Not for long, but long enough, we hoped. The downhill slope had helped, because Bruce had uncoupled the guard's van at the rear and levered aside one of the loosened rails. Then, when the rest of the train pulled clear, he had managed to shove the van forward down the slope until it became derailed. An armoured car might possibly shoulder it aside, but in darkness infinite care would be needed to avoid disaster on a viaduct high above dry stones. So we ought to gain the time we needed, an hour at least to load four trucks with heavy crates of food.

One instant and we were safe; soon, another instant and we should be plunged back into mortal danger.

Timcal was standing very straight and square by my side,

his head thrown up, arms slack, one hand holding his bloodstained machete. He looked satisfied. Satisfied and proud, with a fraction of a long debt paid. Juan was grinning delightedly; I grinned back at him and we both laughed out loud.

Neither my terror nor my relief mattered very much; I was quite simply glad for them. Tonight at least, the Picachos were back among the winners, even if winning might not last for very long. I remembered an earlier echo too, of Bruce saying that to them it would not matter if triumph did not last, so long as their world marvelled at what they had accomplished. Well, this story would flash across the foothills, regardless of Mozon's censorship.

I felt my own confidence begin to glow in response to theirs, luminous and strong. I had been wrung out by endless fear; now I was all sparks and fire because, incredibly, we had made it, until the next part began. My hands no longer gripped hostile metal but gratefully acknowledged the debt we owed it for our lives, and as we racketed through the darkness I discovered I was singing in time to the clack of rails:

> 'We took the coach to Bamborough
> An' she wor heavy-laden . . .
> An' when we got to Scotswood
> The wheel she flew off theor.
> The lassies lost their crinolines
> An' the veils that hid their faces,
> I got two black eyes an' a broken nose . . .
> On the way to Bladon Races.'

16206 and I were treating Comayagua to the immemorial anthem of the Tyneside Geordies.

9

We nearly missed the rendezvous point because, of course, the trucks weren't there. Overshot it by more than a mile and had to shunt back, the carelessness of success making any manoeuvre seem simple even though the freight trucks made a fearful clashing.

There was no way the trucks could have been waiting for us, for the Picacho drivers had orders to see the train go by before they moved. All the same, it was a relief when they lurched across the ploughland a few minutes later, but three of them only.

'Where's Techuac?' called Bruce. Techuac was the man who had been willing to try driving a truck after no more than a few practice gear changes in the *arroyo*.

Dimly, I heard the babble of reply, but by then was kneeling beside Aztlin where we had bundled him aside when there wasn't time for anything else. All the same, I could have taken time from singing 'Bladon Races' to look at him, and was ashamed to realize that from the moment we left the freight yard I simply had not remembered he was hurt. And he was badly hurt: in dirt and darkness I dared not probe far but his shirt was soggy with blood, and he screamed when I touched his ribs.

'There's a clean cloth in the first truck. You'll have to strap him up as tight as you can and if he lives we'll see what we can do in daylight,' said Bruce beside me. 'I've brought a combat surgical pack. I'll put a double shot of painkiller into him so he won't know much about it.'

'He's lost too much blood,' I said. 'I don't see how he can survive a journey.'

'Do the best you can. Until we reach the valley, he'll have to take his chance.' He knelt to say something to the boy; I saw him smile weakly in the furnace reflections and guessed that Bruce had praised his courage. Pride was what had mattered most to Aztlin in life, and memory of pride vindicated would help at the time of his death.

When I climbed down from the footplate, the track was already scurrying with figures, the trucks backed right up to the wagon doors, which made loading far easier. Techuac was working faster than anyone; he had dug a wheel into a rut and not been able to back out again, stalling the engine each time he tried.

We worked in darkness and froze where we stood whenever headlights flickered on the road above, sweeping overhead but leaving us in shadow. Now that the derailed guard's van prevented motorized pursuit directly along the rails, the Quihuli garrison had no way of knowing whether we had taken the train all the way down to San Bernardo, or whether we had stopped on the way. Until morning, surely the searching troops would look for us farther away than the impudent half-dozen miles we had travelled from Quihuli. Perhaps, perhaps. Everything guesswork and assumption, on which our lives depended.

As I helped with the loading I still felt nerve-sharp and good, not tired at all. Yet of course I was tired, and simply functioning on nervous excitement. The crates were heavy and packed closely together, the sacks very awkward in the dark. We all toiled breathlessly under a rising moon, its light an enormous help which soon would betray us to anyone passing on the road.

Two trucks were packed and the third very nearly so, Bruce bouncing down towards us in the fourth which he had managed to salvage out of its rut, when a dreadful scream paralysed us where we stood. A crate had slipped as it was being heaved from freight wagon to truck, and crushed one of the men's feet against the open tailgate. Bruce came running – he had heard the scream even from the truck – and between us all we soon had the crate lifted clear, but the damage was done. The man lay sobbing with pain and I could feel his foot swell even while I held it.

A couple of pieces of packing case made a splint, but I couldn't help wondering whether Bruce's combat kit was the total medical provision in the mountains: if so, then this man might never walk again. 'Can't we leave him where someone will take him to hospital in the morning?' I asked.

Bruce turned from where he had been driving the others back to work. 'No. He's Picacho, and we're making sure they get blamed for this, remember? They'd have him stripped down at Seguridad headquarters –'

'A doctor might guess how he'd been injured, but surely he wouldn't –'

'He almost certainly would, the day after a coup. Or have no choice except to give him up. It's too great a risk to take. We'll have to abandon the fourth truck now. Pedro here was our best driver, and Techuac certainly can't take a truck through Quihuli.'

Apparently Techuac understood, because his teeth gleamed in darkness and he answered in Spanish. 'No time for Señor Broos to pull me out of a ditch in Quihuli.'

I looked at open freight cars spilling sacks and crates, our frantic haste showing in the way anything dropped was left. 'There's a great deal left.'

Bruce shrugged. 'We can't help it.'

'I can drive a truck.'

'Don't . . . *What?*'

'I can drive a truck,' I repeated. 'At least, I've driven trucks not much smaller than these at home. Combines, too.'

'How much smaller?'

'Smaller.' I wasn't going to be drawn into details. 'The gears will be different but otherwise I should be all right. So if you'll just show me –'

121

'For God's sake, Faith. Don't you realize we have to break through Quihuli and then drive up a goat track to a pass eleven thousand feet high, quite possibly pursued until we reach guerrilla country?'

I could feel a chill beginning at the base of my spine and spreading upward to my heart, but alongside it still remained the remnants of that mad recklessness I had lived with ever since we outpaced the soldiers by the watchtower. Soon it would be gone, and only cold fear remain. 'No, but now you've just told me. What else do you suggest? Going with a truck short and starving through the winter?'

The Indians heard our quarrelling voices and were beginning to listen instead of work. Bruce turned to curse them and while he did so I ran over to where he had left the fourth truck. It started easily, the controls much what I expected even though there were more gears than I had ever used. I revved up the engine, but gently, just enough not to stall it, and moved off as if that truck slid through butter. No hurry to change up on such a jolting trip over the ploughland to the train, turn carefully; then into reverse, hoping to God that reverse was where it ought to be.

The gear went into place with a solid clunk but the truck reversed neatly. It wasn't articulated, which was lucky; I'd never achieved the knack of reversing articulated vehicles without a great deal of trial and error.

I switched off and jumped down, to find Bruce there waiting. 'Well?'

'Faith . . .' he said, and gripped me by the shoulders. 'Faith . . . you goddam crazy maniac.'

And he kissed me, while the Indians stopped work again to watch.

I felt the tremble of his body, the swift movement as he clamped control tight again, although he still held me as if we were alone and time waiting to be wasted. I would like to say that I felt then even an inkling of what was to come between us, but the truth is I was still riding my high; emotions spinning wildly so that I was incapable of sensing anything more at all. A crazy maniac, Bruce had called me and he was right. Like the Indians, I had seen and done too little to stay entirely rational under the impact of events which only weeks before I could not even have imagined. One thing at a time, that was the most I could manage, so I bobbed along above the tempest like a balloon on a slack string.

'You'll let me drive the truck?' I said.

He laughed. 'Yes. We need that fourth load badly, in case Yono's guerrillas force us into splitting the loot with them. And you, my sweet, are going to be with me in the mountains. I couldn't bear to watch you starve, when I love you just the way you are.'

I suppose he was high too, or he would never have said it quite simply as a fact, when after so short a time even instinct could not make it true. We all were in a state of euphoria, because the Indians fairly threw boxes and sacks into that fourth truck, while Bruce drilled gear discipline into me in the cab. He had stamped emotion flat again, except he was very fierce with me; his voice levelly insistent to ensure I would not forget what he said when I tired, and sharply snapped if I fumbled even for an instant. He was different again from the way he had been only minutes before, a man of so many facets I felt dazed instead of comforted by his presence.

Soon we must leave such safety as this dark cutting offered and hazard the passage through Quihuli.

'How long?' I asked, and my lips felt stiff.

'Since we left the freight yard? An hour and a half perhaps. Too long, anyway.'

What had they been doing in Quihuli while we sweated to load trucks here? If they guessed we might come that way, then we had no chance at all of getting through. I jerked my attention back to Bruce: he was standing on the ground looking up, while I sat in the truck cab with my hands gripped so tight on the wheel that the knuckles hurt. He was smiling, his face all shadow and moonlit bone. And this time I did feel something, lips softening and any wariness I had

123

learned forgotten, as I looked at him and began to understand a little of what waited for me if ever we reached the Picachero Valley.

'Listen, Faith,' he said quietly. I discovered later that he was always quiet when things were worst. 'Listen, and don't forget. I'm going first, then you, then Raphael and Ixtapa. Follow me exactly, very close. Don't worry about anything except staying close. I'd like to be last in case anything goes wrong, but there are several ways through Quihuli and we can't tell until we get there which will be the safest. They ought not to expect us to break through the town, but if anyone is suspicious, then speed is our best hope. Once we're through, I'll stop and wave the three of you by: Raphael and Ixtapa know the track up to the pass and both did some driving in the army.' He grinned. 'They'll drive like they were on a circuit, all the Comayaguans do. So let them go past, and after a while all you'll see will be their dust. Don't try to keep up. Take it slowly even if we're pursued. That track is lethal and not designed for heavy trucks. Okay?'

'I follow Raphael and Ixtapa once we're through Quihuli,' I repeated obediently. I needed to clear my throat to speak, and my high had quite definitely vanished.

'I shall be ahead until we're through, then right behind you. Don't look around or worry about me once you've pulled past.' He reached up and prised my hand off the wheel, climbed on the step to kiss it, held it gently against his cheek. It sounds corny, but in the foothills of Comayagua while waiting to run the gauntlet of Colonel Mozon's Seguridad, it felt right. 'We play everything by ear through Quihuli, just keep close. Afterwards, take it slow. Real, real slow, right down through the gear shift. I'll block the track if necessary to make sure you have the time you need.'

I nodded, wanted to say something, swallowed, nodded again. Remembered something – someone – I must not forget a second time. 'Aztlin? Rodrigo, too.'

'Sure. I'll put Aztlin in one of the trucks and cut Rodrigo loose. He can walk from here.' Bruce ran for the engine, still wreathed in steam on the line, and emerged with Aztlin and then Rodrigo. I watched while he climbed up on the footplate one last time, heaved over the regulator and jumped down. Very slowly locomotive pistons creaked, hesitated, ground the wheels into one full rotation, two. Pressure and water both nearly gone, my Tyneside hinny ghosted away in a cloud of vapour as the downward gradient added to its momentum.

As its last act of assistance, 16206 would confuse pursuit by not revealing until daylight where we had stopped. With luck, it might go quite a way, and set the radio waves crackling as far as San Bernardo.

Under Bruce's orders, we all kept our lights switched off as we ground the four trucks in low gear across the bumpy ploughland, then one after another swung up on the road, its surface white under the moon. It curved away round a bluff but for the moment seemed quite empty. Bruce was leading and immediately ahead of me; he had Techuac with him, who spoke army Spanish and could yell easiest at a challenge. Bruce himself was filthy, but close scrutiny would immediately reveal him to be a gringo: facially he did not look in the least like a Comayaguan. I smiled at the thought, the red of his taillight only five yards away. We were driving on sidelights now, and Bruce on headlights; darkened trucks would be immediately suspicious, even though everything depended on the army not having discovered that four of their trucks had disappeared. Or if they had, then not connecting the theft with a hijacked train.

Beyond the bluff the road still stretched emptily ahead. Surely Quihuli ought to be like a kicked bee skep, so just where was the Comayaguan army?

The emptiness suddenly seemed threatening. I had Juan beside me and smelt terror on him too: no way for either of us to escape it.

I turned and smiled at him, jerked my head as if trying to pretend that fear must wait outside. Tremulously, he smiled back. The time when we had laughed together on the footplate was already an incident in the past, and yet it formed a bond between us. I could not speak a word of Picacho, he only a few of Spanish, but when we smiled we both knew that if we tried hard enough, then fear could be forced outside. Where it would wait, and watch, and come again very soon.

It was easier for me, needing to concentrate on changing gears smoothly and following Bruce without a gap as he picked up speed. Juan could do nothing except wait, and hiss between his teeth.

Not far into Quihuli now, and as I thought it I saw Bruce's stoplights flash, dull again, come on brightly. He would not stop for anything short of a barrier, but I couldn't see what lay ahead – his tailgate filled my windscreen.

We rolled forward, brakes squealing, not quite stopping yet. Bruce intended to keep moving towards anything less than a tank across the road.

'Techuac,' said Juan, and gestured with his hands.

I strained my ears, heard shouts which might be a challenge and reply, or something very much more threatening. Our trucks were almost stopped, a glow of light ahead. I bit my lip, muscles jumping in my arms; the menace was worse, seeing nothing. I was filthy like Bruce and wore an Indian straw hat, but also would not pass the simplest check. None of us could. The moment we stopped, then four trucks full of Prodam food would immediately betray us. Yet surely, surely, no one would guess that downtrodden Picacho Indians might carry out such an audacious hijack, and then dare to drive stolen trucks calmly through Quihuli to their mountains? At the moment, Quihuli garrison must be suspecting Mendoza supporters or ejected *campesinos*, anyone but who it was, and we must not do anything which might set loose quite different thoughts.

Bruce was picking up speed; God, he was picking up speed again. In my relief I drew back my clutch foot with too much of a jerk and the engine stalled.

The sudden silence was appalling and I was stranded facing half a dozen armoured cars and fifty soldiers stretched on either side of the road as Bruce pulled away. The men immediately turned to stare, the nearest shouting something rude. I ground savagely at the starter and for a heartstopping moment the engine refused to catch, then it fired, screeched angrily as I jerked at the throttle, unable to do anything smoothly any more.

From ahead came the sound of a crash and for a precious instant all those faces turned to where Bruce must have deliberately sideswiped a parked vehicle. He had seen something wrong in his mirror and was trying to give me the seconds of grace I so desperately needed.

I was pressing the clutch with quite needless force, terrified of getting it wrong again, drew back my foot so slowly my knee went into spasm and the engine nearly stalled again. Frantically, I revved up and threw that accursed truck forwards so the soldiers who had jeered were forced to jump for their lives, but Comayaguans normally drove like that so everyone else merely laughed.

A sergeant fired a shot in Bruce's direction, but in fury at his bent vehicle rather than in suspicion, and then we were past. Sweet heavens above, we were past.

Quihuli next, some two miles ahead.

I tried to relax, breathe deeply and allow tense muscles to slump for the few minutes before we reached the town, but it was impossible. Probably dangerous, too. I needed to stay tense, because this was the kind of thing which only the instinctive reactions of extreme stress might possibly accomplish.

As we drove through the outskirts of the town, I could see a great deal of activity in the station and along the track, flashlights bobbing, a searchlight directed at the freight yard. Juan and I exchanged smiles again; the more troops who wasted time searching there, the better. I wondered what they thought they might find, when the one fact the authorities possessed was that their freight train had disappeared down towards San Bernardo.

The refuse-filled *barranca* and roadside straggle of railwaymen's cottages was coming up now, all the huts shuttered and dark, although I was sure everyone inside would be wide awake. Troops in steel helmets patrolled the road but scattered when Bruce's horn blared at them; a burst of gunfire echoed from somewhere across the town.

Left here up the approach road to the station, then right for the main part of the town. My palms slipped on the smooth, flat-angled steering wheel as I dragged at it for the turns. Distances and clearances were difficult to judge when perched so high above the road.

The plaza.

I could feel sweat on my face as well as my hands, along the edge of my hair, salt on my lips. The plaza was full of soldiers milling about, other squads of them being chased into personnel carriers in a great flurry over something. One man called out as we passed and I caught the Spanish: *El tren . . . descrubido.* My heart leaped. They had found the train. At the exact moment when we most needed a diversion, a patrol must have radioed in that they had seen 16206 panting through the night somewhere quite different. No one was worrying about trucks driving north through Quihuli and, providing we were not stopped, then no one might ever work out exactly what had happened. Bumper to tailgate we went fast down one side of the plaza, Bruce's hand on his klaxon. The scene was like a barnyard when a fox has broken in: a frantic flutter of protest and leaping for endangered lives. Comayaguans must be trained to dodge traffic or they wouldn't survive for long in a land of such reckless drivers, but they needed their skills in Quihuli plaza that night. Somehow, they all seemed to escape, but no one in front of us was thinking of anything except his life.

Once through the plaza, Bruce swung sharply right. I was nearly taken by surprise because the way to the mountains lay straight ahead, but as we turned I saw why. The main street was blocked by a tank, and a command vehicle bristling with radio antennae which must be coordinating the search for us.

They ought to know – must know – that four army trucks should not be driving this way through the town. But as we turned I could not see whether the alarm was raised or not, because we plunged into a maze of narrow streets, klaxons blaring, walls so close on either side that I could hear chipped adobe showering on the roof. We would need to turn left again very soon, and then again to reach that single wider road which led to the mountains. By going this way . . . I struggled to remember what lay in this part of Quihuli. This way lay the cemetery.

We were able to make one left turn by the cemetery wall, but then were caught in cross-hatched streets like tunnels, our speed dropping to walking pace. We crossed a deserted market where the surface was so rough I felt myself leave the seat completely when Bruce immediately accelerated across even so minute an open space.

Stamp on the brakes as his lights glowed danger red, wrench at the wheel as we turned again, but right instead of left. Christ, we had to get back on to that wider road somehow. Quihuli was a small town surrounded by a maze of slums and *barrancas*; only the two roads which crossed the plaza at right angles were suitable for trucks.

A howl of brakes forced me to swerve before stamping on my brakes too, or I would have crashed into Bruce. I saw then why he had stopped. We had entered a small square from which the only exit was down alleys three feet wide. Those on the left must lead back to the road we wanted, ahead lay an adobe church with a high wall enclosing what looked like a garden; perhaps it was a monastery. Only a single goat path led out that way, because beyond was what looked like more enclosures and then open country. To the right, houses. We couldn't turn, jammed together as we were and with a maze of streets behind, but nor could we go forward any more.

Bruce stuck his head out and shouted above the roar of engines. 'Engage your auxiliary gearbox. I'm sending Techuac to tell the others!'

I waved a hand and his head went in again. I couldn't imagine what he intended, but struck back the red-knobbed lever which engaged the second box as he had showed me, and saw Techuac go scorching past. Shutters were clattering open on houses in the square as it fairly shook to the noise of our engines.

Bruce waited perhaps thirty seconds to be sure we were all ready, then launched his truck like a missile at the blank wall ahead. The adobe disintegrated in a shower of dust and a rattle of clay facing, but the wall was high and thick enough for the truck to hesitate, one wheel spinning off the ground, before it heaved forward again. I followed blindly, oblivious of scandalized yells as the houses came alive with people. I felt the wheels of my truck crunch fragments of wall, leap on stubbed edges, and then we were through to kaleidoscopic glimpses of green grass, overgrown beds, a stagnant pool. In such surroundings the truck was a dinosaur set loose and smashing all it touched.

I wasn't quick enough to follow Bruce out on the other side; he spun his wheel to hit the next wall squarely, I hit it at an angle and baked mud exploded in my face. It was swept aside in the same instant as a whole section of wall collapsed from the ferocious double impact: sensibly enough, Juan was kneeling on the floor with his head in his hands and for a flash of time I was driving alongside Bruce across a kitchen garden full of peppers and squash and potatoes, with nothing between us to block the view. He looked across and threw up a hand in mock greeting, and I laughed back in the madness of it all; then we needed to stamp on everything to avoid a row of apple trees and he skidded deliberately in front again to absorb the next impact, this time of an outer wall. He hit it sideways in a blast of adobe, slewed again, waved me past. I couldn't hold the truck, but had to go with it as its momentum drove us through the gap, a fearful clang resounding in my ears as I swiped Bruce's tyre. Bone-dry harvested maize fields stretched ahead, the road to the mountains up on a bank beyond. I threw out the gear and jumped down as Rafael and Ixtapa went past in a cloud of dust, grinning all over their faces. They probably believed in ancient mountain gods and for them there couldn't be a better way of breaking out of Quihuli than by crushing the Catholic usurper under their wheels on the way.

Bruce was stuck – slewed sideways and canted into some obstacle I couldn't see.

He couldn't, mustn't be stuck. But I had known he was, and stopped because of it. Yet I was helpless. I didn't remember seeing a towcable in any of the trucks, and Bruce was still trying to free the trapped wheel. I screamed at him to leave it and come, began to run towards him, knowing how little time must remain until the story of four trucks bursting through Quihuli's monastery spread like a flash fire. The army might believe we were no more than drunks run wild, but they would certainly pursue us now.

I heard Bruce's engine change note, saw the front wheels thrash and then bite sticky earth. Each sound of the engine came to me in its separate parts, the power built into it barely sufficient to drive the cumbersome, laden truck out of stinking mud: the monastery cesspit, I realized now, amusement completely absent. There was something wrong with the truck, too: a screech which hadn't been there before and the windscreen was shattered; still, it had driven through three thick walls and now was sluggishly heaving itself out of viscous black morass, so Detroit need not feel ashamed of their design.

I hurled myself back into my truck, and slammed in the gear almost carelessly. The road lay ahead and Bruce had wanted me to lead once we were out of the town. I looked in the mirror to make sure he was following and stopped to disengage low ratio the moment we had climbed the bank. Another truck was there but I waved it on: either Rafael or Ixtapa had waited for us. I felt unreasonably happy that one of them had cared enough, or felt enough pride in himself, to wait.

Now we must all drive helter-skelter for the hills, as fast as possible until we reached the steeper gradients.

I kept glancing in my mirror but it was difficult to see anything, there was so much dust. I was worried about the screech in Bruce's truck, and also about pursuit. Juan was laughing beside me and tapping the speedometer with his finger: we were doing sixty kilometres an hour and at that

131

speed could outrace half-tracks but not armoured cars or jeeps.

Bruce dropped farther and farther behind, but I thought it was because of the dust, his truck seemed to be going well enough. He ought to be ahead of me now he'd lost his windscreen, but there wasn't time to stop and argue. Better to keep going, when every mile of our lead was precious.

Five minutes must have passed since we regained the track out of Quihuli, and I began to count. Six. Eight minutes. Eight and a half.

Juan was leaning out of his window, and turned to yell something and then gesture. Infuriating scarcely to understand each other at all. 'Señor Bruce?'

He shook his head vigorously and waved his hands as if he held a gun, pulled an imaginary trigger. The army had reacted at last.

I pressed harder on the throttle, feeling the cab shake on the corrugated track. As the moon sank I could see the mountains as a great black wall reaching down towards us. I switched on the headlights and quite a long way behind saw that Bruce had done the same. The faster I went the faster he could go, although the road's surface was deteriorating all the time; bends snaked more sharply and with less warning. At least the dawn wind was beginning to blow and Bruce closed up slightly as it swept my dust aside. The wheel kicked in my hands and the headlights threw fantastic shadows from every ridge and pothole; a steeper corner was coming up and then another: no matter how closely I tried to take the bends, our speed was dropping away remorselessly.

Take it real slow, Bruce had said. Fortunately, I was waiting so tensely for shots from behind that I scarcely thought about how narrow the track now was, how I had never driven a vehicle this size at breakneck speed before. I thought only of how much time remained before the pursuit caught us, understanding now why Bruce had insisted that I should pass him once we were out of Quihuli.

I gripped the wheel in anger, staring with gritted eyes at steep hillsides tumbling shadows all around. Although I could not guess how high the army would dare to follow us into guerrilla country, we were very close to safety.

Yet still fatally far away from safety, with pursuit snapping at our heels.

10

I heard the first rattle of automatic fire two or three minutes later.

The track had become a mule trail, the truck wheels jolting off it first one side and then the other as I tried desperately to find a driveable route. Open grassland had given way to stunted pines and grey rocks; in the headlights I caught glimpses of hollows and miniature cliffs streaked with darkness. In daylight and different circumstances, these foothills would have been very beautiful.

Then, without warning, my lights flashed across rock and I spun the wheel until they steadied on the first hairpin bend. It might have made a good breathing space for mules, but surely was impossible for trucks. Yet there was no sign of Rafael or Ixtapa, and if they could manage to drive a truck up there, then somehow I would, too. But quickly, that was the snag. My eyes were glued to the rough surface reflected in my lights so I couldn't see the pursuit, but it must soon catch Bruce even if aimed shots were impossible from vehicles travelling over such ruts.

The hairpin wound between rock on one side and a sheer drop on the other, the track rising precipitously in between. I stopped and engaged the auxiliary gearbox; wiped my hands on my knees, started to wipe them again and swore aloud at myself. I had to go now . . . now, or it would be too late.

The engine roared and shook as I took it too fast for such a low ratio, the cliffside tyre so close to the edge I felt it slither on loose shale. I simply could not hurry, had to take it at less than crawling pace, my teeth gripped so hard together that my jaw ached. This truck was a massive and dangerous beast, and Comayaguans with guns something I could not think of now. The lights lit rock at the far edge of the curve, and I swung out a fraction farther to get full lock on the wheel. Otherwise I should stick and the next five minutes see us cut apart by bullets.

I gave that engine every ounce of the power built into it, the track becoming almost perpendicular just at the worst point on the hairpin. Squeezed tight into jagged cliff, wheels churning over the chasm on my right, the bonnet like an outthrust stubborn jowl before my eyes as that brute of a truck refused to obey the wheel crammed over between my hands. Juan shouted, I shouted, as noise boomed off rock and dust enveloped everything except that one narrow trail we had to take, or die. Headlights predatory in darkness, the truck a self-willed animal taking us to disaster. Tight, tight, tighter into rock; an echoing clang from scraped steel and a spark flicked up and past my eyes. Then we were round, the gradient flattening and the engine shaking from surplus horsepower.

Second gear, third; then second again as the next bend came.

Then the next.

As we took it I caught a glimpse of Bruce immediately below me on the second of those three killing bends. Techuac was standing in the loaded space at the back, and as I watched, he heaved a crate over the tailgate and into the road. It burst in a spray of maize, and he followed it with a couple of sacks of dried beans, which also spilt. There wasn't any sign of pursuit although I could see right down to that first appalling bend. Bruce must have left a trail of cases behind him and on such a narrow surface any chasing jeep would have to stop while men jumped out to kick and heave the obstruction aside. There was no question of being

135

able to hit anything safely on such a precipitous track as this.

After that third hairpin, the way levelled slightly and swung over a ridge, dipped down, then rose in a series of cliff scrambles before running across a rock plateau, the going so much easier for a mile or more that I had time to think, and at once felt stupefied by fatigue. My eyes burned, and my back ached so badly I could scarcely bear it another moment.

Dawn was coming, and against the paler grey of sky I saw the notch infinitely far above which must be the pass we had to cross; a long way below it were some pinpricks of light which I supposed were Rafael and Ixtapa. I felt like putting my head on the steering wheel and weeping when I saw how far we still had to go.

Another hairpin coming up, steeply down this time and with a boulder like an island sticking through the track surface. The truck canted dangerously as I tried to squeeze past with one wheel climbing, and I looked straight down to a rockfall far below. A shuffle of falling dirt and a breath-stopping lurch; instinctively, I tried to steer higher up the slope but the wheel was still climbing the protruding boulder and we tilted even more terrifyingly. I could not make myself look away from that space to my right, from white-spotted granite and grit showering from wheels I could no longer see on that lethal downward curve.

Juan screamed. But my mouth was too dry for screams.

Slowly, slowly we were going, tilting down and outward until we would fall, somersaulting as we went. I croaked at Juan to jump; he might have a chance even though on my side of the cab there was only space. Despairingly, I stabbed at the throttle, felt the roar and lurch of power, something bite on shifting surface. A dreadful howl and spatter of debris, another lurch which hurled me sideways.

Rock and dry earth swam sickeningly into sight again, where only space had been.

We were back on the track, with another hairpin showing just ahead.

Gradually the ache in my arms and legs ebbed, I became

136

aware that I had switched off the engine, and Juan was still crouched on the step, coiled as if to jump. I shook my head, trying to clear the waves of vertigo. I had to restart the truck and get us going again.

I was terrified of the engine, and did not want ever to touch it again. I could not, dared not, touch it again.

Juan was back in the cab and tugging at my arm. I realized he must have been trying to attract my attention for some time. He stabbed a finger in the direction we had come and gabbled something, his lips still loose with fear.

My mind was so stagnant that for a moment a quite different horror swept over me, because I thought he meant that Bruce had been caught. Then I heard his klaxon blaring to attract attention and Juan nodded, miming hooting with his lips.

So it was relief which nearly took my senses next. A huge relief that Bruce was still safe, and a craven relief that I had an excuse to leave the cab, even if only for a moment. I opened the door, still trying to grasp what was going on. The ground looked so far away it took several seconds before I made up my mind that I could reach it; when I did, my legs buckled under me.

Wind was pouring off the peaks, and its icy strength whipped my thoughts back into some kind of order. Somewhere on that first set of bends and perhaps a thousand feet below, I could hear engines and shouts, the racket of automatic fire. I suppose they were firing at us, but if so then folded rock protected us for the moment.

Bruce and Techuac were crouched by the front wheel of their truck on the not-quite-hairpin immediately before the one which had so nearly killed us. The ground fell away sharply there on both sides, leaving the track isolated on a narrow ridge. I had felt the axles scrape as our wheels scuffled down shale on either side. I couldn't see what Bruce was doing, and whatever might have happened to his truck, we couldn't afford to waste time over it. I laid my head against the cold steel.

Then I heard a crunch and saw the silhouette of his truck

137

change shape, lurching as a foundered elephant might, down on its knees. Soon, Bruce and Techuac came toiling up towards us, forcing their pace as best they could over such difficult ground.

When they reached us Bruce held me, breath heaving in his lungs. We had not gained much altitude yet, but the air felt thin, and we were so tired that each extra effort was like a little death.

'My sweet,' he said, voice rough, 'climb back in that cab and we'll get out of here.'

The next part is hazy in my mind and I think I dozed for a while, because the next thing I remember clearly is full daylight on a tremendous landscape of mountains all round. Wind was beating against the side of the truck and the sky showed sharply blue, the range of peaks every shade of grey and purple. Juan and Techuac lay coiled together across seat and floor, sleeping, and Bruce was driving.

I struggled slowly back to a sitting position, horribly stiff, my eyes on those mountains and blue miles everywhere; on the loveliness of an earth I had not thought to see again. The wind in steep valleys, sweet green grass along the Tyne, and laughter by the fire on winter's evenings. It was the Border hills my mind's eye saw and not the Picacho Mountains. They say your life reels past in panorama when you're dying, but I had known only terror; now it was over the memory of a gentler landscape helped set hideous memory aside. For nightmares to feed on later, probably.

I looked across at Bruce, still needing to swallow tightness before I spoke, and even then I only managed trite banality. 'You must be exhausted. Bruce, for God's sake, let me drive for a while!'

'I suppose you aren't tired at all,' he said, and smiled. 'Talk to me and I guess I'll stay awake. Another thousand feet up to the pass, and we should find Rafael and Ixtapa waiting for us there. I haven't seen any wrecked trucks, and if they've got as far as this, then the last hairpins to the Windy Place shouldn't bother them much.'

'The Windy Place?'

'That's what the Picachos call the pass. It is ten, eleven thousand feet above sea level and the bleakest place on God's earth. I told Rafael and Ixtapa to wait there until we came.'

'We aren't being chased any longer?' I discovered that it was an enormous relief to talk, and the more ordinary the words the better.

'No. They won't shift my truck in a hurry. We might even risk going down to see if they have left any food after a week or so.'

'What did you do?'

'To the truck? I took the front wheels off and released the hydraulic jack. Which should be broken, and the axle bent. That section ought to stay blocked until they bring up a tank to shove it aside.'

I shivered, remembering that slope again. 'I wouldn't like to be the tank driver.'

'I doubt whether its tracks will last far over such rough ground; we don't have to worry, anyway.' He covered my hand briefly with his. 'Even if it hadn't been essential to block the way, I should have ditched my truck. I wanted to before, but you didn't hear when I signalled. I couldn't have lasted any longer, watching you drive with one wheel over a precipice.'

'Two wheels.'

His mouth tightened, although I had meant it as a joke. The kind of joke that gets stuck over gaping holes. 'I must have been crazy to let you try it.'

I turned my head and studied a face which three days before I had not known, but now was part of my life, whatever happened. 'You let me try because we had to have that truck. You knew then you would probably lose one, blocking off the chase.'

Words. Flat and useless, but this was not the moment for anything except the commonplaces which would keep our exhausted senses functioning, our minds on reaching the Windy Place by a track which continued to be so tortuously difficult that it was no longer even fit for mules.

But neither my mind nor my senses responded well to the

139

idea that grinding up a mountainside was still the only thing that mattered. I seemed conscious of each breath Bruce drew, the tremor of his muscles as he fought recalcitrant metal up that last slope to the Windy Place, the shape of his hands and the set of his head.

Yet I did not know this man, and he did not know me.

We found Rafael where the track widened just below the pass. He was alone.

Bruce heaved on the brake and climbed down stiffly, calling up to him until he shouted something back.

I scrambled down to join him. 'What happened to the other truck?'

'Ixtapa decided to go on alone.'

'He's all right?'

Bruce stretched carefully, and scraped his hands across his face. 'He was. I guess he's dead now.' He walked away alone up the slope towards Rafael, and stood talking to him.

After a while I climbed back into the cab. Up here the wind was so violent it was hard to stand in it for long, and so cold my face was already numb.

Then Bruce came back and climbed in, needing to squeeze circulation back into his hands before he started the truck up again. He looked bleakly angry.

'Tell me.' I didn't even know him well enough to judge whether I was behaving like a clod to ask.

He did not answer, concentrating instead on manoeuvring the truck in an amount of space which made it a simple operation after all that had gone before.

I took a deep breath. 'Look, I'm not trying to interfere, but sometimes it helps to share. If this next bit is difficult then you ought not to drive it in a rage.'

The line of his mouth relaxed, and he turned to look at me. After a moment we both looked away again, which left me to face the discovery that anything I thought I knew about my own emotions was out of date. 'In some ways this part isn't so difficult as the section we've just driven,' he said eventually. 'But it needs more care than any Latin American driver I've ever known will give it. And somewhere on the way we shall run out of fuel and have to finish coasting on the brakes. If I go first I can make sure they take it slow enough to survive, a yard at a time if necessary. At this time of year there isn't even any water to throw at the brakes to stop them going up in flames.'

His words conjured up hideous images of breakneck bends taken at accelerating speeds, but though I was apprehensive, the worst of my fear had gone. I wasn't alone, and Bruce Shryver had become a man whose judgement I trusted. I understood exactly how he felt though, when we crossed the plateau which was the Windy Place, and saw below a greasy smudge of smoke where grass still burned around some twisted steel. Ixtapa had accomplished so much of which his people could be proud, and then thrown his life away for no purpose at all, taking a truckload of food with him. It made no difference that he had ignored instructions; Bruce was the kind of man who would consider himself responsible for those who followed where he led.

Beyond the pass the ground fell away in a series of precipitous rock steps, and in places the track was hardly marked at all. Beyond the rock was empty air and a valley far below. I laced my shaking hands around my knees and reminded myself about how the worst of my fears were past. The ridge of mountains opposite was encased in cloud, and wisps of mist blew across where we were, too.

'Cloud nearly always closes in as the day goes on,' Bruce observed, and set the truck down that monstrous staircase. It was certainly no route to drive in fog.

It took us all the rest of the day to reach the valley floor, as mist poured off the peaks towards us. We stopped only once, on the ridge above where Ixtapa had crashed. Perhaps he lost a wheel, or just enjoyed leaping boulders once too often. Anyway, the truck had cleared a twenty-foot ravine, hit the cliff opposite, and somersaulted until it caught fire. A few burst crates and sacks were scattered about, which might eventually be salvaged, but nothing else remained except a black stain in the scrub.

We ran out of fuel soon after; Ixtapa had been unlucky in

one way because he must have had very little except vapour left in his tanks to catch on fire, but I don't suppose it made much difference.

Several times I needed to get out and beckon Bruce down places I would never have imagined a truck could go. Twice we all had to labour to build loose stone into a causeway which would smooth one rock step into the next, and after the fuel ran out it was much worse. As Bruce had said, we had to trickle down a yard at a time, and even so the brakes stank of heat.

As dusk came, we reached the valley floor and that was that. The trucks would roll no farther, and no one came to meet us. Aztlin was dead where he lay on crates in the back of Rafael's truck, as I had known he would be, but we had to take turns helping the Indian with the broken foot, walking the last stretch of the way. It all seemed endless, mile after mile of rough grass, the Indian in agony although he never once complained. It was also bitterly cold; we had taken all day to come down from the pass but were still far higher than Quihuli.

And safe.

I had not quite understood before why Bruce had been so confident that the Comayaguan army would not pursue us here, it was a province of their country after all. But even helicopters would find those mountains hostile, with their gusting winds and sudden downdraughts; lifting assault troops over an eleven thousand foot pass was a job which could be accomplished only in the most settled weather. We'll be safe until spring, Bruce had said, and I believed him.

So until then, my home would be the Picachero Valley, with Bruce Shryver and several hundred Indians and guerrillas for company.

11

When I woke it was daylight again, and I lay in a small room shaped like a sliced melon, with a low roof curving towards a point and constructed from some kind of scrub. All the rest was mortared stone, pierced by a single window, through which I could see a chink of blue. It must be tomorrow, I thought hazily. I didn't remember much of our arrival the night before: scattered huts, a slashing wind, Bruce holding me upright while he, too, stumbled with exhaustion.

I was covered with woven rugs and felt warm but very stiff. I moved my hands over my body and realized I was still dressed in filthy jeans and wore a jacket under the rugs. The cascading events of the past few days seemed oddly blurred, which suited me when they contained a great deal I wanted to forget. What I saw was more than enough to think about for the moment.

I grimaced at the squalid sight I must make, and then grinned. Black as a coal-heaver from the steam engine and striped grey with dust, I supposed. I got up and went over to the window, hearing my muscles creak, but could see little except rough grass and some conical huts, which must be like this one. No crops, no animals, no movement. Time suspended by the silence of high altitude.

My sleeping cubicle was curtained off from the rest of the hut, and I ducked under draped material to go in search of water and something which might do as soap. The hut was about twenty feet in diameter, with a rough plank table, some shelving, bench seats and a fireplace. Some Indian cloth on the walls, nothing else. Bruce was sprawled on the floor, fully dressed but muttering and twisting in his sleep. He lay on a kind of reed mat but had no coverings; he looked cold and worn in the light striking through the uncurtained window. I went back to the hutch where I had slept and ripped blankets off the bed to put over him, but when I came back, he was awake.

'You gave me all the covers,' I said. 'And the bed.'

He rubbed his face, annoyed at being caught off-guard. 'If you call it a bed. Rawhide strips on poles aren't much softer than the floor.'

'But warmer.'

He grunted, and stood warily. 'I've gotten used to living at eight thousand feet. I'll go heat some water.'

He went out, leaving me feeling blank; this morning he was different again. It was going to be wearing living with a man who was never the same from one moment to the next. The only odd thing was that temperamentally he did not strike me as in the least capricious.

Living with a man. I stood in the doorway of that hut and faced the fact that very soon I was going to live with Bruce Shryver in every sense of the word, and probably I wanted to, very much. Yesterday I softened to his touch and felt glad; it was only how he was today which made me suddenly uncertain. Yet under the impact of our great danger, he, too, had shown himself far from indifferent to me. I smiled ruefully at myself: danger is a great enemy of thought, a father of emotions and flatterer of illusions.

Well, that was his affair, wasn't it? Today I was simply happy to be safe in the Picachero Valley, and to be safely there with Bruce; we would have to take it on from there. I couldn't start agitating now about how different he could be from my memory of a man who laughed and said he loved me in the steam-filled cab of a hijacked locomotive.

So I went out into the sun feeling buoyantly cheerful, and

saw that on this side of the hut there was a scrap of cultivated ground, a shrunken lake in the distance, and some scattered smudges of smoke across the floor of the valley which marked where the Picachos lived. There didn't seem to be a village as such, nor tracks, only a few foot trails wandering through yellowed grass. Bruce was in a small cookhouse, and showed me a place at the back of it which he had rigged up as a kind of shower. Hot water, too. Hooray for American plumbing, I thought, firmly putting first things first.

It was marvellous to feel clean again, even though I had to dress in Bruce's spare clothes afterwards; it was fortunate that he was lightly built and not particularly tall, but even so I must have looked like a child who has been at the dressing-up box. Perhaps in compensation, I brushed my hair until I could feel the spring in it.

Standing in that glorious sunshine with luminous mountain air tingling against my skin, I felt exhilarated, oddly restless and also nervous.

I told myself this last was simply a hangover from past strain, or hunger, or altitude, but no excuse was true. I was nervous. When I went back into the hut at last, my blood was thumping erratically and something had happened to my breathing.

There were clay pots on the table and almost immediately Bruce came in behind me, carrying something hot. 'You'll hate the food up here, but for the moment we have enough. Tomorrow we must start ferrying the crates from where the trucks are.' He pulled out a bench for me, his manner so detached that my nervousness vanished, and a grey flatness took its place.

Looking back, I can see how reaction from the violent days I had lived through was sloshing erratically through my emotions, changing them from one moment to the next. During the meal I was conscious only of feeling short of air. My lungs worked like bellows but they never seemed to fill; I put it down to altitude, but it was other things besides.

We ate a kind of mush made from beans and flavoured

with herbs, followed by apples and gritty tortillas. We didn't talk much, although Bruce did say that there were a few fertile folds in the mountains where the Picachos kept some sheep, and a few hardy apple trees thrived. Apart from these, they grew maize and beans and potatoes on the valley bottom but the yield was always poor.

'In Aztec times this place was rich,' he added. 'They dug channels along the contours of the mountains to catch the rains and stop erosion, but no one has bothered with the system since and the rock here is very porous. Even heavy rain disappears almost instantly unless it's trapped, and for eight months of the year there are seldom more than showers. I've been trying to resurrect the Aztec system, and the Indians are just beginning to dig out some channels for themselves now they see what can be done, but it's a long project.'

'And you intend to stay for years to see it through?' I looked at bare hut and the single shelf of books, then back at him. We had instinctively tried to avoid each other's eyes during that awkward meal. 'I just can't see the fit.'

'Which fit?'

'You and this place. For heaven's sake, Bruce. You aren't the hermit type, and I've watched while you led a pack of amateurs through a complex hijack. You can't expect me to believe you've spent your life as a farmer.'

I saw his hands tighten and he looked away again. 'I should like to be one, oddly enough.'

'But not here.'

There was a long pause. 'No, not here,' he agreed at last. 'I don't find the Picachos enlivening company. Faith – '

Our eyes locked, huge silence all around. The evening mist was pressing down from the mountains and the sun had vanished: Bruce had lit the fire but it was becoming very cold again.

'Faith,' he said again. Slanting eyebrows drawn down in concentration, a vein beating in his temple, hands clasped on the table. 'You know I did not want to bring you here.'

146

Abruptly my mind abandoned illusion and crawled back to the present. 'Why not?'

He grunted and stood, whether from annoyance or discomfort I could not tell. 'Because it is the wrong place for you, and I'm the wrong man. Unfortunately, there wasn't anywhere else for you to go, and it won't be safe to move out now before the spring.'

'I like it here. I could do with peace for a while, after the way my time in Comayagua has been spent.'

He grinned unexpectedly, and came over. 'My sweet, I don't know quite how much peace will have to do with it.'

I stood, and we faced each other. Neither of us spoke.

The trace of a smile remained on his lips, but otherwise there was still that inappropriate look of concentration, as if he was studying some problem and I was only incidentally of relevance to the solution. Sharp-angled bones and pale northern eyes made an unrevealing façade when that was the way he wanted it. Except for tension he could no longer hide. That and the way his eyes softened now, when I refused to look away. I might have been mistaken about some things yesterday, but not all.

He relaxed suddenly and held me, our stillness slowly filling with what we both wanted. His mouth on mine and the shape of his body under my hands. Distantly, I remembered how he had said that he was the wrong man for me. I tried to consider it, but I forgot. Forgot everything except Bruce and how he wasn't wrong for me. Then forgot that too, as I was taken unaware by the urgency of a man who had been twenty months alone. Yet even in urgency the shadow of grace remained, of care and skill, until my inexperience did not matter any more. When I ceased to forget, it was a joyful splendour I remembered.

Bruce slept much later, lying still in my arms, and in my conceit I believed that this was a peace he had not known for a long time.

It remained quite strange to remember also what we had become together, when still I did not know him. It didn't seem so important any more, and after a while I slept too.

147

He was awake when I stirred, so in the morning I discovered a man who was again different, but this time because of me. The edges of his face had eased, the sense of strain vanished. He shifted slightly, and kissed me. 'My dear. Do you know the exact moment when I began loving you?'

I shook my head. I didn't want pretence about love to spoil what we had gained, simply because he thought I was a romantic innocent who expected hackneyed phrases. I was, of course, which didn't help.

His fingers drifted across my face and came to rest across my mouth. 'When you stood in a locomotive steaming away from bullets, and sang that absurd song. Your lips laughing and those hazel eyes not giving a damn for anyone.'

'Coal on my face,' I said helpfully.

He laughed, a rocket of uninhibited delight which finished the conversation until later. Over breakfast (of the same gruel and tortillas) he was still extravagantly cheerful, laughing easily, talk leaping from one irrelevance to another. He looked much younger, as if a great deal about him had never been let off a very tight leash before.

I watched him covertly, wondering.

I did not believe that such unthinking ease could last, although I enjoyed it enormously, and it didn't. I was almost pleased this time when he changed, because it showed I understood a little of him, even if only hesitantly as yet.

The moment we went outside after breakfast, he sobered up. Head slanted as if he was tuning in to danger, body poised as if at any time he might need to leap for his life; answering for a while in monosyllables. He looked again a man who had not known security for a very long time.

He felt me watching him but turned away without responding, and together we went to search for enough Picachos to trek up to the trucks. There were mules in the valley but no vehicles, nor fuel to restart the trucks. There was usually a little diesel, Bruce said, for pumps and the like, but disturbed conditions over the past few months meant the tanks were dry. It was infuriating that we and most of the Picachos would have to make half a dozen trips of at least ten

148

miles, heaving boxes and sacks, when a couple of gallons of motor fuel would save us all the bother.

There was nothing for it, however. The Prodam maize and beans (more maize and beans, I thought despairingly) would soon deteriorate if they were left for long in open trucks.

To my surprise, Bruce received a surly response from the Indians we visited; even the one with the broken foot preferred the attentions of the local bone-setter to Bruce's offer of drugs. One or two invited us in for aguadiente and no one seemed to be doing anything in particular, but very few thought it a good idea to set off for the trucks today. Even Rafael and Juan were doubtful; they came, but showed their resentment by dawdling annoyingly behind.

'Do you think they will simply slip off home when you aren't looking?' I asked Bruce. The clouds were thickening on the mountains but the view was still magnificent: the sun glittering on immensities of blazing rock and yellow valley bottom. Some of Bruce's reactions might be unexpected, but mine were not: I gazed about me as if I could never see enough, and was quite simply happy.

'Not now they have come,' he answered after a moment. 'But their chiman – who is a kind of medicine priest – says that this quarter of the moon is not propitious for a journey, which may have something to do with everyone feeling ill after twenty-four hours on aguadiente. They had one hell of a party to celebrate their success.'

'Without you?'

'Sure, without me. You don't think they like a gringo any better just because he happens to be on their side at the moment, do you? Rather the reverse, in fact. They know where they are when they can simply hate, and feel unsafe when those they accept as enemies suddenly act like friends.' He jerked his head at lines I could see on the lower slopes of a nearby mountain. 'Take my Aztec channels, for instance. I first came through here several years ago and thought then that, if I ever had time to spare, resurrecting an Aztec system would pay a fraction of the debt our peoples owe to theirs. So I came back when I needed a place to go. It is technology they can understand – their ancestors invented it, after all – and would double their living standards in five years. Then once I had shown them how, they could run it for themselves. Sure, they were grateful to me. After living twelve months here I was invited into most huts, and some of them even accepted my advice instead of chiman spells when they were sick. So what happened? Their first improved crop attracted in guerrillas. *Ladinos* mostly whom they hate, and who will exploit them blind. Without the extra crops I taught the Picachos how to raise, no guerrilla leader could have thought of regrouping through the winter here.'

'But for heaven's sake, Bruce, you didn't bring in guerrillas!'

'So who did, if you were a Picacho?'

I stared at the great barrier of mountains. 'They must be able to understand about the *campesinos* being hunted off their land. They've lost enough themselves over the generations.'

'Sure, they understand. But, for the first time ever, uprooted *campesinos* came here, don't you see? So now they remember how their chiman threw his mixes when I started digging out the channels and said it would bring ill fortune.'

'Mixes?'

'Divination. They do it with red beans, or bits of rock kept in a bag. But ill fortune came just the same, so now the chiman is riding high.'

I glanced at the file of Indians. They talked occasionally among themselves but seldom looked at us. 'And Prodam's food didn't make any difference?' I could see now that his need to win back confidence in himself and so in his project had been another reason for risking so much on a chancy scheme.

'It might, tomorrow. They've all gotten hangovers today. And that's another social difficulty; when I was invited around, their idea of a ball is to compete on how quickly they can drink enough to pass out. It's not my business and I'm no abstainer, but alone up here drinking rotgut by the quart means you're seeing red snakes crawl up the wall in no time at all. I don't intend to take that way out, but moderation isn't a habit the Picachos admire.'

There was something in his tone which told me how close he had come to seeing those red snakes. Told me too just how difficult it had been to stop gulping aguadiente by the quart, alone for so long; how he wanted to tell me about it, pour more words out of loneliness and be rid of the need for good. But he stayed silent, the mood of this morning now completely vanished, so I simply touched him and hoped he knew I understood but didn't mean to poke about where I wasn't wanted. I was also glad of the excuse to touch him. 'Like me. No easy ways.'

He jerked under my fingers as if I had touched an open wound, and did not answer.

We could see the trucks clearly now, stranded where their momentum had left them, quite close to the bottom of the scarp. The Indians were becoming more animated, slapping each other on the back and shouting so the sound of their voices bounced off rock. When we were close, Bruce called out sharply to them and stopped dead, looking around him.

The Indians stopped too and after a while I saw what they were looking at. All around the trucks the ground had been trampled. We went on again more cautiously, and found what I suppose we had all known we would find once we saw those marks. Forty or fifty men at least had come here to trample so much grass flat, and between them they had taken everything. All the food. All the tools. Even loose boards and cloth and upholstery.

Only two stalled and empty trucks remained to show for all our efforts. A shadow swept across spiky yellow tussock-grass and I looked up to see a vulture floating overhead, like a partly collapsed umbrella; irrelevantly, I wondered what we looked like to it. Puny figures in a scraped-out valley, gaping at empty steel.

'Guerrillas,' said Bruce flatly, the word universal. He added something in Picacho but the Indians remained motionless and blank-faced.

151

I stared at the mountains. 'Where are they?'

'They have a camp on the other side of the lake, but I guess they've left some pickets close by, watching.'

Several of the Indians were fingering their machetes and looking around uncertainly; the silence of that valley was extraordinary and now seemed spooky instead of peaceful. Nothing happened though. The silence remained complete and after we had milled around for a while there wasn't anything to do except tramp back to our separate huts.

A stooped and dirty old man met us before we reached them, his hands clasped over a stick for support. The Indians immediately crowded around him and talked with their heads together, excluding us.

'The chiman?' I asked.

'Yes. There are two of them this end of the valley, but he's the one who matters. We'd do best to leave them to it, he'll be trampling on our tails quite soon enough.'

So we walked on, and left the knot of them arguing in the dusk. It gave me an uncomfortable feeling to think how completely we had been put on one side, while anger grew out of the blades of their machetes. I was fairly certain Bruce wasn't armed, which presumably was how he wanted it; but with guerrillas in the valley and now the Picachos turning hostile, it seemed a little foolhardy.

'What can they do?' I said, into that enormous stillness.

'Nothing. They have machetes and the guerrillas have guns. I'll go talk to Yono in the morning – guerrilla camps aren't places to visit in the dark. The chiman knows I'll go, but he'll want to cast his mixes first. So we shall both play out a charade that the decision was made in his goatskin pouches.'

'Yono is the guerrilla leader?'

'*Yo no* means I don't, in Spanish. The bastard never agrees with a goddam thing anyone else says, so the nickname stuck. I fixed with him that if we could pull off this operation, then he could have the credit but the food was ours, since he had helped himself to most of the Picacho crops. And though a bastard, so far he's kept such bargains as he's made.' His voice sounded abstracted, as if he was thinking already of tomorrow and the guerrilla camp.

As well he might. 'Bruce, why should you go? Surely Comayaguan guerrillas are more likely to kill a Yanqui than – than an Indian chiman, for instance, whose valley they need to use.'

'Yono made the deal with me, so I am the only one who might shame him into keeping it.'

'If anyone can.' Fear was back, and greater than before. 'Bruce – '

'You'll be okay,' he said quickly. 'Short of food perhaps, but the Picachos have strict notions of hospitality, and you would be a guest.'

'Thanks.' I was coldly, furiously angry to find that he could believe that my own safety was all I cared about. After last night he must be blind, indifferent and passionless to think like that, surely. Or was I no more than the original, gullible fool?

We had reached the hut as I added, 'You must remember to tell me about their funeral rites before you go. I wouldn't like to muck up my chances as a guest by doing the wrong thing if you die.'

I went over to the fireplace and threw split ocote pine on the ashes so they blazed up almost at once, ocote being resinous and very dry. The flames blurred for an instant and then steadied; it would be the last gut-wrenching straw if I wept now.

'I have to go.' Bruce had stayed over by the door. 'We need that food and unless I go, Yono will keep it.'

'He'll keep it anyway. I don't suppose he carried it ten miles for fun.'

'My guess is that one of his subordinates spotted it, and saw his chance to outsmart the rest. They're a pretty raw bunch up there, with half a dozen guys each wanting to outbrag the rest. So if I don't even dare to go and remind Yono of our deal, he'll let junior get away with it and chalk him up a score. He needs enterprising lieutenants for next

153

spring. But, at the least, I think he'll split with me if I throw our contract in his face.'

I shrugged. He had made up his mind and wasn't going to change. It wasn't so much the fact of him going to see the guerrillas which upset me, but what he'd said.

The door pushed open and the chiman came in, no nonsense about knocking. He surveyed me speculatively through powerful eyes set close together, and kept spitting on the floor while he talked, emphasizing his words with jabs of a stick. Otherwise he took no notice of me, Indian women being even less regarded by their menfolk than *ladino* or Spanish ones are by theirs.

He went at last, leaving a stench behind him.

Bruce propped open the door. 'Most Picachos take sweat baths once a week, but chimans are sworn to dirt as well as celibacy. I don't think they take the celibacy as seriously as the dirt.'

It was dark outside. The yelp of coyotes and drone of the wind was the only sound, the temperature plunging with the draught. I felt as wretched as I had recently been happy, and told myself it was delayed shock from the past few days. I turned back to the fire and fidgeted unnecessarily with wood and ash.

'I have to go,' Bruce repeated. He shut the door and came over. 'Faith, I don't know whether I could have explained things better, but it's been a long time since anyone cared what I did so long as the results came right.'

I piled ocote blindly on the fire. 'Yes, I suppose so.'

He crouched beside me and caught my hands. 'You wait until you have backpacked ocote out of the hills, you'll count each log then. My dear, you're crying.'

I wanted to ask him what the devil he expected, instead I put my head in my hands and wailed like a baby. At last weeping for Ulate and Señor Mendoza, for Aztlin, and for myself a little, too. Because this man whom I had believed I was just beginning to know was still a stranger.

Bruce was tender in a way he had not been the night before, and after a while my misery eased.

154

I did not sleep well afterwards though, and neither did he.

Instead we lay scarcely touching, thinking our secret and lonely thoughts.

12

It was nearly a full morning's walk to the guerrilla camp on the other side of the lake, and we covered most of the way in silence.

We had quarrelled bitterly when Bruce realized I meant to come with him, and he used every weapon he could think of to dislodge me. I understood this, and did not take too much notice of the hurtful things he said, but memory is less easy to control. Stupidly, I found myself unable to forget them afterwards and sulked resentfully, although I do not usually bear grudges.

The one thing he dared not do was order the Picachos to hold me prisoner while he went alone, because once they saw that the Yanqui despised his woman, my position would be gone. If he did not come back, they would no longer regard me as their guest and I should count for even less than their own women. So in the end I won, because Bruce might speak cruelly but was disarmed by his own scruples, which meant that I found the winning singularly bitter.

The guerrilla camp straggled along the lake shore; there were children and a few turkeys running about, women thumping clothes in freezing water, and quite a lot of young men drilling haphazardly. We passed one group squatting intently round a stripped machine gun. Some of the men wore olive denims, others *campesino* shirts under goatskin jackets; they all carried machetes and about half had guns slung across their backs, a few of them modern with automatic magazines, the rest quite old. Flat patient faces stared at us, all looking alike to me in their graduated shadings of yellow-brown, reddish brown, coppery brown. What did they hope for, I wondered, or was hatred and suffering all they knew? Certainly, I could sense their hostility enclosing us, and one or two spat as we passed.

Bruce put his hand under my arm, the first time he had touched me all morning: the proprietorial gesture which said this woman is mine, to take her you need to kill me first. A gesture as old as time, and as unmistakable.

Two armed *ladino* youths stopped us before we passed the first hut beyond the open drilling space. '*No pasado aquí.*'

'I have an appointment to meet El Capitán Yono.' Confidence was vital, and Bruce Shryver a naturally confident man.

The boys exchanged covert looks; an appointment was an unexpected thing in the Picachero Valley. 'No one may pass this way.'

'I have passed before, and will again. Send to tell El Capitán; he is expecting me.'

After an argument one of them went, and while we waited a group of children gathered round us. One of them was Rodrigo.

He grinned at my astonishment. 'It seemed tame to return to Quihuli when the señor released me, and I knew the señorita was a friend whom it might be worth my while to follow. I hid in the back of your truck, and was asleep when the Freedom Guerrillas came. Now I will fight with them and never shine shoes again.'

'You are too young to fight, Rodrigo. In a few years –'

'No one is too young,' he said proudly. 'Already a *sargento* has instructed one of his men to share a rifle with me. I will learn how to fire it, and how to garrotte with wire; then very soon I shall win a rifle of my own.'

I swallowed. 'I expect to be living in this valley during the winter. If you would like to come sometimes I could teach you to read and write, then in the spring you might be able to enter an *escuela gratuita* in Quihuli.'

'*No, gracias, señorita,*' he answered politely. 'In the spring I shall fight and kill our enemies. When we have won, then I will go to school.'

The guard came back and jerked his head for us to follow him, but all I could think of was how I should be guilty of Rodrigo's blood. No matter that I had intended nothing of the sort: but for his acquaintance with me, almost certainly he would have returned to shining shoes on the steps of Quihuli station. Now he would become a killer and probably have only weeks to live.

'Very likely he would not have survived long in Quihuli.' Bruce picked up my thought with uncanny accuracy. 'You have to accept that we influence others simply by existing, and go on from there.'

'Good intentions in heavy hob-nailed boots,' I said bitterly.

'They're better than the other sort. Keep close to me but stay quiet in front of Yono, okay? These may be Freedom Guerrillas but they surely have not gotten around to sex equality in the ranks.'

As we crossed the camp, we were followed by a thickening crowd of idlers, mostly children but some adults, too. At the far side we stopped in front of a hut. One of the guards went inside, then reappeared and beckoned Bruce in. He tried to block me when I followed but Bruce shouldered him aside and he wasn't quick enough over thinking what to do about it. Inside the hut were two Prodam crates used as chairs, and parts of others roughly nailed to make a table. Behind it sat a man with thick-lidded Indian eyes and a mouth like a pair of pliers: narrow, tight and roughened at the edges.

'Sit down, Señor Broos,' his voice was a surprise, quiet and not unfriendly. He snapped his fingers. 'Another crate for the señora; I did not know you had been so fortunate, *amigo.*'

'I find that difficult to believe,' observed Bruce. 'It would

158

surely be the first tale of my doings which hasn't come running around the lake the same day it was born.'

Yono laughed, showing teeth sharpened like a picket fence. 'Perhaps you are right. Señora, you are welcome to Freedom Camp. Rodrigo told us how you came to Comayagua wanting to help our people.'

These courtesies were so different from anything I expected that I felt remarkably foolish and fumbled the flowery Spanish which was needed for a suitable reply. It didn't matter, in fact was probably a good thing; Yono did not expect me to take an active part in the proceedings. He turned back to Bruce and put a bottle on the table. 'We will drink to the spring, eh? Then I would like you to explain to me the mechanism of a portable missile we have received through friends. *Hombre!* I could scarcely believe such a thing could be packed into a carrying case.'

Bruce shook his head, smiling, and I had the impression that this was an argument which had been thrashed out many times before. 'I have come with a request of my own today. One of your lieutenants took food which belongs to the Picachos. By right of arms, and because you and I agreed it should be so.'

'We agreed it?'

'*Sí, mí capitán*. That was our agreement.'

Yono stroked his chin, enjoying himself hugely. 'I cannot recall it.'

'I think your lieutenant did not recall it. You, *mí capitán*, I understand to be a man who does not forget; even as you are also a man who never overlooks his own advantage.'

Yono roared with laughter and threw his shot of aguadiente down his throat. '*Ayí, hombre!* I told Estaban when he brought in those crates that you would not beg, but come here to demand.'

'What was his reply?'

'He said it was all the more reason to kill an insolent Yanqui.'

Bruce swirled aguadiente in his glass; he had not drunk any of it yet. 'And your response to that, *mí capitán?*'

159

'I said I would see.' The mouth pinched shut, laughter vanished.

Bruce did not answer, still swirling his drink, but I felt my muscles knot. There were other men listening in the shadows of that hut, and they were tense, too.

'Well, what are you thinking?' demanded Yono.

'I am thinking,' answered Bruce, 'of a man whose word was considered trustworthy in these mountains. If Yono said kill, then we knew it would happen and feared him in consequence. If he told his men not to kill, or steal, then they preferred to die rather than disobey. And if he said it shall be so, then that was how it came to pass.'

There were indrawn breaths around the hut, and someone cursed aloud. Yono smiled, but it was a different smile from before: lips peeled back as the corners of his mouth lifted, and nothing at all to do with humour. 'The food is yours. I told Estaban so, but he is impulsive, which is good in a soldier.'

'A soldier needs many qualities,' Bruce agreed noncommittally.

'Including a knowledge of weapons they may capture or receive as gifts.'

'No,' Bruce repeated. 'I understand very little about missiles, and would not teach you if I did. I thank you for justice I expected to receive, yet am honoured in receiving it just the same. I will ask the chiman to send Picachos to carry the Prodam food back to their huts.'

'Not so fast, *amigo*. According to one bargain the food is yours, yes. By another, ours.'

'What other bargain?'

'The bargain struck by a captor over goods he seizes. So I have a difficulty, eh? How do I decide between you and Estaban, so you both feel my justice has been done?' He reached into the shadows and hauled out a good-looking *ladino*, who scowled at Bruce and hooked his thumbs belligerently in his belt.

Bruce stayed sitting on his crate but put down his untasted drink. 'I think you have already made your judgement.'

'I think perhaps I have.' Yono's voice rose in savage mimicry and everyone chuckled dutifully. 'You claim a bargain, Estaban claims a conquest. So the two of you may put one against the other, then my word will never again be doubted in the mountains.' He picked up an automatic off the table and gave it to Estaban. 'Shoot him.'

We were all so flabbergasted that for an instant no one moved. There were, I suppose, seven or eight people crammed into that small hut, and as it dawned on them that in such confined space bullets could go anywhere, most dived for the floor. Except Yono, who picked up a cigar and began lighting it; and Estaban as he poked the gun forward, giggling a little with shock and delight. Bruce and I were seated a yard away, his hand on my arm keeping me where I was.

I yelled and instinctively tried to pull away and lunge for Estaban; I hit the edge of the table and then the floor as Bruce hurled me from him with all his strength and the crack and stink of explosive split air above my head.

'The food is yours, Señor Broos,' said Yono placidly, and struck another match.

I leaped to my feet in a lather of fear to find Bruce looking infuriatingly calm, still sitting on his packing case. He drank his aguadiente, and stood. 'Your word is good, *mí capitán.*'

Yono blew out smoke and cuffed Estaban good naturedly. 'He is brave but still has a lot to learn. *Salud y conquista, amigo.*'

'*Y la vida para gastarlas,*' Bruce replied drily.

I followed him into the sun dazedly, tagging along like any dutiful Indian wife, to find most of the camp waiting for us. The shot must have brought everyone running and they formed a hostile, jostling palisade of faces through which we had to fight our way to the edge of the camp.

When we were free of them at last, with grass and space and silence all around again, the earth had never seemed more beautiful than the Picachero Valley was to me that afternoon. The sun was warm and welcoming on my back, sky and lake cobalt-dark, the mountains soft behind mauve haze.

'Would you mind telling me what happened?' I asked,

when the last of our escort had gone. I was conscious of breathing deep grateful gulps of air and my bones felt loose.

'Estaban learned that a single bullet in a heavy and unfamiliar gun is not always as decisive as he thought. Yono had a hell of a good laugh on us both, and I grew a few more grey hairs.'

'Me, too,' I said feelingly. 'For God's sake, Bruce – '

'Yono set us up. He'd decided how to wriggle out of an awkward spot without losing face before I ever showed up. If he'd put more than one bullet in the magazine the result would have been different but, like I said, he keeps to a bargain.'

'Up to a point.'

'Oh, sure, the Picachero Valley isn't the City of London. Like a bullfighter, Yono's fond of blood as well as being a born showman. He also has discipline to keep through a difficult winter, and didn't want to spend it listening to Estaban boast how he'd forced his boss into busting a deal.'

Bruce didn't seem to mind, that was the extraordinary thing. He'd been forced to dodge a bullet at three-foot range, and apparently accepted it as a normal way of doing business.

Again, he came very close to reading my thoughts. 'I don't enjoy dealing with gangsters, but over the years I have learned a little of what it takes to get a drop on them, if that's what I have to do.'

'I apologize.' I prefer to perform unpleasant duties as fast as possible and, any way I looked at it, Bruce deserved an apology. The fraction of a second he had taken to send me sprawling could easily have cost him his life. 'I ought not to have come. You were quite right, you would have been safer alone.'

He stopped, so we turned to face each other. 'My dear, I don't believe any other woman would have said it without excuse. I would apologize too, except I don't want to remember the things I said. It helps now to have you here.' He held up his hands so I could see how badly they were shaking.

162

Mine were too. So we laughed and kissed, caught in the slipstream of reaction after desperate danger. Then, until the altitude made me gasp, we ran together along the lakeside, delight in each other and in our escape inextricably intermingled.

That evening when Bruce went out to tend a goat he kept, I found some paper and almost guiltily began to write. I had mentally turned so much that I had seen into scenes for a book – no, short stories, I thought now – that my fingers twitched to discover whether I could make them come right on paper. Just for a few minutes while I was alone, to see how it went.

Yono, I thought. Yono in these vast and silent mountains, followed by hating men. A violent man breeding violence, and surrounded by predatory greed. Now, that should make a story. Yet it was his character that interested me, the mixture of pride, cruelty and inconsequence I had glimpsed today in a crowded and squalid hut. And Rodrigo, yearning for a rifle. Señor Mendoza, seated imperiously in his chair, embracing death as if it were his mistress.

As soon as I tried seriously to peer behind the face each showed, I began to make new and exciting conjectures about them all, to wonder how each might eventually reflect a fraction of what I had seen in Comayagua.

The paper was rough and the ballpoint half-frozen. I looked up, searching for a word and saw Bruce sitting by the fire.

'I'm sorry,' I said guiltily. 'I didn't hear you come in.'

'What is there to be sorry about? I'm enjoying the view.' He was completely relaxed, interested, grey eyes intent, as if finding something unexpected in me mattered to him.

I looked down at my hands, instinctively curled across paper as if to hide what I was doing, and laughed. 'I have written really bad stories for a long time, and certainly didn't want to admit to anyone that they were mine. If I can ever write something I really like, then I shan't mind everyone knowing. It was one of the reasons I left home, although it seems presumptuous now. Arrogant, too.'

163

'Because you came to look at suffering, expecting to weigh up its use to you?'

'Something like that.' I was not entirely pleased by being understood so well, then looked down at my handwriting on the paper. 'Yes. Exactly like that.'

'I doubt it,' he said drily. 'But now you think you know how it was, you still want to write?'

'Yes.'

'Why?'

I stared at my spread fingers. 'I don't think I can prevent myself. It is just that what I want no longer seems so important, when measured against what is happening here. Nor do I like a good deal I have discovered about myself. Although perhaps I needed to discover it. If I had really looked at the people I knew at home, for instance, then I ought to have been able to write better about them than I ever shall about Yono. I think I was too dissatisfied to look.'

'You will write well about both, surely. If you are any good. Then afterwards look at yourself again, and remember how quickly you were able to set ambition in its place, even though you are still ambitious. I wouldn't call that arrogance.'

I stretched, thinking that I had been arrogant with Willy Charlton. He was nice; and though I could never have loved him, I need not have used him simply to reflect my pride in being wanted. 'I hope you're right. I doubt it, but there can't be many women who don't prefer compliments to a bed of thorns, and I'm certainly not one of them.'

He came over, laughing, and bent to kiss me, hands on my shoulders, roughness of cheek against mine, the way he stood and his hands on my body becoming a violent physical pleasure I had not felt before. This must be where my inexperience showed, I thought vaguely; that I should feel like this for him after two nights and a week of days.

Recognition; knowing; certainty; for this was the one great passion of my life, though it might be incomplete and short. How could one possibly know, or was this romance again? Yes, I could and did know; no half-hearted wondering for me.

Fool – when the one thing I completely understood about him was that he did not want me to love him.

The rains continued intermittently for a week, then settled into downpours which lasted for hours, or even days, at a time.

The Prodam food which the Picachos ferried back from the guerrilla camp whenever the rain eased would help them through this time of annual near-starvation, but in spite of Yono's word not all of it was released, and we had lost two truckloads on the way in. Day after day, all we had to eat were beans which tasted and looked like red clay, maize mush, a little turkey meat, greens like acid spinach, some apples, and more maize, this time burned to make bitter coffee. Even with the utmost care, there was insufficient to maintain vitality at the cold, wet altitude, and it would run out completely before next year's crop ripened.

Bruce and I climbed each day to the slope of mountain where he had begun to resurrect the Aztec channels which were designed to store and deflect these torrential rains, but the task was enormous and, once the bad weather came, few Indians came to help. The atmosphere between us and most of them was a compound of mistrust and suspicion which daily became worse. Rafael and Juan still spoke to us, and also the Indian with the broken foot to whom Bruce smuggled antibiotics when the injury became infected. So did their families, but the Picachos were not neighbourly in the usual sense of the word. They lived scattered over the valley in separate distrustful groups, and prejudice was a way of life. You couldn't blame them when their existence was so unremittingly harsh, but, fenced in by expressionless faces and turned shoulders, I found it difficult to keep my sense of proportion.

Of course they grudged each mouthful we ate, and the fact that none of the Prodam food would have reached the valley without us made no difference. Instinctively, they hoarded

165

energy and went into semi-hibernation as supplies ran short, while our reaction to adversity was to work harder on the channels and try to hunt scarce game. Remorselessly, the points of contact between us and them diminished, even though the crisis we faced was the same.

'Go home, Yanqui,' said Bruce one night, after about five weeks of rain had passed. 'I guess we shan't be able to stay here right through the wet, after all.'

I sighed in relief. 'Thank goodness for that. I don't know how you lasted for so long, up here on your own.'

'It wasn't so bad before. I won a sort of acceptance while they believed I might help them. That finished for good when the guerrillas came and seized their reserves; overnight I became the traitor at the gate and nothing will change it now.'

'My arrival made it a great deal worse.' I had picked up a few Picacho words and realized quite quickly that while they had not feared a man alone, they did fear settlers. As soon as the Aztec channels ceased to be something which might help them, they became instead a symbol of what could be done to make this valley rich; and once land became rich in Comayagua, the Indians lost it.

They resented me above all, because they were terrified of the settler children I might breed. Although we took what care we could, I, too, was beginning to be frightened of the children I might breed, since Bruce clearly had no intention of being around once this sodden, cold, unhappy winter was past. This joyful splendid triumph of a winter which I didn't want to end, even if the Picachero Valley had ceased to be a refuge.

Bruce did not deny what I had said, but held me to him; we were lying together in darkness and under all the covers we possessed, although it wasn't late. There was very little oil for lamps, or fuel for the fire. 'It will be tough going out over the mountains at this time of year, but soon it must be riskier still to stay. The chiman tried to give us one half share between the two last time around, and I guess that soon he won't listen when I object. We could just about have afforded to lose one truckload of food on the way in, but never two.'

Outside the rain was slapping down. 'If we wait for a good day – '

'It will take five days at least to cross the mountains, another two to reach Quihuli. It won't stay dry for more than a few hours of that time, and we shall need to backpack all we can carry to survive. The rains will be easing on the Quihuli side already, but not here for another three weeks or so.'

I took a deep breath. 'And after we reach Quihuli?'

He lay slack, no longer holding me. If, during these past weeks, I had learned how splendid love could be, then I had also discovered how much it hurt when the man I loved was not content. The dangers we faced had nothing to do with it: he was not content with me.

There was of course no reason why he should be, except that my love was left desolate by his discontent, nor were answers any easier to find as he became more familiar to me – I can't say that I came to know him better, when those weeks only made me more aware that something essential about Bruce Shryver remained beyond my reach.

On the purely practical level he was amazingly easy to live with, and we had only to begin to discuss almost any subject for it to flare into interest. I don't remember a single hour when we were bored together, although frequently on edge. Our passions did not stale, although we were so different; we never found the time long, encased in grey mist and rain with only ourselves for company.

Sometimes I was convinced he must love me too, completely, but those were also times when afterwards he left me; often I wanted to force some crisis I scarcely comprehended, yet each time my courage failed. I treasured my dreams and wanted to keep them for as long as I could: I must have been pathetically easy to deceive – I wanted so much to be deceived and knew so little.

'Faith,' Bruce said now, and then again as if he had intended to say something quite different, 'Faith . . . after we

167

reach Quihuli, I will get you out of Comayagua. I haven't worked out how yet, but it's a promise.'

'I expect you will.' I felt sadness coming like a storm at the finality of his voice. I would have given anything to stay in the Picachero Valley now, because once we were out, he would leave me.

'Oh, Christ.' He moved sharply, almost with revulsion. 'This isn't any good, is it? After all the years when I could have stayed with the woman I loved for as long as she wanted me, I have to wait until now to find her in Quihuli railroad depot. Faith, when I leave this valley I shall be on the run again, because somewhere out there is a man who wants to kill me, as slowly as he knows how. If we married he would kill you instead of me, because he wants his fun to last. Stalk and threaten you, not quite killing perhaps, and the same with any child we had. That's how it is, and like I was with Yono, I'm safer left alone.'

My mind at last made the connection it had been struggling a long time to make. 'Pete Zeller,' I said. 'It's Zeller, isn't it, Bruce?'

'Just what the hell do you know about Zeller?' he asked softly.

I explained, hesitating often because I'd hated what happened in San Bernardo so much I'd shied from thinking of it ever since.

'He sure doesn't change,' Bruce said, when I stumbled over telling about Zeller in my hotel bedroom. 'Okay, let's skip that bit. He was going on to Costa Rica and El Salvador, you say?'

'He'll be back,' I said wretchedly. 'He was certain you were in Central America and meant to look until he found you. Mozon – I think he got on fine with Mozon. Now he's dictator, probably Zeller would come back to Comayagua anyway.' Just possibly he might be glad of the excuse to come, and pay off a score against me.

I felt Bruce nod, although he agreed for different reasons. 'Sure. Mozon will want US military aid, and as soon as the Seguridad reported that a Yanqui was mixed up with the

168

Quihuli hijack he'll send word to Zeller. Mozon won't care whether his Yanqui is the one Zeller's looking for or not; information is always a cheap way of paying for an arms deal.'

'And it is the Yanqui Zeller is looking for,' I said flatly.

'I figured he would expect me to go to South America, where we both once operated.'

'He knew you were up here somewhere.' I frowned, trying to remember. 'He said when he caught you he'd give you to the Comayaguans to fix.'

'I expect he would. Unless he found me with you, when he'd soon think up some better ideas.'

A killer, Zeller had called Bruce, which was impossible to believe. 'You'll have to tell me why.'

'It doesn't make any difference,' he said wearily. 'Except we need to get the hell out of here even faster than I thought.'

'And after we have, I'll wake up one morning and find you've gone?'

'Yes.' He was lying completely still, not touching me at all.

'Don't you think that eventually you might get tired of running?'

He gave the ghost of a laugh. 'I am tired of it.'

'Why go on doing it, then?'

He moved, so violently that I nearly fell out of the narrow bed; a moment later I heard him across the room fiddling with the lamp. The wick caught, sputtered, burned in a stink of animal fat, lighting the muscles of his thigh. He pulled on his clothes with an angry jerk; I had never seen him so obviously disturbed.

I dressed too, neither of us speaking; I did not intend to let him disappear as he sometimes did, and walk off his agitation. Because this time he had said he loved me, and I believed him, even though I had not when he said it once before, a long time ago when we were strangers to each other. And Bruce Shryver loving me meant infinitely more, was incalculably more important, than Pete Zeller stalking us with a gun. Yet Bruce had said it almost dismissively, as a fact beyond dispute, which would not influence what he did.

169

The most important answer of all was coming right, but this did not mean that the rest was simple. Once Bruce left me, I should never find him again, even if Zeller did. I needed to forget elation and be very careful now; one mistake could destroy everything I had gained.

'I'll heat coffee if you kick up the fire,' I said, and nearly laughed at my own lack of inspiration.

He hesitated and then went over to the hearth. 'Don't worry. I started this tonight because we couldn't go on any longer the way we were; I won't leave things half-explained now. I'm sorry, Faith. I tried to keep away from you at first, but when I realized there was no place else for you to go except here with me for the winter, I gave up. I don't think you believed me when I said I loved you from the time you sang in that locomotive, but it was true, though only a fraction of what I feel for you now. I was a shit to say it all the same, and until tonight I haven't said it again. I wanted you from the moment I saw you in Quihuli. I was so goddam lonely that to turn away and leave you was one of the hardest things I've done. Then Colonel Mozon's revolution made sure I couldn't turn away, and I loved you, and you came here. Until you did, I never knew how much simpler wanting is than loving.'

'Simpler, but not better,' I said smiling. 'Tell me about Zeller, Bruce.'

'He came to Ecuador six years ago. Young, very tough, seeing everything straight. Good guys and bad, period.' I nodded. I could imagine a younger Zeller like that; he hadn't changed much except, probably, not to believe in good guys any longer. 'I was controller on station for fourteen agents through Ecuador, Peru, Columbia, Bolivia. Not quite the spy stuff people imagine, but digging for influence and information where it counted, dollars rather than hit gangs. Most of us tried to believe we weren't criminals, but if you cared enough to think then it got harder after a while. I went out to South America when I was about Zeller's age and thinking much as he did I guess, wanting to do a good job for democracy and the U S of A. It doesn't work out that way too

170

easily down here.' He nodded in the direction of our labour on those mountain channels: when we left they would soon crumble back into Aztec dust.

'Well, Zeller was trouble from the start,' he added. 'He wanted results and didn't care how he got them. I had to clean up a couple of his messes fast and sent him home as unsuitable, but the next year he was back. In Bolivia, where he tried to blackmail a couple of guys who just helped themselves to a strike.'

'Helped themselves to a strike?'

'Bolivia's full of skin-poor miners who starve when there's a strike, but conditions are so bad it's still easy to stir up trouble. If you're in a position to buy stockpiled tin and then discreetly start a strike – well, you can clear up a lot of cash. A couple of guys Zeller knew had done this and he told the Department up in Washington that if they sent him down again, he could lean on them and stop the strike. Washington doesn't like sky-high tin prices and revolutions in the mines. So they sent him down. I was in Peru at the time but when I heard he was back I flew to the States and told them I refused to have Zeller on my ground. He went, or I resigned. So they agreed to pull him out and I went to Bolivia myself to make sure he left.'

'You must have been very sure he was dangerous.'

'He'd killed three men in six months while under my control. I couldn't prove it, but I knew. He'd gotten results though, and the Department weren't happy when I threw him out.'

'But they backed you all the same.' I stared at him across exaggerated shadows thrown by the oil lamp; Bruce had been Zeller's boss and infinitely more valuable than an inexperienced young man who thought muscle or a bullet solved everything. Yet Bruce had ended as the fugitive, while Zeller dealt in American military aid with men like Colonel Mozon.

'Yes. Then. When I reached Bolivia I discovered the strike was over. The strike committee had been offered safe conduct for talks on pay and conditions in La Paz, and the hotel elevator crashed while they were in it. Six were killed and the others badly injured. Accident, of course. Zeller had tried leaning on the guys who bought up the tin, but they were too strong for him and not the sort you kill, since middlemen of their breed come in useful next time around. So Zeller fixed the strike committee instead. He laughed in my face and didn't mind being pulled out. Sure, Washington would be angry – there are plenty of men up there who are horrified by murder. But there are others who don't mind too much so long as murder works, and Zeller knew that in his trade they are the ones who count.'

'What did you do?'

'I gave him to the Bolivian police. Set him up and let them take him, though I made it look as if he was in it for money and not American interests; he had cover as a mining engineer. He pleaded guilty as part of a deal our people made with the Bolivians to keep everything quiet, but of course he knew I was the reason he'd been caught. The Department placed enough dollars where they counted to make sure he wasn't executed: US citizen, pan-Americanism, aid to friendly nations – all the usual strings were pulled. Three years later the Bolivian military deported him, which was nearly two years ago.'

I thought about it while rain slammed against stone and dripped through the roof. Zeller's hands, which had laboured so harshly that the callouses still hadn't faded; Zeller, who would never forgive three years in a Bolivian jail, and whose revenge was hounding Bruce to places like the Picachero Valley because a straight killing was too easy. 'You have to stop running from him some time, so why not with me?' I said at last. 'You're playing Zeller's game, coming here. Twenty months alone in a hut – he must be laughing now he knows where you are.'

'I expect he is.'

'But don't you see, Comayagua was a crazy place to come? He can do anything he likes here, especially now there's a new dictator in San Bernardo wanting dollars. A dictator like Mozon too, who understands Zeller's sort, I'm sure. You

172

ought to go back to America and wait for him there. If you set him up for the police once, then surely you can do it again, only this time where the law won't let him go.'

'I told you, he wouldn't – didn't – come for me. I resigned, of course, after I'd sent Zeller down, there was one hell of a fuss anyway. I'd wanted to for a long time, but somehow the time is never right when you're so much on the jump you haven't a moment to think. I'd kept quiet over a lot of things I ought never to have gone along with, and told myself that U S policy made it right. Other killings beside Zeller's, not directly by my people, but you're in very dirty water with the others you use in that kind of situation. I had some money, so I pulled out when the dirt settled and bought a place I liked up in Wyoming. I told you once that I fancied being a farmer. I wanted out, I guess.'

I nodded, wondering how old he was. From some of the things he'd said over the weeks, I had guessed at late thirties; with me, sometimes, he had seemed much younger. Now he looked drained and sick, a man who couldn't fight any more. Old Señor Mendoza had been younger at heart than he. 'You stayed in Wyoming until Zeller came looking for you?'

'I thought I had covered my trail but he was taken straight back into the security machine. He made it work for him, and found me in six weeks. The first I knew was when the house burned down, killing an old woman who cooked for me. I thought it was an accident until, next day, I saw Zeller in town. He wanted me to see him, made sure I did. Then I believed he'd bitched it up, not known what time I usually came in when he fired the place. But that afternoon my dog was shot, and a week later a woman I was seeing broke her back in an automobile accident. Zeller was the witness who reported the smash and was commended for pulling her out of the wreck. I knew then. He isn't interested in killing me, only in something slower and crueller than a Bolivian jail was to him.'

'So you have to fight. You can't dodge him all your life. If you are sure of this – '

'I'm sure.'

173

'Then he's a killer, probably more times than you know. You have every right to defend yourself against him.'

He looked across at me, smiling slightly, sloped eyebrows drawn together in pain and resignation. 'I can't, Faith. That's what I have to tell you. I came to the end of it in Bolivia. I had started by believing in what I did, you see. My father was killed on Iwo Jima before I was born, and I never had much of a home, so I believed in America instead. Justified things I ought never to have justified because that was the trade I was in: dirty perhaps, but vital for the kind of world Americans want to build. That the best in America wants to build. I don't think that way any more, and after Bolivia I refuse to hire my life for easy excuses. A private citizen who kills is a murderer, and I couldn't kid myself into seeing it differently, just because this time it happens to be my skin laid on the line.'

'You would let him shoot you?'

'Not if I could help it, but he surely isn't planning on doing that just yet.'

'So you would stand aside and let him shoot me instead?' I said brutally, hating myself for still staying across the table from him, for trying to make him face the meaning of his words, but this wasn't a time to be ruled by emotion. I'm safer alone, he had said earlier, but it wasn't true: he intended to make certain that he suffered and then died alone, when Zeller caught him next.

A muscle jerked under his eye. 'No. Of course . . . no. But don't you see, Faith? With Zeller you have to be in there first. Lay for him and kill him when he's thinking of something else. I can't do that. But he can, and will do very soon. If we stay together then you'll be the target in his sights.'

I took a deep breath, trying to bring splintered thoughts into some kind of order. Bruce meant every word; he might run, or even fight, but if he could not kill then he was defenceless against a man like Zeller, and the farther he ran the more vulnerable he became. I wanted to yell at him, to insist that this time he had to put me first, for both our sakes, since scrupulousness was surely out of place when dealing

174

with the Zellers of this world. Somehow I had to force Bruce into killing him, and then we could be happy. And yet . . . and yet . . . I could not do it. Bruce had been so long alone; I could not now use love as a weapon too, and if I won then so diminish him with guilt that he would remain solitary all his life, even though we lived together.

I went round the table then, and held him tightly. 'I couldn't kill Zeller either, unsuspicious in the street. No matter what he'd done.'

I saw his astonishment, how he looked at me as I had so often wished he would look. The quiet and secret look which seals one spirit with another. 'I don't deserve that after what I have done to you. The gift of understanding to take away with me. I was afraid you loved me, but did not know how much before.'

'It isn't a parting gift,' I said cheerfully, since it wasn't a moment for high emotional temperatures. 'It's an engagement present. You said you would like to marry me, remember? Well, I've just accepted, and Zeller isn't going to change my mind. When we reach Quihuli, I've decided to take the train to San Bernardo if I can, or walk there if I can't. I'd be surprised if you feel free to leave Comayagua while I'm hob-nobbing with Zeller in the Hotel Miragloso. I suppose it's called the Hotel Mozon now,' I added. 'I don't know how the hell we're going to fix Zeller since I doubt if he possesses better feelings, but somehow that's what we have to do.'

'No!' said Bruce violently, taut as wire in my arms. 'I thought you had a right to know why, after all you've given, I was still unable to make much come right between us. To understand why I have to go, even though I love you. But there isn't any way you can stop me from going.'

The door banged open, letting in a blast of wet air, and Yono came in, shaking rain all over the place. 'Ah, Señor Broos, how a woman helps in the winter! Perhaps you can spare some coffee and aguadiente for a half-drowned man, eh?'

13

Yono made himself completely at home. His soaking poncho, boots and hat were thrown on the floor, skunk-smelling feet put up on the table, cigar smoke puffed in our faces. His arrival took us so much by surprise, and the effort needed to switch our minds from our affairs to his was so great, that for a while we simply did what he said: we boiled maize coffee and poured aguadiente, then sat down as far from his feet as possible. Not that we could have done anything else: he had a machete in his belt, a holstered gun under one arm and a machine pistol across his knees.

'Ah, Señor Broos,' he said, slapping the pistol grip, 'I know better than to rely on one bullet, eh?'

'Sure,' said Bruce. 'Where did you capture that?'

Yono winked. 'No capture. All nice in crates from El Faro. We have good friends who remember us often, and send presents.'

I stiffened, thinking of Calderon. It didn't really matter where the guns came from any longer, but I disliked leaving unfinished business niggling away at the back of my mind for ever. Yes, it did matter; if Prodam and agencies like it got a name for gun-running, then most countries would allow their peasants to starve rather than open their frontiers to such suspect aid.

Bruce went over to the fire and stood with his shoulders against stone and his face in darkness. 'Why did you come here on a night like this?'

Yono drank scalding coffee at a gulp, followed it with aguadiente, and waved his hand for more. 'You are direct, *amigo.*'

'I find it sometimes pays.'

Yono idly clicked a catch several times, then hefted the machine pistol one-handed and pointed it straight at Bruce. 'This is the payment which counts.'

My throat dried as I understood why Bruce had moved. Away from me. But this time I must somehow keep my nerve, believe he knew how to deal with men like Yono, and not get in the way.

'*Pues, sí. A la vejez, viruelas!* To hell with old age,' Bruce replied sarcastically. 'You can fill me with bullets whenever you want without walking in the wet for half the night. The Picachos would be delighted.'

Yono hooted with laughter, seized the bottle I was holding and tipped half of it down his throat. 'I would not kill you, *amigo*. See, the catch is safe all the time.' He threw the gun at Bruce. Luckily, he caught it and with the muzzle pointing upward; the jerk sprayed bullets through the roof with a shattering roar.

Yono spat on the floor. 'I forget sometimes which way to put so small a catch. Sit down again, Señor Broos. We do not need guns between us, eh?' He touched his machete and grinned.

Bruce leaned the gun carefully against the wall and came over. 'My answer is still no, *mí capitán.*'

Yono raised his hands in exaggerated surprise. 'I have not asked a question.'

'Not yet.'

'Señor Broos, I come this time alone and at night so no one know how I, El Capitán Yono, came to the Yanqui asking for a favour. You do not love the swine who rule in San Bernardo, who took our land and starve our brothers in cages they call camps. *Seguridades* fester like the pox in

177

Quihuli nowadays: questioning, beating, shooting. Why will you not help us?'

'Because I'm not at war any longer, *mí capitán*. I can't believe the winner wins, only that men die and others weep for their dead. If you should take Quihuli, then you will burn alive any *seguridades* you catch, in bonfires on the street, and they will burn you when they recapture it.'

'They will never take back Quihuli once we have it.'

Bruce shrugged. 'Guerrillas need to be very sure of their strength before they tie themselves down in towns. But you asked me why I wouldn't fire missiles or instruct your men in the ways of war, and I just told you.'

'We can't lie down and let them stew us in our own lard for supper! What do you expect us to do, Yanqui? To live like slaves for ever in Comayagua, so your people may enjoy their peace and profits? You would have more of our blood on your hands than if you stormed Quihuli with us! But bodies do not stink if you are far away, so that is how you prefer it, eh?'

'Yes,' Bruce said quietly. 'That is how I prefer it.'

Yono slammed his hand down on the table. 'You are the one who should be crucified on a bonfire.'

'Perhaps. Yet at the end of it I would be dead and a woman weep for me, but your cause not be helped at all.'

'How is it helped if I leave you alive?'

'You are about to tell me, *mí capitán*,' Bruce answered, sitting very still. 'You did not walk so far in rain and darkness to hear another refusal over guns, when you understood very well that my mind had not changed since we spoke last on this.'

Yono spat full in his face, drawing his machete in the same instant. 'Do not move, except to put your hands on the table. Slowly, Yanqui.'

Carefully, Bruce wiped the thick gob of spittle off his cheek first, then put his hands on the table. He appeared impersonal and calm, the insult made to look trivial. I had become familiar with that professional mask of his, but scanned it anxiously for nonexistent clues to what he planned and felt.

178

Yono was utterly ruthless, and would be very difficult to trick, impossible to bluff.

'*Bueno*,' he said now, watching Bruce like a vulture. 'I am not Estaban, a boy pegged out to be taught a lesson. Or a pig of a *campesino* for the gringos to despise. I speak and you do as I order, eh?'

'I am listening, as I was before.'

Yono flicked a thumbnail at his machete, the ting of metal soft though it was, completely separate from the many sounds of water all around. 'The boy, Rodrigo, who came in your trucks, he went back to Quihuli some time ago. He may go where a man cannot without suspicion, and sends back news of all that happens in the town. The numbers of soldiers and where they go, and what he can see of their plans. I want you to travel with our next messenger, and listen to what Rodrigo has to say. Then act on it.'

Oh, Rodrigo, I thought. How proud and happy he would be, sent alone against Colonel Mozon's Seguridad to win recognition, and perhaps a rifle of his own.

'You intend to attack Quihuli before the rains end?'

'The army intends to attack us, here, as soon as they do,' replied Yono grimly. 'With machines flown in from your country. We have no choice. We must strike first or be slaughtered in a valley without cover. We starve at this time of the year if we scatter into the mountains.'

'So why do you want us to go and meet Rodrigo outside Quihuli?'

'You. The woman stays here. How else could I trust you to do what I want? The boy wanders freely in the town, but the bombs and helicopters brought ready for an attack on the valley are guarded at a base set up near the Agosto road. Rodrigo says there are Americanos there, uncrating equipment and swearing at ignorant Comayaguan *bastardos*. Only another gringo might bluff his way into a place so closely kept.' He smiled unpleasantly. 'You, *amigo*. I want those *materiales sangrientes* destroyed the night before we attack, and since you will not help us willingly, then I keep the woman as I said. You may have her back when you have finished.' He sighed. 'Holding the woman of a man you need is an old trick, but it still works, I think.'

Bruce sat like ice. 'I could very easily try, and fail.'

'It is sad, but possible,' agreed Yono amiably. 'The woman would then be of use to us before she died. Just because this trick is old, everyone understands how it works. Perhaps you try now to tell me you do not care, eh? Women are everywhere. But I do not think this time I believe you.'

'No, I won't try to tell you that,' Bruce said curtly, and turned his head to look at me. The colour had drained from behind the weathering on his face, leaving it oddly patched.

'I keep her for you, *amigo*. It is a bargain, and Yono keeps these bargains of his, eh? She is safe if you are good, and before you go, you will also change your mind and teach us how to use this missile we have received. Then if you do not destroy the bombs and helicopters, we shall fire it and see how much damage it will do.' He flicked his machete carelessly at me, and the sting of it was oddly dry, the steel too sharp for instant pain. Blood slid from my wrist to the boards of the table. 'She will remain for afterwards, when we settle what each owes the other.'

I suppose I must have been staring at my blood and perhaps Yono was too, since neither of us saw Bruce move. We kept a machete by the ocote wood; he had it in his hand and nearly reached Yono before he could react. Nearly, but not quite. Yono threw himself aside and came up standing against the farther wall, his own machete held shoulder high and poised to slash. He had a gun in his shoulder harness, but it was beneath his left armpit and out of reach unless he dropped the machete or changed to holding it left-handed, and Bruce gave him time for neither.

It was as if a fog had lifted from the air, leaving it thin and polished. Argument, uncertainty and crude bullying vanished, a single deadly danger in its place. The light was bad, the space confined, machetes cruel weapons at such close quarters: the curved, honed blade heavier than any sword, the unguarded hilt exposing an attacker's hand.

To both men, existence was the other's eyes and arm, the

180

flicker of his steel. A single mistake and the price was not just blood or tendon but probably a limb. Yono understood machete fighting because it was the usual weapon for cantina quarrels, the more drunken combatant often left to bleed to death. He started slowly, guarding himself and waiting for the opening he needed. He looked very strong: barrel chest, thick legs and shoulders; when he did attack it was with driving blows which could break an opponent's blade or slice through half a dozen ribs.

Bruce fought much faster; intensely, dangerously fast. He had to keep Yono away from the holstered gun, and relied on flustering him before his own strength was destroyed by using such a heavy and unfamiliar weapon. My heart was frozen by my eyes, as I watched him. His back was half turned to me and I could do nothing to help, terrified that if I moved, the distraction might kill him. Yono wouldn't care whether I was in the way or not, would welcome any use he could make of me.

I saw Bruce's muscles whip taut as he turned the full force of his shoulder and extended arm into driving the flat of his blade against Yono's, point slithering down toward Yono's hand until each man was exerting every ounce of his strength, arm against arm, blade against blade, their faces only inches apart. Breathing raucous, concentration a vivid and frightening thing. Slowly, slowly, Yono was forced to give way, the point of his machete ground aside a fraction at a time. Sweat poured down both faces, into their eyes, gathered on jaw and nose. If Bruce could only force Yono's blade just a fraction farther to the side, then his body would be unguarded. A swift disengagement and downward flick would gut him where he stood.

Bruce could do it now. Another inch for safety perhaps, then he must not wait another instant. This was a test of muscle and in the end Yono must surely be the stronger: I was already astonished how much power Bruce's slight frame could produce. And then with horror I realized why he still waited: even in this extremity he did not intend to kill, and in so savage a fight softness of purpose meant defeat.

Yono would kill at the first opportunity, and not care that he wanted Bruce's help to take Quihuli.

Even so, Bruce's move when it came was so swift it defeated the eye. I never knew another man who could move so fast, and with machetes speed is quite as important as strength. There was a slithering whine as he disengaged, and before Yono could recover from the suddenness with which such great pressure was released, Bruce struck downward at his exposed hand. Too late, Yono attempted to leap out of range: all he could do was turn to take the blow on his arm instead of his fingers, which would have meant instant disarming. He howled out loud but was wearing a goatskin jacket and though blood dripped from his wrist to the floor, he was less hurt than he ought to have been.

He had also grasped that Bruce could have killed him, and had not. His teeth showed as he smiled, and he sprang straight back into the attack, looking strong despite a chest heaving for air, and blood spattering through the loose ends of his cut sleeve.

Bruce, too, was breathing in rasping gasps; he had been the one to burn up strength faster. As well as being stronger, Yono must also now be the fresher, his familiarity with the machete about to give him an overwhelming advantage.

Head up, elbow held high to balance the weight of his blade, Yono now looked every inch the tamer of turbulent guerrillas. He flicked his blade almost contemptuously in Bruce's face before dropping the point in a castrating arc, calling out loud to taunt his enemy, enjoying the exercise of his skill.

Bruce was forced back instantly, dangerously, almost trapped against the table edge, then within seconds forced into the darkest corner of the hut. He left it desperately late. Then, poised, meticulous still, though the end must be very close, he drove his fist into Yono's unsuspecting throat, and leaped aside. Yono shook his head, dazed, then was back at him again, slobbering a little from the blow he had taken but still full of murderous fury.

When wielded by an expert, the machete forces a man to

182

guard himself on two sides at once, the clash and snicker of steel made even more brutal by the blood it draws anywhere it touches. Yono was bleeding from jaw and chest as well as from his arm, Bruce from arm, the back of his hand, and neck; both were shaken with effort, their movements becoming less certain, breath ragged.

Bruce was still defending himself desperately, and since in defence he had an undivided mind, his flash-swift reactions made him a formidable opponent so long as his strength remained. I watched Yono's satisfaction turn into frenzy as he failed to reach bone, while Bruce continued to give ground with such skill in the cluttered conditions that once Yono was nearly caught by a kicked bench.

I had snatched up the machine pistol from where it had been propped against the wall, and held it poised for use as soon as a clear chance showed. I had said that I could not kill Zeller unsuspecting in the street, but I could and would kill Yono if it might save Bruce's life. In any case, terror and instinct swept thought aside, because the next few seconds would inevitably bring the bright spout of arterial blood. I just held the gun and waited. I had no idea of the spread of bullets from such a weapon, and the fight was now a mêlée of reddened steel and twined bodies, lurching movements, grotesque shadows on the wall.

Bruce was very nearly finished, the point of his machete dropping lower as even his extraordinary agility faltered. But when Yono stepped back for a killing blow, he was still forced to miss by a thickness of skin; the difference was he then had time and space to lift his arm and chop down with all his gathered strength at Bruce's unguarded side. And Bruce made no effort this time to avoid that lethal edge; instead he tensed his remaining muscle and drove his machete back-handed to block a stroke which certainly would have killed him. Sparks showered in the air as the blades splintered from such combined and savage force. Bruce immediately dropped his haft, as if this was a move he had long anticipated, and seized Yono's throat with his free left hand, Yono's wrist with the other, ruthlessly forcing it back so the wound on Yono's arm caught across the table edge.

Yono growled deep in his throat and threw himself backwards as the only way to release his arm from crippling pain, took Bruce with him as he tripped and sprawled on the floor. They rolled into the glow remaining from the fire so I saw the end when it came, as Bruce used feet and legs to outclass Yono in a kind of fighting he did not know, all the time keeping relentless pressure on his throat. Bruce Shryver was not a soft enemy when he simply fought to win.

Yono's mouth opened, gasping for air; blood came to his eyes and bulged in the veins of his face; his muscles loosened and the snarl slid from his lips. Bruce released him the moment his body went completely slack, and groped blindly for a machete. Then he held the ragged remnant of blade across Yono's throat.

Breath shook in his ribs so he could not speak, but somehow I grasped what he wanted. Quickly, I went to the bed and pulled off coverings, using the other machete stub to slice thick Indian weaving into strips. I was shivering violently and my bungling hands plucked at the job of tying and gagging Yono; I was also unfamiliar with secure knots, and Bruce beyond clear explanation. By the time we had finished Yono was conscious again, and glaring at us out of hate-filled, bloodshot eyes.

Bruce went over to stand where the automatic shots had ripped the roof, holding his face tipped to dripping water, his eyes shut. He had not spoken beyond isolated, necessary words since the fight began, and still did not when I held him. I was wordless too; I had believed that I would witness the execution of my love and couldn't hold him tightly enough to convince myself he was alive. Until he flinched and some kind of sense returned for me to use.

'Sit down so I can see what he has done to you.' My voice shook and it was an enormous effort to let go of him, to turn away and find the surgical kit, to bring it over without falling on the way; my legs felt so remote they scarcely answered the orders of my brain.

He shook water off his face and sat, but mercifully more from the need to sit than because he was badly hurt. The exposed fighting side of his body was cut: right arm, hand, right side of neck and chest, but only a slice at the base of his neck was deep, where I could see what looked like an artery pulsing under a flap of skin. 'It ought to be stitched,' I said, feeling sick.

'Stitch it, then' he answered, eyes closed again. 'What about your wrist?'

I had not thought about it since the moment I looked at my blood on the table, but now I felt it throb at once. The cut was about four inches long, the blood sticky on my sleeve. 'It's all right'.

Bruce opened his eyes again. 'We have to get out of here tonight. Into the hills before Yono can set up a chase, and we can't do it still losing blood. Whatever he said, he won't have come here quite alone, there'll be someone sleeping with a woman in the nearest hut who will come looking for him in the morning.' He fumbled among wadded medical packages. 'There's all the medical gear we need here, including antibiotics. You fix me first, then I'll do that wrist of yours.'

I knew all about sickroom foulnesses but had never done anything quite so gut-wrenchingly horrible as setting cobbled stitches into the unanaesthetized flesh of the man I loved. He put his head down on the table, gripped its edges with his hands and managed nearly to keep still; I felt so dizzy that all I saw was blood, all I knew was that I must not faint until I'd finished. My senses slid as I cut the needle free, and I plunged into a vortex shot with pain which did not seem like any escape at all.

When I struggled to consciousness at last I found that Bruce had finished stitching my wrist and had the bandage fixed. I came to my feet with a rush and stood, feeling light-headed and very strange. 'Bruce, you can't go into the mountains tonight.'

'We have to go,' he said flatly, and then added, 'I think we'll go down the valley. It will be easier, and Yono won't expect to find us down the valley.'

185

I opened my mouth to warn him that Yono was conscious; though he didn't understand English, a word like valley wasn't difficult to translate; then I realized how Bruce had repeated it, and gestured as well. 'Okay, the valley it is. Yono won't expect us there.'

I saw the glimmer of a smile in his eyes, the tinge of colour returning to his face, and while he packed two rucksacks, I heated soup and beans. We sat to eat, consciously hoarding our strength, ignoring Yono and the rain still slopping down outside. We argued as convincingly as we could about the valley and which frontier we should aim for, and all the time I thought about those mountains. We would be run to earth within a day along the valley; safety lay in the crags and *arroyos* of the Picacho Mountains and then beyond again to Quihuli, where we must also evade Colonel Mozon's Seguridad, and perhaps Pete Zeller, too.

The confidence I had felt – surely it could not be only an hour ago? – about facing and fixing Zeller had evaporated. No one was granted an escape like the one we had just had from Yono twice in a lifetime; if we met Zeller, then the luck must run his way.

We left as soon as we had eaten everything in the pot and drunk a good slug of aguadiente, the spirit so raw I felt as if I'd drunk barbed wire. Bruce injected some kind of drug into Yono before we went, and then untied him. 'He'll invent a story for his men if they find him simply sleeping,' he observed. 'Guerrillas would never respect him again once they knew he'd lost to a Yanqui with machetes, and everyone will be the loser if they run wild.'

I doubted whether Yono would thank him for compassion, but at least we could afford it now.

Outside, it was completely dark and probably not yet midnight: we had perhaps eight hours in which to reach the hills and then climb high enough to hide from watchers once daylight came. We wore most of the clothes we possessed, as well as US Army slickers against the rain, and carried uncomfortably heavy packs containing all our reserve of food, surgical kit and aguadiente.

We walked in silence and saw no one. Bruce had a compass, or we should have found it difficult to find the way in such utter darkness, heads down against gusting rain. I lost Bruce once and froze in ridiculous terror until he found me again; I couldn't help reflecting on how I'd managed to survive on my own before I met and loved him, and in nearly as alarming situations, but aloneness was scarcely endurable any more.

Bruce showed no particular signs of exhaustion, but he was very abrupt and stiff in manner, hoarding his reserves of energy. A fight of such extraordinary savagery would have undermined the strength of men more physically powerful than he. He was tough, though. Tough, vigilant, and with a will to match. As the night continued in unrelieved misery, I began to be afraid that I might be the one to collapse. My arm hurt and I suppose that I, too, had lost a lot of blood. I would damned well refuse to let it be me, and set my teeth to slog through mire for as long as he did, my ears straining in the darkness for the squelch which alone showed where Bruce was. I scarcely noticed when, at very long last, the flatness of the ground broke up and we began to climb.

'Not much farther,' Bruce said softly, and put his hand under my arm. 'Another hour and it'll be getting light.'

I shook loose from him, although God knows I didn't want to, but he needed all his strength for himself. 'We shall have to lie up all day?'

Although I was so deathly tired, it wasn't an attractive prospect while such rain continued.

'Today, yes.' He didn't elaborate, so I wasn't sure whether he was unable to travel any farther, or whether it wasn't safe.

We climbed with single-minded concentration then, aiming to reach as high as we could in the short time which remained before dawn. The rocks were slickly dangerous and the slope soon became very steep, footholds difficult to find among tumbled boulders and outcrops, which often forced us into detours. Everything ran with water. As the light grew, the mist thickened, but the rain stopped at last,

187

an enormous relief when the force of such a downpour alone was something which must be fought. Conditions remained wretched all the same. Eventually we found a rock shelf which should dry quickly if the sun shone, and where we ought to be protected from observation. From there we watched a jonquil mountain dawn glimmer through the mist, feeling too tired to eat and too wet to sleep.

14

We were lucky, because the sun did shine for a while on that first day. Without it, I don't know how we could have survived, as shock, blood loss and utter weariness rolled in on us and our bodies refused to warm even though we lay close together. But when the sun broke through the mist at last, everything changed.

We were able to lay out our clothes to dry and doze naked in its warmth, to wake creakingly stiff but with energy again to eat. Bruce had brought some combat rations he had hoarded against emergency, and the gluttonous pleasure of not eating maize or beans was indescribable. I expect the US Army complains about its rations, but powdered milk, cold reconstituted beef, and chocolate seemed the most marvellous meal I had ever eaten.

Bruce lay for a long time watching the mountainside, and eventually identified two sets of watchers higher up. A few figures beat through scree and undergrowth at the foot of the slope, but otherwise no one came near us. In the valley we thought we heard distant shouts, and certainly some shots; the lake glittered in the sun, and mist blew across folds in the ground, I hoped Yono would look for us all the way to the frontier, and slept again, deeply this time. Cold woke me and I discovered we were in shadow, the sun vanished behind wild-looking clouds. Bruce lay beside me

189

on bare rock, his skin crinkling from the cold but sleeping the hefty sleep he needed. We were both still naked and I lay looking at him, not minding much about the cold.

He woke shuddering quite soon, and laughed when he saw I preferred to freeze so long as I could watch him sleep; we made love swiftly and strongly then, driven perhaps by the need to believe in life instead of the death which still enclosed us, the lack of a future even if we did survive.

Bruce was a trained and efficient man who had been intent on covering his tracks when he bought a place in Wyoming, yet Zeller took only six weeks to find him. There wasn't much wrong with the U S Security Service's ability to find those it wanted, and Zeller's position enabled him to use its expertise for his purposes. We might outrun him for a while by living in places where its efficiency faltered, but we should never be secure and Bruce above all knew it. So he refused to let me live with him, and whatever I had said, I could not see how to force him into changing his mind without destroying more than I gained. We had to get out of Comayagua, but each step we took meant one less moment together.

That second night was better than the first. It didn't rain so heavily and we seemed to make more ground climbing than stumbling over the plain; also, we were both much stronger. My arm still hurt but the throbbing was gone; and Bruce was apparently suffering few ill effects from blood loss and my crude stitching.

We crossed the spine of the mountains above the Windy Place on the third night, as the moon showed fitfully through clouds. I looked back to where the Picachero Valley lay and thought how utterly my life had changed during the weeks I had lived there. On the far enclosing slope the Aztec channels showed as diagonal scribblings of shadow: perhaps the sole memorial of our lives would be a few Indians deciding to shovel dirt for themselves when the rains ended. Most probably they would do nothing.

Then we started on the immense downward trek to the foothills above Quihuli, no longer needing to be quite so cautious because guerrilla outposts here were unlikely to know that we fled from Yono. The next dawn found us still very high, and buffeted by a strong cold gusty wind. Mountain piled on mountain all around; torrents flashed down gulleys which were normally only boulders, and far away in the glowing east the plains rolled on and down.

We camped all day again, partly this time because of Bruce. His neck and some cuts on his ribs had become inflamed, and though he carried his pack strapped sideways, the drag made matters worse.

'It's no good being pig-headed,' I said, annoyed he hadn't told me earlier. 'It's more important for you to be fit than for us to reach Quihuli ahead of the chase.'

'Yono will have realized by now how we fooled him into thinking we went along the valley.'

'So what? He won't come pelting over the Windy Place just to beat a wilderness of rocks for us. He's got Quihuli to assault, or don't you think he'll try it now you aren't there to blow up the dump?'

'He has to, or wait to be rounded up in the Picachero Valley.'

I sighed. My sense of proportion had returned, and I was glad now that Bruce had not left Yono tied up for ridicule. 'Surely they deserve to win this time, and take back a little of their land. I hated him when he tried to kill you, but . . . Did you know that if I could have seen a clean shot, I would have pulled that trigger?'

'Sure.' He was lying flat on his back, face as unreadable as a hatchet blade. 'And I jumped him with a machete because as soon as he said it, I knew he wouldn't keep a bargain which involved a woman. To Yono's kind they're pack mules, only cheaper. He understood he could twist me up by threatening you, but wouldn't care enough to guard you from the rest once I'd gone to do what he wanted.'

'I would have killed him,' I repeated, forcing him to understand.

'Oh, Christ,' he said wearily. 'So would I, if I'd had to.'

'But you didn't.'

'No.'

191

I hugged my knees, staring at barren stone. We both knew that because of his almost inhuman humanity, Bruce had taken enormous and scarcely justifiable risks. If Yono had won, and cold judgement must have reckoned him the likely winner with machetes, then I inevitably would have become the victim: deprived of protection and forced perhaps to kill in Bruce's place; abandoned to an existence of grief and violence.

Incredibly, Bruce had won, and I felt weak with love, relief and admiration each time I thought about what he had done to achieve such a victory, and what he had endured since. But it did not alter the fact that he had salved his conscience at my expense and probably would again, since he could not help the way he was, nor would I want him different. After all, probably he was right. Except that in such matters there is no right and wrong; only more violence, which makes all things harder to forgive.

I heard sounds and realized guiltily that I had been hearing them for some time: the click of stone on stone and voices, some of them quite close. Bruce was asleep. We had halted in a gully which was better hidden than most on that slope, so there wasn't any point in moving. I crawled to where I could see out and at once spotted several groups of men. We lay to the south of the track up which we had driven the trucks, protected from above by a sheer spur of cliff; on either side of us rifle-carrying guerrillas picked their way, jumping sometimes down drops so steep I envied their surefootedness. They were obviously patrolling ahead of others, and called to each other as they moved; down the track itself an advance party of six men was trotting quite fast towards us, and just in sight beyond them two bigger groups were winding down from the Windy Place. Yono was moving to take Quihuli.

It took quite a long time for the first of the larger groups to reach the track opposite where we were. I dozed while I waited for them, being very tired and in no danger unless inconceivable ill luck revealed our hide. I roused to the thud of feet, the clatter of equipment and talk blown on the wind.

About fifty guerrillas were swinging past below me; shabby, unmilitary, scattered over the track. Their heads were up though, and they looked about eagerly, unwearied by their long march and moving fast. They were strung to a purpose, the contours of their faces standing out against the hazy distance as they laughed and chaffed each other. There were some Picachos among them, although class distinction still marked them out: the *ladinos* all carried automatic weapons, the Indians mostly shared Mausers or carried boxes.

They were soon out of sight and the next group moving down towards us: the same eager bearing again, a mix of arrogant hope and noisy babble which boasted of how they were not victims any more. I had been two months in Comayagua, and saw now how little I had learned about its peoples, who hid behind many masks. Their crops were sparse, and they drank in order to become unconscious, or to quarrel. They were rapacious and mistrustful, made cruel by poverty. They bred too many children too young, and remained sluggishly anchored to old superstitions and irrelevant habits. They had also survived by clinging to what they understood, which in this new time included their chance to take hold of revenge.

I no longer made the mistake of believing that such sympathy and understanding as I might feel towards them would be reciprocated.

I slept after a while so did not see Yono go by although I'm sure that he was there, and when I woke it was raining again. A drizzle which rapidly thickened into a downpour and turned the mountainside into a waterfall. Bruce woke too, and seemed better; I told him what I'd seen but we decided to go on. Our food was running short and conditions were too bad to lie up through a night of plunging temperatures. The wind was strong and cold, the rain showed no sign of stopping; Bruce said that even towards the end of the winter it often rained for thirty-six hours at a stretch in the mountains. We needed to get lower, and fast, while our strength lasted.

We also needed to do it without falling on greasy rock,

193

which meant using the track; in such roaring blackness we should just have to hope to be accepted as stragglers from Yono's column if we were spotted.

In fact we saw no one and heard nothing except rain and wind. Shoulders bowed against the force of it and tripping frequently in disintegrating boots, I have never felt so physically wretched in my life, and was only able to endure so long because Bruce was beside me. We seldom spoke and it was too cold to stop, but he was there and it made the difference between lasting and not lasting, between believing this night would end and that it would end only when I reeled into a gully and died.

I knew, too, that I must not even look as if I was nearly finished, when he had no strength to spare for helping me. Zombie-like, I walked straight into him when eventually he stopped.

'We can't risk going any farther on the track.'

'Oh, God,' I said, and shivered deep in my soul. 'Where, then?'

He did not answer, but held me instead, his hand guiding me down some invisible slope. The rain was merciless – no wonder sensible Comayaguans stayed where they were at this time of year. Daylight when it came was no more than greyish fog, with visibility under twenty yards. Which made it safe, probably. Because we had to go on; exhausted, blistered, sliding dangerously on shale slopes. We would die if we stopped now.

So we ate standing up, gulping greedily at the last of the chocolate and feeling it pour a fragile energy back into our drained bodies. My throat closed against sodden beef squares and disintegrating maize but I could have eaten a chocolate block the size of a one-volume *War and Peace*.

I nearly tripped over the first guerrilla we saw. He was lying face down in a boggy hollow and was obviously dead. Bruce turned him over and cleared mud off his face. 'He must have fallen and been too exhausted to get up.'

I stared at the man, too numb for pity. 'There will be others close.'

194

'A few lookouts, perhaps. Unless my compass has gone haywire, we're well south of Quihuli here, and Yono should have most of his men gathering on the town. I aim to cut between Quihuli and Agosto, and hope they're too busy to look so far for us.'

'The railway?'

Bruce shook his head. 'If Mozon is stockpiling for an offensive out of Quihuli, then the railroad will be taken over by the military. Yono's probably planning to cut it even before he attacks. It takes longer to walk, but we'll get there in the end.'

Where? I thought. San Bernardo, where Zeller might be waiting? Or Mexico, where I would wake up to find Bruce gone?

We moved on slowly; even so short a stop made it doubly difficult to keep going. The inflammation on Bruce's neck and chest was less, which possibly was one benefit of the rain, but neither of us could last much longer without rest.

The relentless procession of rockfalls and gullies eased at last, and became rough gradients, but I gaped at the first tree when it loomed out of the mist towards us. The lower slopes of the Picacho Mountains are a landscape by Salvador Dali: bushes and crippled pines and exploded rocks hurled from the heights above, but not difficult walking after the wilderness we had negotiated.

We picked up speed again and came at last to trees which were really trees. Tall hemlocks and firs which might have come from the Northumberland hills, even a few flowers where pine-needle mould gathered in hollows.

The rain stopped.

Words can't describe how we felt when eventually we grasped that it wasn't raining any longer.

We remained as miserably exhausted as before, and it was still too cold to think of resting, but it became possible to imagine warmth and rest; when we broke out from the trees to a patch of ground which once had been cultivated, the change from wilderness seemed extraordinary, and we understood that caution had at last become more urgent

195

than the need to keep moving. Almost immediately, as if it was planned, we came on an abandoned adobe hut; it was awash with mud, but shelter of a kind. The brushwood sleeping platform was dry and there was even a little firewood by the hearth.

'We must be lower than I thought,' Bruce said, piling kindling in a prodigal heap. 'I guess these people are among those cleared off their land and into camps, or else they fled to avoid the round-up. No *campesino* abandons anything willingly, even a brushwood bed.'

'What about smoke if we light a fire here?' I scarcely cared though, we had to rest and might never wake if we did so while still sodden, without a fire.

'It's misty still, and we're on a lucky streak at the moment. We just have to hope it lasts, and enjoy it.' He stood and kissed me, holding me so a glint of warmth began at my lips and flashed across dulled nerves. 'My love.'

He didn't say any more, but all we had become together was in his voice. Alone, he would have lacked the ultimate, desperate edge he had needed to take on and then defeat Yono with machetes. Alone I could not have lasted over the Picacho Mountains in the rains.

15

We rested as best we could all the next day, disturbed only by bugs, and when the time came to leave we picked up our packs and went, moving circumspectly, not speaking about how our luck had lasted. As if we feared to tempt fortune, and bring armed men running from the trees.

By the end of the following night we had left the hills and were quite close to Quihuli. Closer than we intended, in fact. Bruce had planned to circle well clear of the town, but we were confronted by such an unexpected complex of lights sprawling out from Quihuli itself, and stretching across broken ground towards Agosto, that a detour began to seem tiringly expensive.

We lay up for the day in cactus scrub where we could watch what was happening and decide on the best route for the following night. It became gloriously warm as the sun rose, while behind us the mountains remained lost in storm clouds; I turned my back on them and was thankful.

I slept curled up in sand and woke feeling lazily content. I lacked energy to worry about the future any more; the present was enough so long as Bruce was there, and between us we had defeated the mountains. But he wasn't there: I panicked unreasonably for a moment, then saw him lying behind a shallow ridge where the cactus ended. He turned when I crawled through spikes to join him, and made a gesture of caution.

I was astonished by what I saw on the other side of the ridge. Away to the left Quihuli straggled along its gullies, the note of its church bell making me think of Señor Mendoza in his courtyard, which had been shadowed by the bell tower. The difference lay closer at hand. Where there had been a single dusty track leading to Agosto some ten miles away, there were now dozens of tracks weaving in and out of each other as rain opened up fresh quagmires, yet heavy traffic continued to pass that way. The tracks mostly led to a wired-in, heavily defended compound which was completely new. Arc lights on poles dotted the plain and the enclosure itself was filled with coloured drums, tarpaulin-covered stores, and a few makeshift huts. To one side were two large helicopters painted black but with Comayaguan flashes on the fuselage. While we watched, another landed and began unloading more containers. These were painted yellow and we were close enough to see some kind of red lettering on the side. Then one of the helicopters took off, so we froze face downward into grit until it flew away in the direction of the coast. Trucks were moving briskly between Quihuli and this mushroom-growth of a base, howling horns at each other and skidding in muddy ruts. Most went directly into the compound, a few circled the wire and went on towards Agosto.

'They've done a lot in a few weeks,' I said softly, and saw the muscles of Bruce's face tighten. Comayaguans alone would never have achieved so much, nor could they have afforded it. Those were American trucks and helicopters, almost certainly American drums and crates.

'Mozon looks a tougher and better bet to the Pentagon than El Miragloso,' he answered after a pause. 'They've decided it's worth helping him to stick.'

'An anti-communist is an anti-communist, and who cares about his prisons anyway?'

'Do you think they'd be emptier with someone like Yono in control?'

198

'It was true what you said? About throwing *seguridades* on bonfires in the street?'

'And how the Seguridad revenges itself when its turn comes. Sure, I've seen it. Not here yet, but that's only because they haven't had the chance. Or you can put thorns in a man's genitals and pitch in his mouth, there isn't much difference between one atrocity and another when you see them.'

I was silent; when I watched Yono's guerrillas coming down the track, I had finally understood how it was too late, and also perhaps too soon, to look for solutions here.

The sun shone all day, the colours of Comayagua like spilled paint as the land flowered in the aftermath of rain almost while you watched. In the distance some caterpillar tractors were pulling multi-furrow ploughs across the drying earth, turning *campesino* plots into plantation-type fields. Much closer, on the flatlands between the base and Agosto, troops were practising on a makeshift range. The crackle of fire and thump of mortars sounded deadly in the clear, spring-scented air, although their American instructors must have been sweating blood over the Comayaguan army.

Because there were certainly Americans here, as Yono had said. Not many and not fighting troops, but even at a distance I could pick out the difference in the way Americans walked and how they towered over those they supervised. I thought the helicopters were piloted by Americans too, possibly mercenaries since they did not seem to wear uniforms.

Bruce hardly spoke, his face as inscrutable as an Indian's. And that kind of Indian face hid impotent hatred, as I also now understood.

I drowsed quite often although I never saw him do so, until eventually I became worried. 'Bruce, you're not planning anything, are you?'

He looked at me consideringly, and then smiled. 'It's strange not to be able to hide my thoughts any longer.'

'You can,' I said frankly. 'But – '

'I know what's in those drums and yellow containers, Faith. Defoliant and napalm. Yono was to have been burned

199

out of the Picachero Valley, and if Mozon doesn't discover that he's gone then the Picachos will be napalmed instead. Probably they will be anyway – Mozon's a careful man. And using a defoliant on these hills may deprive guerrillas of cover, but will bring ruin on the whole province next year, when the rains come. Once the trees and scrub go, the remaining soil vanishes.' He stared across at the ploughing caterpillars. 'Flash flooding will sweep out beyond here, and they're stripping even the gullies and windbreaks between separate *campesino* patches.'

'You said you weren't at war any longer,' I said helplessly.

He rolled over and stared at the sky. 'I'm not. War finally defeated me, as you saw with Yono. But you were the one who told me I couldn't run all my life, and of course you're right. Sooner or later you get cornered with no place else to go. Mozon is ready to attack as soon as the storms lift off the mountains: I can't leave him to blot out the Picachero Valley and destroy the livelihood of everyone in the foothills, just because he wants to flush out a few hundred guerrillas.'

'You can't stop him!'

'Not if the United States continues to back him, but that's a low-profile mission down there. No fuss, and no questions wanted. The administration may have different ideas but Vietnam's still a dirty word to most Americans. But napalm is inflammable stuff, and they've stacked it like they were kids at a picnic; if I can put Yono's missile where it ignites either fuel or napalm, then defoliant and a good deal else will go up as well. Those helicopters are gunships and they're expensive, sophisticated things; no one is supposed to hand them out as a favour to tame assassins just because they happen to have grabbed power. I doubt whether any agency could mount this kind of operation twice without someone noticing; we've gotten ourselves a pack of curious newsmen in Central America nowadays, and watchdog committees in the Senate, too.'

I swallowed. 'Yono's missile! For God's sake, Bruce. You can't go looking for Yono now, and ask him politely to hand you over a missile.'

'No?'

I bit my lip. Just possibly Yono was enough of a leader and possessed sufficient grasp of his present perils to set private revenge aside for a while. He would not forgive Bruce for defeating him, but wait for retribution if waiting suited him. 'And when you have succeeded?'

Bruce gave a gasp of laughter. 'My sweet, such confidence is the hell of a burden for an uncertain man to carry. I haven't found any answers, you see. But if I can do this, then I think the choice about our future has to be yours.'

I took his hand, still scabbed from Yono's machete, and held it against my face. 'There isn't any choice. You understood that in the end, didn't you? It has to be together, or we only spread destruction further.'

Bruce went alone to find Yono, while I stayed hidden and tried not to worry about him. He was safer alone when I was part of the revenge that Yono would want eventually to exact, but the risks to Bruce remained very real, so I worried all the same. He had asked me to keep the base under observation and it helped pass the laggard hours, as did thinking about the splendid victory I had won. Strictly speaking of course, I had not won at all. In the end, Bruce had yielded because we had passed from one understanding of each other to the next: as I accepted that he must be allowed to risk both our lives in an attempt to destroy napalm which was no concern of ours, so he had come to realize that I must be allowed to share in the threatening chances of his life. We wanted very much to live, but if we could only survive by parting, then mere survival was not worth its price of a lifetime separation.

Traffic between Quihuli and the base, and also the training range beyond, continued to be very heavy all through the day. Columns of men in combat fatigues tramped past, carelessly trailing guns; trucks whirled by in clouds of dust as the ground dried, although I thought it was the same forty or fifty making repeated trips; the three helicopters annoyed each other by always wanting the same airspace over the base. There must have been some organization to it all as the base had sprung out of nothing in such a short time, but there seemed a great deal of energy running to waste in screamed orders, fingers stabbing at klaxons, people and equipment shuttling from one place to another.

People asleep, too. I think the Comayaguans found American hustle very tiring, and whenever they thought their Yanqui instructors weren't looking figures drifted away behind stony ridges and piled stores. Since there were certainly less than a dozen Americans, I could see a great many recumbent figures from where I lay.

The sun moved very slowly after Bruce left. Shining into my eyes, then hot on the back of my neck, eventually throwing shadows across the earth as it vanished behind the usual clouds boiling over the mountains. Bruce could not return before dusk made it safer to move, even supposing he found Yono. If he returned. If Yono did not kill him, and providing he did not walk into the patrols trudging haphazardly about. Foreboding lay like sludge over my earlier elation; I must have been insane not even to try to stop him doing what he planned.

Sunset. Military activities eased as the floodlights were switched on. A staff car escorted by two jeeps came fast from the direction of Quihuli, and when it stopped by the entry to the base, the blaze from the floodlights and the diagonal sun lit the interior as if it was a stage set. Huddled in the jeeps were some terrified *campesinos*, and sitting to one side with his arms tied was Rodrigo. Napoleon Espinoza was in the staff car with two others whose faces I couldn't see. When Espinoza got out to show papers to the guard, I realized that one of them was Pete Zeller.

He was leaning forward, the bulk of him dark against the radiant sky, his head lifted towards the mountains and where I lay, as if he sensed an enemy hidden close. Then the gate swung open, the car and jeeps drove inside and drew up between a huddle of huts where I couldn't see them any more. Lights came on in one of the huts, flickering sometimes as people moved about inside.

Zeller, I thought. Here of all places, and now of all times. Yet on several counts it wasn't really surprising; such a quantity of expensive American equipment lying around made it easy for him to come, and he must have guessed that the Yanqui reported in the Picachero Valley was Bruce. It might even be imperative for him to come, if he dealt in arms with Colonel Mozon.

Rodrigo caught, and in there too.

Dear God, what shall I do? What can I do?

The poised avalanche of dread which had been building in my mind all through the afternoon broke loose, and took with it any illusion that the worst was now behind us.

The wind began to blow strongly while I lay in anguish, thinking about Rodrigo. And Zeller. The air chilled, and high in the mountain peaks I heard thunder. It would be another murderous night up there and, what was infinitely worse, a killers' and a torturers' night down here. Without any warning, time had become a shark gliding past and sizing up its prey, while I remained helpless, clutching at the ground.

Bruce returned so quietly that the first I heard of him was my name whispered against the wind, the squeak of earth as he lay beside me just below the skyline, cold lips to cold lips. 'Okay?' he said against my ear.

I nodded, overwhelmed by relief that he was back, and also sick with fear. 'You, too?'

'No trouble.' I felt him smile. 'We shall need to make a slick exit when we've finished, though. You could have filled a beer can with Yono's sweat when he realized that he'd have to wait before chopping me.'

'The missile?'

'I'm not sure. The instructions must have been translated from Russian into Spanish by an illiterate using a kid's dictionary. It is also smaller than I expected. I didn't let on about any doubts I had or Yono would have killed me on the spot, but I guess I shall have to go down there first. I need to start that napalm burning, it doesn't ignite just with a match. Then, once there is a fire, a missile in the right place will scatter it all over the place. Defoliant, napalm, gunships, the whole lot ought to blaze.'

'We both go down,' I said, and put my hand across his mouth to stop protest before it came. 'Listen, Bruce. I would come anyway, but Rodrigo is down there. I suppose they caught him somewhere he ought not to have been, but they must be more than just suspicious to bring him here.' I stared at the lighted bulk of that base, which Colonel Mozon's ruthlessness and American money had created within a matter of weeks. Down there a child called Rodrigo was probably already screaming for the mercy he would not find. Words became a whispered torrent as I told Bruce what I had seen, including Zeller. If Rodrigo had not been taken, I would never have told him how Zeller had come so close.

Bruce listened quietly, lying with his head on his arm, his body slack. He must have been very tired after a sleepless day full of strain, and backpacking a heavy missile too; Zeller at Quihuli something he could scarcely bear to imagine.

He simply grunted when I had finished, then moved to rummage in our packs for food: we had only some dried maize and a few vitamin pills left. If we survived tonight, then food would be the next problem we had to solve. 'You realize that if we try to do two impossible things instead of one, the most likely result is that we fail in both?'

'Yes,' I said helplessly. 'I'm sorry, Bruce. I know you'll say it isn't my fault Rodrigo is down there, but if I'd never come to Quihuli, then he'd still be polishing shoes instead of – ' I swallowed. Instead of suffering horrors I could not bear to think about.

'Which hut exactly do you think the boy is in?'

I pointed it out as best I could; thank heaven Bruce wasn't the kind of man to argue once he understood my mind was – had to be – made up. I was also thankful that I hadn't argued either, when he was caught in a similar trap earlier in the day. This endless day, which now we were not likely to survive.

'The jeeps?' he asked.

'Parked outside the huts. I'm sure I would have seen their lights if they'd been moved.'

'How many men altogether inside the perimeter by nightfall?'

'Two or three hundred. Another eight hundred or so under canvas by the practice range.'

'Americans?'

'I'm not sure. Inside the perimeter not more than five, I think. Three helicopter pilots, and a man who kept shouting at the Comayaguans while they stacked stores. Another doubling as mechanic and petrol bowser operator. Plus Zeller, of course.'

'I could do with him up here right now. Assaulting a camp at odds of a hundred and fifty to one would just about suit him. I'll fix this missile ready to fire before we go, supposing I read some Moscow clerk's Spanish right. We might not have time to do more than set a switch on the way back. The snag is, I need some light.'

He had brought a flashlight with him from Yono, but using it was a nightmare, however carefully we arranged shading. Bruce set everything he could by touch and moonlight, checking and rechecking each circuit until my nerves screamed for haste, though I knew it wasn't something which could be hurried. Because of his counter-insurgency background, Bruce knew more than he had admitted to Yono about portable weaponry, but too little electronics to take anything for granted. He said that this missile wasn't complicated, being wire-guided and intended for unsophisticated hands; all the same, it wasn't designed to be set in darkness by someone uninstructed in its mechanism.

The stretch of time while we had to have light was the worst. I shivered in the bitter wind, stripped down to a ragged shirt, holding a screen of jackets while he fiddled endlessly and showed glints of light each time he moved.

Once, I thought I heard voices, and lay flat to stop him moving and to blank out any possibility of light. Nothing happened, except that I lost concentration and muddled some connection, so Bruce had to start again.

205

We left the missile partly hidden by cactus and drew ourselves over the edge of our protective ridge at last, going carefully down towards the wire. My fears faded as we moved, because anything was preferable to waiting any longer, imagination crucified by what Rodrigo might be suffering. Thinking too of trigger-happy Comayaguans waiting for us in their bunkers by the wire, and Zeller on the other side.

From the hills, the base had looked like a large illuminated postage stamp, surcharged with gleaming equipment and postmarked by shadow, barbed wire forming the outer perforation. But for all the complicated menace of its appearance, we didn't experience much difficulty getting in. The patrols moved under floodlights which made them easy to dodge, and the rest of the guards seemed to be asleep: they stood only to urinate and occasionally to fire at shadows, which turned them from being an active deterrent into a nerve-racking sideshow. The tussocky terrain offered cover and prevented the wire from fitting snugly to the ground; careful reconnaissance and a great deal of wriggling did the rest. It was a slow business all the same, and getting out again after an alarm had been raised was something I did not dare think about.

Our first requirement was a gun. I didn't know how Bruce felt about killing, now so many lives might depend on what we were able to do here tonight, but we couldn't even begin without some kind of weapon. The side of the base where we had broken in was mostly filled with tented sleeping quarters and men were walking about holding mess tins and laughing together; there was also a fine voice singing and unmistakable sounds of conviviality quite close. These men were waiting to go on the offensive with weapons they believed would give them easy victory, consequently they were strung up and boisterously excited. Bruce led the way while I stuck to him like a burr, trying to imitate his fluid, silent movements.

Light sprayed from a hut door as it slammed open. I glimpsed combat gear inside, deal tables, stacked mechanical spares. A man came out, holding a towel and humming to himself as he went past. Bruce did not move from the shadows where we stood: someone wearing only trousers and singlet probably wasn't armed.

I could feel my heart accelerate while we waited. Waiting was what flaked at courage and brought nightmare visions crowding back. At the far end of the canvas alley from where we stood, two men stopped to talk. One wore a steel helmet and clattered when he moved, the other was stripped to the waist and had lather on his face. Let the geared-up one come, and not the other. I felt my lips move as if I intended to say it aloud. I was useless in this kind of situation, when a few minutes' wait made me shiver with nerves. I was also the only help Bruce had; I simply must not allow myself to be useless.

The two men parted, and the one wearing the helmet came towards us. He moved lightly and cautiously, some kind of gun resting across his arm; a more sensible guard than any we had so far seen. A boy, handsome in the reflections from the arc-lights and with soft stubble on his cheeks. I saw him clearly as he passed and was still thinking about the pride of his expression when he fell. Bruce had taken him from one side, the edge of his hand under the steel rim of his helmet: I don't think the boy saw anything at all.

We did not speak when Bruce dropped him in the deep shadows where we had been hidden. He thrust the helmet and a combat jacket in my hands. 'Pull the helmet forward over your eyes.' Words almost too soft to catch. When we moved off again I saw he was carrying a long-snouted automatic rifle, and wearing a canvas belt with a holstered automatic on one side.

Both the helmet and the jacket stank of sweat and were too small for me, but probably would deceive a casual scrutiny. . . . And in that instant, without any warning at all, I was suddenly overwhelmed by the bizarre unbelievableness of everything that had happened, and was still happening, to me.

This was me, Faith Milburn, scuttling from one shadow to

the next in a Comayaguan military base, wearing ludicrous fancy dress and expecting to die before the night was ended. Each step which brought me from the North Tyne to Mexico, from San Bernardo to the Picachero Valley and now into Colonel Mozon's camp, had seemed logical at the time, but now the reality of my situation was almost impossible to accept. This couldn't be me, nor could strong male voices singing drunkenly nearby be Comayaguan soldiers who would kill instantly if ever they saw me clearly.

'Allá en la noche calláda
Para que se oiga mejohor,
Amamemú choquea siá moyó . . .'

' . . . Love me with all your might, as I love you . . .'; the trite words scrambled reality even further. To where I had once eaten out with cheerful fellow-students in Newcastle's Spanish restaurant and . . . 'What is it?' I said aloud, very loudly; perilously and crazily in an ordinary speaking voice, when Bruce put back a cautionary hand in warning.

I saw his face as he turned, startled, and then everything slid together again, illusion peeling off my consciousness to leave me aghast at what I'd done. We had reached the place where the tents ended and there was an open space before stacked crates and drums began. Some men stood there, arguing over a steel trolley they were pulling.

'Wait,' said Bruce swiftly, and without breaking stride he went on towards them, although his gesture had originally been intended to keep us under cover. But the men had turned to the sound I'd made, and concealment was impossible.

Bruce held his rifle easily over one arm and called out to them in Spanish. 'Having trouble?'

I'd seen five Americans around the base, before Zeller came to make it six, but would a collection of mechanics ever accept another Yanqui as something only to be expected?

I stood where they could see my helmet and not much else, wondering frantically how I could make restitution for my lunacy. Exhaustion and inexperience do strange things to

208

the mind, but few of them more dangerous than what they had done to me. One of the men seemed to be questioning Bruce; I watched with sick anxiety while they crowded round him, gigantic shadows thrown on trampled earth . . . one of them taking Bruce's rifle.

I opened my mouth to shout; all I could do was attract attention and trust that his speed would achieve some miracle of escape. Then I realized he was shoving them good-naturedly aside, saying something to make them laugh, crouching together over whatever they had on the trolley. He straightened after what seemed an enormous length of time, went with them a little way, pointing where he wanted them to go. What looked like money changed hands as he took his rifle back – the man had only held it to be helpful. ' . . . *de explosivos en cantina después!*' Their light-hearted parting floated back to me.

He stood to watch them out of sight, one turning to lift a hand as they went.

Then he came back to me. 'They weren't sure whether they should stack that ammunition or use it to arm a gunship. I told them to arm it, then go get drunk.'

'I can't think . . .' I began wretchedly. 'Oh, God, I can't believe how I could be such a fool.'

Bruce grinned. 'I think you may just have given us a chance, so don't dare apologize. I give them five minutes before they high-tail it to the cantina – they'd be crazy to try arming gunships in the dark without anyone to see they do it right. They were too proud to admit to me they didn't know how themselves, but with the pesos I gave them to spend it shouldn't be long before they decide to take the easiest way.'

We were speaking quietly but standing without conceal-ment, no one was close, confidence our best armour here.

'There are phosphorous, fragmentation and cannon shell on that trolley, uncased and ready to use. If I can't start something worth watching with raw material like that, then I deserve to provide meat for Zeller's choosing. Of course, those guys ought to check it back into stores and not leave it lying around, but I'd bet the Federal Reserve against the Comayaguan banana crop that they don't.'

'Rodrigo?'

'After. It will be like a campus during a protest rally around here when my fireworks start.' His hand closed over mine, briefly. 'It has to be this way around, Faith.'

I nodded. If Rodrigo really had been brought in for interrogation, then too much time had passed already for there to be much left of him, and many more lives than his would be destroyed by the gleaming drums I could see piled close to where we stood. Yet a child's life was something I could grasp, while bombs and napalm remained a horror story for the press.

We also needed as much diversion as possible, if we were ever to get into the huts where the Seguridad held their prisoners.

16

After that everything became infinitely more difficult, as if to warn us that we had scarcely yet begun. We left the area where so many men were quartered that two unknowns might pass without remark, and entered a restricted zone filled with military hardware and certainly guarded. Even the Comayaguan army must understand the sense of placing sentries under cover here to watch for intruders, rather than leaving them lounging under arc lights; once we entered that maze of containers and steel drums every movement was hazardous.

Without Bruce, I should have been lost at once. Lost literally, because direction became surprisingly difficult to maintain in higgledy-piggledy blind alleys made up from stacked stores of every description; and doubly lost, because I should have been very quickly challenged. At least I was of some use to him as well, with so many directions to be watched simultaneously. I had to forget everything except the need to concentrate all my senses on the fractional warning I might be able to give of danger. Yet everything I saw seemed menacingly wrong and threatening: light glancing off yellow plastic became a man's face; the flap of canvas changing to the shift of weight as an unseen sentry's finger tightened on the trigger. Later, I would feel terror again, terror which was like a hand clutching at my shoulder

211

from a dark doorway, but I must, must, must, not feel terror now, when terror numbed the senses on which our lives depended.

There was more light ahead of us, where the wall of drums we were using as cover ended. A tap from Bruce's fingers: move now. Pressure left then right, both freeze as I jerked warningly against his grasp, some kind of movement snatching at the edge of vision. A pair of soldiers carrying their guns carelessly over their shoulders came into sight and vanished again across a narrow space. A mutter of greeting the far side of our protecting drums, the shuffle of cloth and surreptitious rake of a match. They were smoking. God. The air reeked of inflammable fumes; perhaps we could go quietly home after all, and leave them to do our job for us. Softly we moved forward again, each foot carefully placed; the North Tyne poachers would have to look to their laurels if ever I returned there.

We reached the place where the drums ended, and stood looking at helicopters parked in a cleared but confined space. They were strongly lit and it didn't take me long to spot three sentries; one looked asleep but the other two certainly were not. There would be more beyond where I could see, too. To our left, perhaps thirty feet away, was the armourer's trolley which Bruce had hoped to find.

Again, we couldn't afford not to wait, to breathe each breath carefully and not shift at all while using eyes and ears to plot each movement in that treacherous space. The black-painted helicopters looked like stranded wart hogs, but would do their job with deadly efficiency once the time was right.

'You remember the canvas we just passed?' Bruce breathed, lips against my ear.

I nodded; it had been badly secured and flapped heavily in the wind, muffling sound as we tried to listen for guards.

'Can you go back and untie another rope? Then it should blow right off one end and take some drums with it. I need thirty seconds while no one looks this way.'

212

I nodded again. I had come because I knew there would be a time when he needed help, unskilled though I was; this was that time and I must not think how far away that canvas was, nor that I might not find it in a labyrinth of drums, or see the guard who caught me in his sights

'Take it as slow as you like. When it's done, come back here. I'll be watching for you.'

I nodded a third time. Words were danger; I also thought my mouth too dry for words.

He held me for a weakening instant when all I wanted was to stay with him; an urgent leaping instant, too, when danger was shut out. Who knows why love is offered or withheld, why it was me and him and always would be, even if one of us lived and the other died tonight? 'If you're not sure, wait,' he said against my face. 'There's plenty of time left.'

There wasn't, though. Not for this, and then to reach Rodrigo across the base from here, while he still lived.

Darkness and then deeper dark; shadow and gleaming moonlight sailing out of storm clouds. I wished the storm would come tumbling off the mountains in the way they so often did, cover that hateful moon and hurl thunder at listening sentries. Probably there weren't many of them anyway, only my imagination peopling every cranny. I hauled sharply at this optimistic thought: I had to believe – I *did* believe – that guards were breathing down my neck whichever way I went.

Turn left here. I remembered this stack of red-lettered drums. DANGER. HIGHLY INFLAMMABLE. OPEN WITH SECURITY KEY ONLY. Countersunk metal screw caps, invulnerable without the proper tool, which was certainly kept elsewhere. I paused, irresolute; retracing a route meant that everything looked different. I knew my general direction well enough, but a single insecure canvas cover was less easy to discover. I heard a scuffling, regular beat of feet coming nearer, followed by bad-tempered commands. Guard change, so midnight, possibly. I was forced to wait a long time while the new sentries settled down, but at least I saw where the nearest were, one of them too close for comfort. I slipped back to a different alley, turned two corners, sure again of where I was.

'*Qué hacéis aquí?*'

I stood paralysed as the challenge came, then dropped to my knees and wormed into a shred of space between some containers, panic-blood beating in my ears. Feet belted past, skidded to a stop some ten yards farther on, which might mean the guard wasn't sure of what he'd seen, or exactly where. I pressed my face into dirt and prayed he wasn't sure.

'*Quién es?*' Another voice calling, a sergeant presumably.

The man shouted some answer, head turned so I couldn't catch his words. I didn't know what to do; the concealment I had found might save me if they mounted only a casual search, but not if they decided to scour the area. Yet movement made discovery more likely now everyone in this section was alerted. I strained my ears, trying without success to make sense of mumbled argument. Another pair of boots tramped past my nose and the noise, if not the sense, of argument grew.

I took a deep breath and wriggled through to the far side of the container stack where I had hidden. If you're not sure, wait, Bruce had said. But three men distracted ought to mean reasonably clear ground ahead and time wasn't running for us, whatever Bruce pretended. I stood at once, because now that I had decided to risk moving, then the quicker I did so the better; I felt horribly exposed all the same and too panicky to keep a proper watch. I'll be glad when I get out of this, I thought, and smiled at such phenomenal understatement.

Twenty feet away across another moonlit alley was the flapping canvas tarpaulin I was looking for.

The guards were flashing torches aimlessly about, one of them sharply slapped down by the sergeant for a flippant remark. Very soon they would be back at their posts, dissatisfied and wide awake.

No point waiting. I stepped boldly across the silvered alley between containers on this side and drums on the other; I was so brilliantly lit that my shadow was etched on piled stores. Then I was back into dimness again, unchallenged. The tarpaulin was cracking in the wind, and from the shape I guessed it covered spare machinery of some sort. Someone had balanced drums on the top to help keep it in place. Bruce was quite right, if I released the last two ties this side, then it ought to billow like a sail and send the drums flying. The knots weren't difficult, in fact the tarpaulin was flapping because it had undone two of the four itself. I stood a moment, straining to hold the last rope against the pull of the wind and trying to calculate where the guards had gone, but the boom of canvas muffled all other sounds. Hurry, it seemed to say, hurry!

I released the rope and it whipped through my hand, bellying canvas high in the air. It snapped heavily twice, then the first drum went; the tarpaulin immediately blew higher and the rest of the drums followed the first. There was the most godawful clashing clatter as they bounded away into the next alley, bringing down something there as well.

The returning sentry let out a shout and fired a burst from his automatic rifle, the bullets ricocheting off steel. One of them must have pierced a drum because there was a terrible fuel stench and the sergeant came pelting back yelling at him not to fire any more. It seemed to me that they were incredibly lucky that nothing had ignited, but Bruce had said that even napalm wasn't the kind of stuff you lit with a match, so perhaps it was safer than the smell made me believe. The released fumes must be inflammable though, surely.

The moment I let the canvas go I had sprinted across that dangerous stretch of moonlight, squeezed past containers again and regained the alley where the soldiers had been talking. They were all reviling each other by the tarpaulin now, and I made my way back towards the helicopters as quickly as reasonable prudence would allow. Keeping to shadow, eyes by now completely attuned to darkness, feeling good; believing this was no longer the moment I might die. Later perhaps, but not now.

Bruce was waiting close to the alley's end. How he knew

215

which way I would come I don't know, but he did, and the touch of his hands spoke for him so clearly that I smiled to myself. This time it had been his turn to be worried sick.

He had drawn the armourer's trolley under cover and bent over it while I waited, surprised to discover how glad I was just to stand quietly, how stupidly short of breath I felt. I couldn't see what he was doing and didn't try. I knew he intended to detonate what was on that trolley so it ignited at least some of the napalm, and if he thought he could do it then I didn't expect him to be wrong. A dump of fuel and combustible stores like this ought surely to have been divided by anti-blast walls at the very least, but the Comayaguans never dreamed that Yono would not stay in the Picachero Valley until the rains ended, and the moment the weather lifted over the mountains, they intended to strike. They had in fact done extraordinarily well to get so much equipment assembled within weeks, and I thought I detected the energy of Pete Zeller at the American end of affairs. I expect he was disgusted by what he saw at Quihuli base when he arrived, but he could not be everywhere, after all.

'Okay,' said Bruce softly, beginning to draw the trolley back the way I'd come. Ammunition here and napalm farther up; fuel, I wasn't sure where. Perhaps that was closer to the helicopters.

We dared not go too far while there was still a great fuss going on around the tarpaulin, so Bruce wedged the trolley against a stack of drums, stood considering it for a moment and then drew an automatic from the belt he'd taken from the soldier earlier. 'Be ready to run like hell. Left, left, right – okay?'

'Yes.' The word sounded loud although I whispered. He, too, had done no more than keep his voice down, clarity more important than silence now.

With one hand he pulled me behind him; I suppose we were twenty feet from the trolley. Very carefully, he took aim at the exposed end of a bomb or shell he had placed pointing inward at the rest. In rising wind and fitful moonlight it must have been a horribly awkward shot, even though the range was short.

The report sounded sharply. Subconsciously I had not expected to hear it at all, anticipating some huge explosion from the trolley. Which if it had occurred would, of course, have blown us into vapour. Instead, a brilliant eye-dazzling flash followed, exploding into a kind of molten yellow core. I felt my arm gripped and together we raced back the way we had come, jinking in case anyone fired at us, knowing we must be seen. My eyes saw nothing except phosphorescently glaring shapes and I tripped when the ground roughened. A volley of reports came from the blaze behind us, cannon shells rather than bombs, I thought hazily. Bruce's hand under my elbow steadied and encouraged me; then a flat roar and suck of air sent us staggering into the sharp edges of a parked truck, threw golden splats of light high in the air. Something whacked into the ground a few feet to one side of us: bullet or debris? Impossible to be sure. No way of being sure. We ran like hell instead, full tilt into someone haring in the opposite direction, all picking ourselves up and pelting on, a challenge not even considered. Ammunition exploded behind us, the glow changing from yellow to deep crimson. I wasn't sure whether this meant that the napalm had caught, or whether it was merely wood from the packing cases. Vaguely, I thought napalm ought to be more spectacular: those drums had to get hot enough to explode, or be punctured by flying splinters and then leak heated jelly. Once that happened, the Comayaguans would run for safety like sensible men and leave the base to burn.

At the moment they were still trying to put out the fire, which didn't seem much brighter; a whole belt of shells hurtled into the air, not into the drums, unfortunately.

Someone yelled at us and Bruce yelled back; a couple of soldiers swept past and almost as an afterthought emptied a magazine of shots in our direction; impossible again to tell whether it was because we looked suspicious or because that was the kind of thing the Comayaguan army did in an emergency. There was pandemonium everywhere. Naked

217

men tumbled out of sleep gaped at the bonfire burning merrily at the far side of half an acre of stores from where we now were; officers shouted and struck out at anyone they could reach, and someone more level-headed than the rest had coupled up a hose although there didn't seem to be any water for it.

We stopped in the first quiet place we found when we reached the huts again. My throat hurt although we hadn't run far, only very fast, and I realized for the first time that thick black smoke was rolling in on the wind.

'Napalm?' I choked on the words.

'Diesel.'

'Will that do?'

'God knows. It means the drums on the far side of that alley ruptured, instead of the ones we wanted. Or they ruptured, but aren't hot enough yet to burn. They mix additives to make storage safer.'

'Rodrigo?'

'Sure. We certainly can't go back and try again.' His voice was inexpressive but such disappointment was crushing. Behind us I heard an American voice yelling for foam and order; already the flames seemed less than they had only minutes before.

We were about a hundred yards from the hut where I had seen the jeeps draw up when they brought their prisoners into the base earlier, and they were still there now. Bruce paused and groped along the dashboard of the nearest for keys, but they had been taken out. He hesitated and then went to the oldest vehicle there, a beat-up Quihuli police jeep. Ancient machinery didn't have steering locks or complicated ignition systems.

'Watch for me, will you?' he breathed.

So I watched, eyes shuttling between sparks still blowing into the sky behind us and the hut I believed we had to enter. The door was shut and a sentry stood on guard outside, though there had been light from an open door as we approached. As if someone had been there watching, until he decided that the fire was being brought under control and

218

other matters were more important. I heard the jeep's engine wheeze softly and immediately die, as if Bruce had just touched the wires he wanted to make sure they worked. One thing was sure, we wouldn't have time for fumbling anything if we came back this way.

In spite of so much commotion, the sentry heard too and called out, not really suspicious. There were too many vehicles charging in all directions for instant suspicion, after all.

If we were to have any chance of success, then this was the moment to be ruthless: to shoot, and be inside the hut before anyone guessed there might be anything wrong. But Bruce called back, bluffing, and this time it didn't work. I don't know why the guard suddenly understood that we were enemies, but he fired without hesitation. When in doubt, shoot: the motto of the Comayaguan army.

I felt a blistering pain across my upper arm, before numbness blanked sensation out. I'd thrown myself instinctively on my face and didn't know where the rest of the burst had gone. I scrambled up calling frantically to Bruce and scarcely thinking of the guard and his rifle any more.

'Keep down,' he said with the desperate quietness I remembered from previous instants of disaster. That quietness of frozen and trained willpower which alone kept panic from bitching everything, when nearly everything was already bitched. The jeep engine roared and its headlamps cut shockingly across darkness, transfixing the guard where he stood, knees slightly bent and his mouth open, weapon thrust forward to fire again. The light stupefied him as the jeep leaped forward, then he yelled and dived sideways for cover. The jeep struck the place where he had been standing, and even before it did, I was up and running, kicking where I knew that sentry was, waiting to fire into our backs as we passed. My boots struck flesh, and he shouted again, his flailing legs tripping me so I fell on top of him.

He was still holding his rifle and the hot metal burned my neck; I wrenched aside and kicked again as if possessed by alien frenzy. I don't know where that second kick landed but something gave with a pulpy squelch and he screamed,

219

instinctively trying to roll away. I tore the rifle out of his slackened grip and staggered to my feet, arm hurting fiercely now. I couldn't see Bruce anywhere and was swept by rage instead of fear for him: he ought to have been there, when our lives were saved only because I had attacked a soldier twice my weight.

Three shots, close spaced, came from inside the hut and rage vanished again, terror back in its place. Of course Bruce had no notion of where I was or what was happening out here. He had taken the only chance remaining and gone straight into the hut over the bonnet of the jeep.

I dropped to my knees and burrowed through the debris under its chassis; the hut roof was half down and there was a lot of broken glass around, a hole punched clean through prefabricated wall by the jeep. Lights were still burning inside the hut and when I had crawled to where one front wheel was cocked up on a crushed filing cabinet I could see the stark interior.

A soldier was sprawled face down close to my eyes, moaning and clutching at blood on his tunic. He had probably been coming to investigate the commotion outside when the jeep struck. Anyway, he didn't look as if he was likely to interfere for the moment. There were two *seguridades* in there, both in shirtsleeves and one of them surprised without his weapons, the other with his hands in the air and a machine pistol at his feet. There was a huddle of bodies at the far end from where I lay, surrounded by a great deal of blood; a terrified *campesino* stripped and bleeding propped against a wall. Lieutenant Napoleon Espinoza sat at a makeshift table looking guiltily astonished, like a boy caught stealing money from his mother's purse; Zeller was standing quite relaxed, gun half lifted as he smiled across towards where Bruce was, although from my position I could only see the lower part of his body. From his stance he had covered Zeller an instant before he could jerk round to fire.

A single shot made me cry out but no one noticed, as Espinoza snatched back his hand with a shout, blood flowing from his wrist.

220

'You're too young for this game, sonny,' said Zeller kindly. 'Señor Shryver could shoot off each of your fingers if he wanted to, so you'd best not try laying for him yet.'

'The same goes for you,' answered Bruce. 'Drop that gun and join your vultures by the wall.'

'Yeah?' Zeller did not move, and still the smile stayed on his face. I felt among debris for the gun I'd seized, although I had no idea how to fire it. Pull the trigger and hope there was something left in the magazine, and that the safety catch was off. But if Bruce could smash Espinoza's fingers, then he could damned well put a bullet in Zeller where it hurt. Except that Zeller planned something, knew something, wasn't in the least worried, although I sensed an odd compound of respect and gloating in his manner. Bruce had been his boss on his first job and nothing since had altered that relationship. Zeller intended to kill him but wanted the manner of it to be fitting, as if even in this he craved for Bruce's approval.

Bruce fired again. He was using single shots from the pistol and not automatic fire where close aim was impossible. Yet this was no longer a private quarrel but a place where guards would come running any second, time roaring past and taking with it more lives than ours alone. Zeller was scarcely important any more, except he was in the way and would kill us if he could. He couldn't at the moment; that was the irony of it all. He hadn't dropped his gun when Bruce ordered him to, but his own respect for Bruce's marksmanship made him hesitate over the next risk he must take. Then he shrugged, made as if to drop it and instead flicked it lightning swift from one hand to the other, rolled and came up on one knee ready to fire a crippling shot angled from the ground. Bruce did not move and the change of hand made no difference to his aim; his shot came fractionally first, the slashing whine of it horrifyingly unexpected as Zeller's gun jarred and spun across the floor.

Zeller stayed on one knee for a disbelieving moment as blood spurted from the torn flesh of his hand, then he came to his feet as if pain was something he did not notice. His

221

expression was murderous and his muscles bunched in fury as he flung himself at Bruce. Since Espinoza chose that moment to dive for his gun, Bruce had to jerk aside and fire at him instead of Zeller. Utter confusion followed, and I lost vital seconds scrambling through the narrow space left between debris and the jeep's radiator to gain the inside of the hut.

Men were yelling outside too, and I hesitated, wanting to fire blind in warning for them to keep away. Deciding to fire high, because two shots fired beside Ulate's body was all I knew of guns, but when I pulled the trigger nothing happened. God knows what I did wrong; I tried to fumble with knobbed steel but then turned in a panic at the sound of animal shrieking, its pitch inhuman. I don't think he really was so agonizingly hurt, but the screeching came from Espinoza dancing about in his polished boots, clutching his shoulder. Since I wasn't feeling in the least merciful towards people who would pull triggers the moment they had the chance, and very badly panicked besides, I drove the stock of the rifle I carried at his head, and the screams chopped off short as he fell.

I turned an instant too late.

Even after shooting Espinoza, Bruce had almost dodged Zeller's charge, then went with the piston force of it and rebounded off the wall ready for the first opening he found. Zeller was much heavier, six inches taller and ten years younger, with beserk rage to make up for the disadvantage of a damaged hand, providing the fight did not last. It ought not to have lasted more than seconds, since Bruce's sidestep meant that as he turned, the muscled thickness of Zeller's belly was exposed to his gun, yet instead of firing, he drove the metal of it muzzle-deep into Zeller's midriff. He had that one clear chance to kill, and when he did not take it, it was too late. Zeller gasped, but at close quarters his weight and strength were unstoppable, and he hurled Bruce towards a man I had not even noticed in the far shadows of the hut, who fired directly at his back.

Some instinct must have warned Bruce, or perhaps he saw

222

the flash of triumph on Zeller's face: he fell clear by flinging himself sideways, but paid the penalty of being crushed by Zeller's driven weight.

I heard my own scream of warning end, disaster so unbelievably swift that I never saw a clear target for the pistol I had snatched from Espinoza's table until Zeller dropped on top of Bruce. Then I was stopped by the man who had been standing hidden in the corner, the man I hadn't been able to identify in Espinoza's car, and who ever since we had stormed into the hut had been the joker in Zeller's pack.

'Put your gun on the floor, Señorita Milburn.' It was Calderon, and although that first shot of his had missed Bruce, he could not possibly miss a second time, since he was aiming directly where Bruce lay pinned beneath Zeller's bulk. 'I worried about you after the fall of the Mendoza dictatorship,' he added, with the same unruffled courtesy he had used to send me to Comayagua all those weeks ago. 'I am happy to see that you are still alive, but really I cannot commend your judgement. Guerrillas are always dangerous company, and see the trouble your rashness has brought on you tonight.'

17

Zeller's face was a mask of fury as he rolled clear and got to his feet. 'What the fucking hell took you so long?' he spat at Calderon.

'I could say the same to you, Señor Zeller. You have one man and a girl come at you, and it is nearly a slaughter-house.' He flicked his gun at the shambles in the hut. 'And you would have been one of the dead, except that your enemy was *quijotesco*, and did not kill you when he had the chance, not once but twice. You are a fool, señor,' he added to Bruce.

Zeller snatched up Bruce's gun and kicked him heavily. 'Stand up. Real slow. Hands wide.'

Bruce came to his knees and then stood, hands spread. Our eyes met for an instant over Zeller's shoulder before he looked away. His face was expressionless; taut muscles forming sharp angles from cheekbone to jaw, eyebrows drawn into slanting lines. He understood what he had done, and offered no defence.

Zeller rounded on the shirt-sleeved *seguridades* who had stood gaping at the tumult since we came. Two minutes ago? A lifetime. I licked dry lips and thought about Espinoza's gun which I'd placed back on the table, instead of dropping it on the floor as Calderon told me. If Calderon's attention should waver even for an instant . . . in some ways he was a more dangerous man than Zeller. Profit and survival were his concern, and he would quite calmly do whatever was necessary to achieve both. Because, of course, his presence here made his part in all this a great deal clearer: an ally of Zeller was an ally of Colonel Mozon. Which meant . . . which meant . . . I couldn't grapple with the intricacy of it all. It must mean that Calderon was interested in money, and nothing else. Mausers to the Indians, something much more sophisticated to Mozon, surely, to help him seize power from El Miragloso. Mozon couldn't have been pleased to guess from Maynard's letter that Calderon was profiting from others in Comayagua besides himself, but with a coup so close had not been able to quarrel with his supplier. I wouldn't give much for Calderon's life if ever Mozon was securely in power, but liked to think that Ulate at least had not known what was happening until too late; then he had argued, and been killed. Now enough arms were gathered in Quihuli to make any dictator lick his lips, and Calderon was here, too.

One of the security men came and stood where Zeller told him, holding a gun in my back hard enough to hurt. The other went over to grab one of Bruce's arms while Zeller kicked him savagely against the wall, and then twisted the other arm so hard I heard the sinews creak.

'Bring the woman here,' Zeller ordered.

There didn't seem any point resisting, especially when going closer brought me within two paces of that gun on the table, which must now be the sole chance remaining to us. I felt slack and cold and stupid, plans fluttering and falling in my mind, none of them making sense.

Zeller slapped Bruce's face with his bloodied hand: it must have hurt him more than it hurt Bruce, but he didn't seem to notice. He had fed his pride with thoughts of revenge for so long, he was half-crazed by the discovery that face to face Bruce Shryver could have defeated him twice over, but for a scruple. And then again, if Calderon had not been there.

He slapped again. 'My hand. Christ. Look what you did to

225

my hand.' The childishness of it was ludicrous, except for the murder printed on his face.

'You were fortunate,' observed Calderon dispassionately. 'You could have lost your fingers if the gun had exploded, and it seems to me that not even one of them is broken.'

Zeller drove his good fist into Bruce's stomach. 'Slowed up though, haven't you?'

'Really?' Calderon raised his eyebrows sceptically. '*Dios.*'

Zeller swore at him. 'He must have been wasting too much juice screwing his woman into macaroni all cosy in the mountains. Is she a good fuck, Shryver, or spoiled already?'

Bruce did not answer, his face grey, still choking from that last blow.

Zeller twisted brutally, hand on Bruce's forearm just above the wrist; the security man was holding Bruce's other arm two-handed, Calderon still covering him from one side. As Zeller continued to twist, there was the sound of tearing muscle and Bruce's head went back, mouth open soundlessly, sweat pouring off his nose and jaw.

'Yes,' my voice was no more than a croak. 'Yes, if that's what you want to hear said. We fucked well together. The best. There's no mistaking the best.' Words unshaped and falling, as I couldn't control them any more.

Zeller jerked his head at the man behind me. 'I told you to bring her close.' And he yelled some answer at the growing clamour of inquiring voices from outside, following it with curses until they scuttled off, a single nervous officer poking his face through torn boards to make sure all was well. No one would interfere with what went on in here, now it was confirmed as Seguridad business.

'We are wasting time,' said Calderon. 'We know that with your enemy here, then that fire cannot possibly have been started accidentally. So probably the boy told the truth when he said the guerrillas would not stay in the Picachero Valley, but would attack us here.'

Zeller showed his teeth. 'Sure. Two minutes will see me finished.' He stared at me. 'For the moment. If some revenges are better kept on a back burner for a while, then others need to be taken fast.' He fastened his bloodied fingers around mine, and jerked me to him. I snatched back and he winced, then jolted his elbow in my face so my teeth snapped together and vision blurred. The sheer savagery of his every movement took me by surprise each time, even though I expected nothing else. When my eyes cleared, he had taken Calderon's gun and Calderon was holding Bruce in his place: he looked contemptuous, but wasn't tangling with Zeller either.

Zeller's grip was like a hawser on my hand, forcing the gun between my fingers, curling thumb and palm over the butt, crushing the wrong finger between guard and trigger. He tightened his hold viciously, cursing the man at my back when I nearly tore loose once.

I watched, hypnotized, my mind spinning dizzily above the horror of seeing my hand forced outward, still holding Calderon's pistol, its muzzle wavering as I fought to scrape strength out of nowhere and throw it against Zeller's bulk.

'Don't, Faith.' Bruce's voice when it came was clear but unfamiliar.

I stared at him numbly, and saw his eyes no longer blank but flickering towards my hand, his lips form three soundless words; then he seemed to brace himself, understanding before I did exactly what was coming. Zeller shoved the muzzle of the gun he forced me to hold against Bruce's spread right hand, and crushed my knuckles across the steel.

I couldn't help it.

I couldn't prevent the spasm which crooked my finger on the trigger. The recoil numbed me to the elbow as Zeller's grip kept bone and steel crushed together; I saw black burning cautery printed on Bruce's palm, instantly wiped out as scarlet burst over flesh and metal. And still Zeller wasn't done. He drove my hand and the gun into shattered bone, forcing a sound out of Bruce's throat which haunts me still. Then he let me go, and laughed.

Calderon also released Bruce's arm, so it swung loose against his leg, blood pouring off his fingers.

'Now perhaps we may get on with more important

227

matters, señor. Tie up your own hand and we will go to look at this fire.' Calderon showed no emotion at all.

'Sure,' said Zeller lightly. 'I guess if I handcuff him now, he won't go far. The rest of what I want from him can wait until later.'

I shot him as he turned.

In the chest, because I was not certain of my aim.

Gun dragging at my hand, this hand and gun with which I had shot Bruce. Recoil this time an inconsequent jolt compared to how it was when Zeller held me.

And so it was that I became the one who killed, and at the time I scarcely thought of it at all.

Get Zeller after. Those were the words which Bruce had shaped, his eyes on the gun I was forced to hold. His mind still coolly judging Zeller, and guessing how the lust of even part-fulfilled revenge would make him careless. He had shoved me contemptuously aside once he had used me as he wanted, and forgotten that he'd left me with the gun.

I shot Zeller again when he hit the floor. Bruce sent the man who had been holding him staggering, so he cannoned into the other, who was standing somewhere behind my back. I can't imagine even now how Bruce patched nerve and thought together out of such great shock; but the others had discounted him as a force and weren't watching him any more, which helped a little, I suppose.

Calderon, the two security men, none of them reacted fast enough as Zeller died, and if I had not been far, far beyond the reaches of normality, I too would have stood gaping at this killing which was mine. But my senses were so stripped by anguish that only hate and love mattered any more, purpose a branding iron in my brain.

I stepped back from Zeller's body and swung round to cover those two soldiers before they recovered from utter stupefaction: they understood at once that I would fire if they so much as moved their eyes. They were so damned lucky I didn't fire they melted where they stood.

I had to try several times before I was able to speak. 'Stay where you are, drop your guns and kick them over here.'

They did exactly what I said, pop-eyed with justifiable fear.

Calderon. For Christ's sake, where was Calderon? He was the deadly danger who had already brought us to ruin once. I had to risk looking away from those two security men for an instant; I looked, and they were looking too. Three of us, transfixed by another death. I had been holding Calderon's gun but he must have kept another small automatic hidden; when I shot Zeller he would have shot me, except that this time Bruce had not hesitated. Weakness and blood loss made no difference, briefly his speed remained.

He had taken Calderon around the throat one-handed, thumb seeking the artery where pressure blackens consciousness within seconds, but he lacked the strength to make it as quick as it had to be. Calderon had already thrashed half free, gun still held in the hand Bruce could not reach, since he fought with a useless arm. While I watched, he loosed his hold on Calderon's throat, hooked his legs from under him, and dropped on his back as he fell.

Then he crooked his elbow around his neck, and broke it.

Bruce Shryver could always have killed efficiently, if he had wanted to.

'Bruce!' I said urgently. 'Bruce – '

I did not think he would ever stand, but he stood and dragged himself to where the *seguridades* were, their eyes dilating as he came. 'Find something for my arm.'

One of them scuttled across the room and came back with a dirty shirt, and all the time Bruce stood there wiping his face absently and dripping blood on the floor. He looked quite dreadful, face already fallen in like a corpse's, blood on his chin where he had bitten through his lip. Almost the worst part of it was that I could not help. The security men were cowed but I dared not leave them uncovered for an instant, and somehow later must tie them up. A great many things would have been easier if I had shot them, and only later was I thankful that I had not. At the time, mercy was simply another complication. At least Espinoza showed no sign of returning consciousness.

I remembered the *campesino* and turned, but he had gone. Poor devil, I hope he made it through the wire, naked and beaten as he was. 'Bruce,' I said again. 'Bruce. Oh God, Bruce, are you all right?' I didn't seem able to get beyond his name, and shock was beginning to make me crumble. I mustn't weaken yet. And what an abysmal question: he was so far from all right that the realization we were still inside Quihuli base and two hundred miles of wilderness from the nearest frontier made this moment a death more dead than death itself.

'Tight,' he said to the security man who brought the shirt. 'Tie a strip as tight as hell below the elbow, and wrap the rest over the hand. Then find me something to drink. The Americano will have a flask.'

Zeller did have a flask, and of scotch instead of aguadiente; Bruce brought it to me after he had drunk. The Scottish Highlands seemed a hideously long way away, and my imagination so loosely held that it soared there on a mist of longing, but at least the whisky spread puff-ball warmth from throat to stomach and held off collapse a little longer. Bruce took the gun from me and sat on the edge of the table, holding it on the security men. 'Go and see if the boy is alive.'

The bodies I had seen when I first glanced inside the hut were those of three *campesinos* and Rodrigo. Two of the men were dead. The other still breathed but looked as if he would never recover consciousness; Rodrigo was alive, but his beating had crumpled the bird bones of his undernourished body.

His eyes opened when I touched him. '*Ayudamé. O Dios, ayudamé.*'

'You are back with your friends,' I said. 'It's all right, Rodrigo. No one will hurt you any more.'

His eyes squeezed shut. '*Ayudamé.*'

I kissed his split lips gently. 'You have been saved, and the pain is nearly over. Do you remember the English señorita?'

'*Sí,*' he breathed '*Sí.* I remember. I tried not to tell them . . . but . . . I did. I am ashamed, when . . . Yono will never believe me worthy of a rifle now.' His eyes closed again, tears glittering.

'No,' I said; how very much I hated that this should be the only comfort he desired. Yet he had earned the right to feel happy as he died. 'When you are better you will have your rifle, I promise.'

Then I went over to fetch Espinoza's gun from the table, and shot him in the head.

I was not naively untried any longer; Comayagua and Zeller between them had seen to that. No hospital here would treat an escaped victim of the Seguridad, even supposing that we could have got him there alive, so that night I not only became an executioner, but also joined the bloodied butchers of humanity.

I went back to Bruce. The two *seguridades* were still standing petrified, but I'm not sure that he saw them clearly, the first merciful numbness of his injury swamped by an incoming tide of pain. 'Faith?'

'I'm all right,' I said. If I lived, the memory of Rodrigo would never leave me.

'Do exactly as I say. Don't think about it except as something which must be done. Strip Calderon of coat, pants, shirt, tie. Fold them and bring them here. Search Zeller. I want his passport and billfold. Any other money or papers he's carrying. And Faith . . . be quick.' He turned to the *seguridades*. 'Go and stand facing the wall.'

They exchanged glances and then fell on their knees, gabbling. The trouble with mercy is that it stays to trip you next time around. Those two had been in shirtsleeves so probably were the tormentors of Rodrigo and the others: one had held Bruce while . . . we didn't owe them anything. Except they, like us, were caught in a trap not of their devising, and mercy remained the only way back to sanity.

They would, they said, be shot if we left them behind alive, or tortured for possible complicity with guerrillas.

Bruce wiped his face muzzily. 'What do you suggest?'

'We want to walk home, señor,' said one. 'Let us go, and I swear – '

'No.'

'I swear, señor – '

231

'Where are the keys of Lieutenant Espinoza's automobile?'

One hesitated and then drew them from his pocket. 'Here, señor.'

'Then you both come with us. I'll let you go after we pass the gate.'

'But, señor – '

'That's the deal. It'll be easier to desert from outside, so what are you complaining of? And since I'm trusting you, you have to trust me. Otherwise you stay here tied up, and recover consciousness in a Seguridad cell.'

They accepted.

Calderon's body was something I scarcely thought about, but Zeller's seemed filled with malevolence. As if he could reach out whenever he chose and destroy our petty efforts, then laugh as he had before.

I could see Bruce's thoughts congealing; he had decided on some plan I couldn't grasp but needed to grope for each move, search for the place where plans were made. Two hundred miles at the very least for us to go. He could not possibly last.

Under his direction, one of the men went to start the car. If he'd made a run for it then, I'm sure Bruce could not have hit him, but they had seen some remarkable marksmanship that night and were not in the mood to take chances. Also, they were terrified by their own inaction, to which Espinoza would testify, and really wanted to desert.

The man backed the car up to the entry and shouted reassuringly at guards irresolutely fingering guns close by. Zeller's curses had prevented anyone from breaking in when the firing started again because these were soldiers, whereas the hut was Seguridad business. I wondered how long it would be after we left before anyone dared squeeze past the crushed jeep and look inside. Not long, probably.

Bruce called out in a reasonable imitation of Zeller's Bolivian drawl for them to go fight the fire, and they skulked farther into the shadows without going far. I gulped deep breaths of air when my turn came to go out: the driver, me,

232

the second security man, Bruce. I climbed into the back of the car and kept Calderon's automatic trained on the man who sat beside me; Bruce went in the front with Espinoza's gun. Automatic rifles were useless weapons for a one-armed man confined by upholstery.

'Let's go,' he said to the driver. 'Remember. Show your Seguridad papers at the gate same as you did coming in, nothing else. Don't speak.'

'Señor, they may ask – '

'Don't answer. Remember that my bullet is nearer than theirs, and do exactly as I say.'

The gate was close by, the base quite small when you weren't fumbling around in the dark. A Quihuli fire tender was being waved through and if I'd been driving, I think I should have stamped on the accelerator and bolted past.

I felt a jolt, as if the same instinct had seized the man in front.

'No,' said Bruce warningly. 'Pull past the tender so one guard has to come, but then stop.' He stuck his head out of the window and yelled at the sentry to hurry.

The man trotted up, unsuspicious, and also nervous of the Seguridad plates on the car. 'A terrible night, señor.'

'What do you mean, terrible? A fire started by a cigarette I don't doubt, and you describe it simply as terrible? It is treason, which men like you are shot for.'

The guard recoiled, but glanced at the driver's papers. 'There is no woman on this pass.'

The driver opened his mouth, shut it again.

'You'd better call your sergeant,' said Bruce.

The sentry called him thankfully, while we sat stunned, wondering whether Bruce's hold on his senses had slipped.

A sergeant stamped up, warily self-important. 'Señor?'

'I am putting this man on a charge. I suggest fatigue duty in full kit, followed by instruction in how to address his superiors with the courtesy they expect. Lieutenant Espinoza will be following in the jeep shortly; you may offer him my compliments and ask him to sign the sheet you will have made out by then. I shall check that you have asked him to

233

do so, you may be sure.' He nodded to the sergeant, still automatically listening to orders, wound up the window and ordered the driver to stop wasting time.

No one fired after us as we drove away.

'Pull off the track to the left,' Bruce said, almost immediately.

The moment we stopped, and while everyone else was still void of thought, he made the two *seguridades* get out, strip off their tunics and sweat shirts, take off their boots. Then he gave them some money. 'If I see anything moving two minutes from now, I fire without warning.'

They vanished into blackness, bare feet scuffling on earth. They had sufficient pesos to buy *campesino* clothes and could not possibly explain the loss of their uniform nor what had happened at the gate without incurring the most fearful penalties, so would have no choice except to disappear. We sat for a moment in the car after they had gone, exhaustion like lead in our veins, while shock from what had happened was dissolving all that remained of will and purpose.

'Can you drive?' asked Bruce thickly, into stupor I had no desire to leave.

'Where?'

'As near to where we left the missile as you can.'

I nodded, forgetting he couldn't see me in the darkness, and straightened stiffly once I had scrambled from the back of the car. The same blusteringly cold wind was blowing, the same sky was there, the moon and smells of damp earth; only I was so different that I didn't seem to belong among them any more. The touch of steering wheel and gear provided the shadow of reality again, although I needed to concentrate each separate sense to conquer them. It wasn't far to where we had left the missile hidden only a few hours before, and driving there a simple matter over stony earth rather than sand where we would stick. In daylight our tracks would show, but my mind was incapable of more than one thought at a time, and while I drove I was thinking that there were still a few shots of painkiller in the medical kit we had left with our packs.

Then I remembered Bruce's original intention to fire the missile.

Probably it was too late anyway: the fire at the base had died to a crimson glow behind a cloud of black smoke. Occasionally there were small explosions and once a yellow flame burst into spray, but for some inexplicably perverse reason no general conflagration followed. The most it achieved was to keep firefighters at a respectful distance and prevent the fire from being stamped out completely.

We left the car and slogged up the shallow ridge to where we had waited throughout the previous day; I stopped and looked back once, but there was so much confusion in the base it was impossible to tell whether we were pursued or not.

'Yono will have watchers here somewhere,' Bruce said wearily. 'I slipped him when I brought the missile, but I guess it hasn't been difficult to spot us coming back.'

It didn't seem to matter. Nothing mattered. If I could only sleep, and forget Rodrigo. Forget Zeller, too. I closed my eyes, and immediately fell. Earth in my face and the torn flesh on my arm crawling pain from elbow to below my ear. Bruce was crouched over that hateful missile and hadn't noticed; he was as near finished as a man could be and still stay conscious.

I picked myself up slowly and went to look for the medical pack, to find Yono standing by the rucksacks, etched black against the sky, watching and waiting, his thumbs stuck in his belt. I stared at him, mind shuttering, then sat and put my head on my knees. I simply could not cope with any more.

I heard the clatter of weapons as he went over to Bruce. 'You took too long in returning here, Señor Broos. The fire is no longer dangerous.'

'Perhaps.' Bruce sounded remote, as if he had not grasped the meaning of Yono, waiting here. 'Do you want to find out?'

'*Naturalmente*, when we have nothing to lose by finding out. But probably also very little to gain.'

235

'And if the napalm burns, you will attack tonight?'

'What is that to you, señor?'

'Nothing!' Raw violence in Bruce's voice this time. '*Por el amor de Dios, nada*. So perhaps you would like to do it?' I took my head off my knees, and saw him indicate the opened and strutted base of the three-foot-long missile, nestling among its dials and switches.

Yono looked puzzled. 'For the honour of it, certainly, if you will show me how. But time is short.'

'I wouldn't show you how.'

'*Qué!* You offered to do this! I kill you if you waste time now!'

'You are waiting to kill when I have done it. So you must choose. A bet, since that will bind your honour easier. If the napalm burns, we take our lives and go.'

'And if it does not burn?'

'It is a bet. If not, then we cannot prevent you from doing whatever you wish.'

Yono scraped his jaw, stubble rasping. 'It is a bet, Señor Broos. The death by machete if you fail.'

'And we go with our lives if the napalm burns?'

Yono's face cracked into mirth. '*Sí, señor*. You understand us too well. You may trust me to keep a wager. Win or loose.'

I knelt beside Bruce, the night wind strong on my face, and everything very real again. 'Can I help?'

He glanced at me, his face no more than a movement in the dark. 'Don't worry.'

'That's what I said to Rodrigo.'

'Yes,' he said helplessly. 'Yes, I know. I hoped you didn't.' Because this time he would shoot me rather than leave me to face Yono and unendurable memory alone. 'Hold this, then, and snap back that clip. Set one-sixty on the scale.' With no alteration in his voice, he added, 'I love you, Faith.'

I swallowed, then nodded. This was fact, like switches and dials and exhaustion; a fact stronger than them all. Also stronger than barbarity. Perhaps. 'So much, my love. So much and always.'

Our final rites and absolution; better than most.

I held the panel of control switches, watched him connect a circuit so red light glowed. The missile did not make the roar I expected as it left its frame, wire-guidance system trailing. I felt the panel I held quiver as Bruce made some correction to his aim, then there was a solid thump from the direction of the base. Sparks shot upward from where the fire still glowed.

'*Gracias de nada*,' said Yono sourly, hand at his belt.

The sparks thickened and burst, flowed together and exploded again. A sheet of fire spilled through smoke before flashing down and across to something else, which burned into yellow incandescence. Smoke like tight-packed jungle hid what happened next, but we heard the noise of burning change pitch, saw the upward surge of heat which meant this fire would now destroy everything in its path.

Yono turned and ran shouting to where he must have men concealed; we could not speak or move, just stared at immense black clouds of smoke reflecting that unearthly glare.

At least it made a fitting funeral pyre for Rodrigo.

18

We could not hurry, but after a while picked up our packs and went down the slope to where we had left the car; behind us I saw shapes loping across the ruts towards the base, guns trailing, but no one stopped us. Perhaps Yono gave orders for us not to be molested, or his followers may simply have been intent on more important matters; anyway, we were safely across the many tracks leading back towards Quihuli before the first volleys of firing started.

We may have been pursued by Seguridad or the army when they discovered what had happened in their interrogation hut, but I don't think so. The disaster at Quihuli base must have occupied everyone to the exclusion of all else, and Yono's guerrillas cut off all communications except radio as soon as they attacked. What we didn't know was whether the alarm had gone out during the brief interval between the time we passed the gate and Bruce's missile struck. If so, then troops beyond the confusion of Quihuli would be looking for us, and road blocks be set up on any tracks that we might use.

But we had no choice; we had to use the car, take the best route we could find and get out fast.

I drove, since Bruce had no use in his right arm at all, the surfaces so rough I prayed he would stay dazed through the hours to come. There did not seem to be any proper roads at

238

all the way we went. Tracks meandered between fields and through farmsteads. The only highway paralleled the railway and was too dangerous to attempt; probably the guerrillas had closed it, anyway.

The firing gradually faded into the distance behind us, otherwise I gained little sense of how far we travelled. The same cactus clumps and crumbling huts went by, the same treacherous descents lay in wait whenever the track we were following petered out completely.

I saw a huge glow in my mirror for as long as the darkness lasted, but the last sounds I heard were the thumping of mortars and a sharp crack of a mounted gun – a tank, I supposed. A fixed position is not easily taken by underarmed *campesinos* who would murder the garrison if they surrendered, even when it was already half blown apart.

Luckily the car was a heavy-duty Dodge; powerful, nearly new, and well sprung. After perhaps an hour of jolting our way down steep slopes towards the plain we hit a very narrow, but straight track which looked as if the military might have built it to open up access to the resettlements in the foothills. I glanced at Bruce; he was conscious but bowed over his arm, attempting to shield himself from the appalling jolts I couldn't avoid over such rough ground.

I simply had to risk it. We needed to put as much distance as possible between ourselves and Quihuli before daybreak, and Bruce could not endure such a brutal progress for very much longer. When I turned on to the track, the improvement was immediate. The Dodge rode smoothly, there wasn't any traffic and the miles flicked uneventfully past. The only trouble was, as strain eased so my own sense of shock returned: trembling began in my bones and spread outward, until I was calling aloud for it to keep away, increasing speed dangerously in an effort to force concentration back into its place.

As a cool and gracious dawn flowed across the sky, I turned into a small wood of knotted trees, switched off the engine and got out of the car. I ached all over and my arm felt as if a fire burned there; my eyes were gritty and as soon as I

239

stood, nausea surfaced out of my trembling bones, thought scrambling as I retched.

I lay on the ground and wept when the retching ended, and eventually tipped into a kind of sleep.

I did not sleep long, my caged mind struggling for release even through such great exhaustion. When I woke the sun just speckled the thick greenery, and was not yet hot. Bruce was watching me, his legs drawn up, sitting with his back against a tyre. I stared at him stupidly, unable to speak; so much foulness had been spilled over our love that, for a moment, I could not see past it.

Then he took my fingers and put them to his lips. 'My dear . . . my dear. Some things are past, and others just beginning.'

Some things are never past, I thought but did not say. He knew, and lived with more of them than I. 'Go home, Yanqui.'

His smile deepened. 'It sounds good, so long as a Britisher feels like coming along too.'

'Yes,' I said, still limply unresponsive and nearly drowsing again. I remembered only how memory was something which must be kept locked away for a long time yet. Then I grasped again how far from home we were, and how out of reach it was. 'Bruce, your hand!' I struggled to my feet. 'Whatever must you think of me?'

'Do you really want to know?'

'Later. Yes, very much.' The foulness had not gone, but love was back where I could see it. I bent and kissed him swiftly. 'Can you stand?'

He could, and seemed perfectly collected, which was a kind of miracle in itself. While I slept he had given himself a couple of injections and gave me one now, saying that infection was inevitable here. He refused to look at my arm; it was only a superficial tear and my shirt had stuck to it and stopped the bleeding. It even hurt less after my brief rest. 'It's best left,' he said, feeling it carefully. 'I hope it can be properly fixed tomorrow, but I shall only let in more bugs by opening it up now.'

I stared at the dirty cloth bandaging his hand; bones were broken there, and muscles torn in his arm. Neither could be left for long, and I felt my senses spin again as memory swept inexorably back, reminding me how those bones had felt.

'Listen, Faith,' he said quickly, brushing aside the beginnings of abject apology as guilt took me by the throat. 'We have to get out of here, fast. You've done so much . . . I can't believe how much you've done. So don't you dare blame yourself for other men's dirt. But you can't last much longer and neither can I. We have to chance our luck at the airport.'

I swallowed, feeling sick. 'The airport?'

'You still have your passport?'

I nodded.

'Okay, then. There will be a call out for me, since Zeller made Mozon search to see if I was in Comayagua, but we brought Zeller's papers along, remember? And you have a return ticket to Jamaica, while Zeller was carrying enough dollars to buy me a ticket, too. Bribe whoever needs to be bribed so we get on the plane today.'

'You don't look in the least like Zeller!' The airport surely was a crazy chance to take.

'God forbid. He had gotten himself some high-powered Seguridad clearances in his billfold, though. I think we have to risk it. The alternative is walking to a guarded frontier, and the nearest must be eight days away, at least. There aren't many roads which don't lead to San Bernardo and we can't possibly risk using a Seguridad automobile there.'

I stared at my tattered jeans, the blood on my shirt, and wondered how awful my face and hair must look. 'Anyone would put us behind bars on sight.'

'Then we just have to clean up,' he answered grimly. 'If we stay on reasonable tracks then we ought to be able to buy enough gas to take us to Progreso; there's nothing odd in a gringo woman wearing the kind of peasant clothes we could buy in a market some place. They'll only think you screwy like the rest. We brought Calderon's clothes along, and we shall damned well have to make them fit me somehow.'

241

'You knew. You knew even back in that hut we'd have to try the airport.'

'I realized we hadn't too much choice once neither of us was fit enough to walk. Using a Seguridad vehicle is a reasonable risk today, but tomorrow when Yono's been beaten off from Quihuli – ' He shook his head. 'They'll piece together what's happened then.'

'Yono won't win?'

'Not this time around. There was the hell of a lot of firepower around that base, whatever we did to the napalm. So let's get going, shall we? The Jamaica flight turns around late afternoon unless things have changed.'

I could think of so many objections I didn't know where to begin, except of course he was right. We couldn't walk, or afford to hide when he would have fever and blood-poisoning within two days, and both of us were exhausted beyond belief. We had practically no food and no clean water, nor means of sterilizing any; if we didn't get out today then there wouldn't be much of us left to try tomorrow.

I drove again through thickening up-country traffic, my nerves screaming each time we saw army markings or I dropped the car into a pothole. We stopped after a while and I gave Bruce another pain-killing injection: there was only enough for one more of those, too. At least petrol was no problem. We stopped again at a sprawling village and an old man sold us cans from a stock he kept in his pig pens. I bought a bright Comayaguan skirt and blouse in the tiny market, but the choice of food was maize, raw peppers and some putrid meat. Even the goat's milk was sour, although we both choked down a little.

Jamaica, I thought.

The route we had taken from Quihuli was a jagged curve down through the hills to the plain, the geography of Comayagua simple enough once the sun gave me an approximate direction. We intended to meet the main highway well below San Bernardo, since we would certainly be stopped if we attempted to pass the checkpoints on the outskirts of the city, and reached it at last during the afternoon siesta. There didn't seem to be any special searches along the section we could see, but not surprisingly a considerable amount of military activity cluttered it even during the heat of the afternoon, with convoys of trucks driving in the direction of the mountains. A few soldiers gave us curious stares, most drivers pulled over respectfully when they saw our plates and the only Seguridad patrol we passed saluted. Their truck had radio antennae though; they might easily check our passage with headquarters. It was likely, surely. So how long before sluggish siesta-bound Seguridad clerks checked out their report, and wondered what Lieutenant Espinoza's car was doing on the Progreso road?

Time was becoming an enemy for a different reason, too. So far as I could remember, the Jamaica flight left Progreso between four and five in the afternoon. 'We'll never do it,' I said into a long silence, as I recalled the hours that road had taken to travel when I arrived. I thought we had struck it well towards Progreso, but recognized almost nothing.

Bruce did not answer, his eyes closed although he wasn't asleep.

Apart from the military, the traffic was light during the heat of the day, and as their convoys were nearly all travelling in the opposite direction I was able to put my foot down, scattering chickens at seventy miles an hour as soon as the surface improved.

I began to feel very sleepy as the throbbing heat of the plains enclosed us like a skin; I also worried obsessively about Bruce, but most other recollections of the night were still blurred by urgency, and this growing, insidious drowsiness. When today was finished, one way or the other, it would be different.

Bruce must have realized that I was about to fall asleep at the wheel, and somehow he roused himself to talk to me. About America and where we would live; making me laugh at the absurdity of six-lane highways on which I could never legally approach the speed at which we were taking these crumble-surfaced Comayaguan roads. His voice hesitating each time we hit a patch rougher than the rest, giddily

243

snatching at some fresh subject as soon as it was past. Then insisting that I answered him, using voice and touch and laughter to help me to endure those last remaining miles.

Only once did he refer to the night before, and then in a way which might eventually help me to live with what had happened. 'Rodrigo,' he said, as we passed some children playing by the road. 'If you are ever to write a book you believe to be worthwhile, perhaps it should be about him. The whole of him. The boy who would have sold us to the army, because that is the way to survive around here, as well as why and how he died.'

'And I am surely an authority on how he died,' I answered bitterly, my eyes on storm clouds billowing above distant jungle. Not far to Progreso now.

'No, Faith. You aren't, whatever you can't help thinking now. The how and why were finished long before we ever reached that hut. But it might just be that you have drawn the job of adding up the balance, and then writing something good enough to make a few others search their consciences about what is happening here. To damn well force them into thinking just once about a courteous, cruel and courageous child who wanted to own a rifle before he died.'

'I shouldn't think I could,' I said shortly. 'For God's sake, what do you think I am? How could I write about Rodrigo, when it hurts even to remember what he looked like?'

'How much would it matter if it hurt, so long as it made a good book? A book which eventually you accepted as accomplishing what you had set out to do?'

I was taken aback, not so much by what he said but by such an apparently ruthless attitude. 'I don't think I could face it,' I repeated.

'Yes, you could. And you won't get any peace until you do. I have been running away from myself for ten years, and I know how futile it is. What's the good of wanting to find reality if you refuse to use what you discover? Why crucify yourself with misplaced guilt and grief, when you are the one person who might give some meaning to Rodrigo's death?'

'You sound like a hack psychologist,' I said resentfully. 'Write it, and forget.'

'Write it, and accept,' he answered gently. 'Then you can take it on from there.'

There was a long pause. The noise of tyres on the road and blaring klaxons from an army convoy, full of other sad-eyed boys on their way to fight. 'All right . . . I'll try,' I said with an effort. 'I may not succeed.'

'I shall be surprised if you don't. Stop at the next village, will you? Wherever you see a cantina, in a side street for preference.'

I found one called the Sunset Friend, filled with bitter wine smells and clashing bead curtains. An old woman stood behind the bar and didn't seem surprised when we asked for water and the use of a room for half an hour. Probably she thought dishevelled foreigners so strange anyway that an apparent need to stop for their lusts every few miles seemed quite commonplace to her.

I changed quickly, Bruce cutting my shirt so as to leave a piece stuck to my arm; after so much driving it was hurting fiercely again. There wasn't a mirror, which was probably just as well for my self-confidence, and drowned beetles floated in the water the old woman brought, so I felt even dirtier than before. Then, clumsily, I did my best to shave Bruce and help him into Calderon's suit. I had to slit the seam of the arm and tack it again with borrowed thread, replace wrapped shirt with less obtrusive bandaging. Once we reached the airport everything would depend on Bruce's ability to behave normally and look unexceptional while he bluffed his way through heaven knew how many checks on Zeller's papers. His hand was a clotted and swollen mess: no other way to describe it. Even though I gave him the last dose of pain-killer, he blacked out before I had finished the agonizing business of rebandaging, and so nearly did I.

It was a great deal longer than half an hour before we left the cantina, and I half expected to find Seguridad standing by the car when we came out, in curiosity if nothing else. Bruce was thinking only of staying upright by that time, but I know I heaved a sigh of relief when we found only a child too young to recognize Seguridad plates, abstractedly kicking at a tyre. Some women stood in doorways watching, and one of them spat when she met my eyes. Traitor, that saliva seemed to say. Only traitors to womenkind associate with Seguridad, those bloodsuckers on our flesh. Absurdly, I wanted to call across and explain, but it was too late anyway; she had gone inside and slammed the door.

Sixteen kilometres to Progreso a stencilled sign said when we swung back on the highway, and the airport was beyond the town. Surely, the Jamaica flight must have gone.

I glanced at Bruce as the first shacks of Progreso came into sight; his eyes were open, but drawn face and bitten lip were a shocking contrast to fresh shaving, clean shirt and carefully knotted tie.

'Wait here,' I said, when I'd found a space for the car which was neither too conspicuous nor too far from the airport entry. 'I'll go and see if the flight has gone.'

He nodded; I think even he had begun to wonder how he could ever make it through that building, and then bully surly officials into allowing us to leave.

The terminal was seething with people just as I remembered it, and the Jamaica flight hadn't even landed. It was expected, but no one knew when. I heaved a sigh of very preliminary relief and pushed my way over to the airline desk. Zeller's US dollars in my hand: the girl began by telling me there weren't any tickets but that, at least, was one fence I didn't intend to fall over.

'How much would it cost if there was a ticket?'

Her eyes flickered to the thick wad of money in my hand. 'Two hundred and ninety dollars US.'

I was certain that this was nearly double what Calderon had paid for my outward flight, but money simply did not matter any more. I peeled six fifties off Zeller's roll. 'I've got a hot date in Kingston tonight.'

She smiled, an uncomplicated grin of delight at her undreamed-of luck. 'Certainly, señorita. But if you want reservations for today's flight, then that is another hundred dollars.'

246

I gave the extra in exchange for two boarding passes, not caring in the least that she thought me the world's most gullible idiot. Let her have some dollars to enjoy; if we ever reached Kingston then I would put anything left from Zeller's money in the nearest charity collection. The ticket was what mattered, and getting on that aircraft early enough so someone else was thrown off if it really was overbooked.

There were two Seguridad guards standing by the barrier, more of them lounging on the terrace drinking. There weren't any signs of above-average security though, and the newspapers didn't mention Quihuli. It was my first experience of the kind of censorship a dictatorship can order if it wants to, and for a moment I wondered whether we had imagined the scale of that fire at Quihuli base, been mistaken when we heard Yono attack.

It is strange how long it takes to accept that some newspapers are no better than pulp fiction: on an inside page I finally spotted an announcement that the Quihuli train would not run until the end of the week as the track was under repair. So perhaps Yono won a little before he was driven back into the mountains.

I stood on the weed-strewn terrace of the terminal to watch the Fokker land, its jaunty Jamaican colours a flag of hope. But we weren't there by a long way, and the idea of Bruce using Zeller's passport and papers became less attractive each time I thought about it. Peter Reinhard Zeller looked out from those passport pages like a vulture of ill-omen: smiling slightly, even his cheeks well muscled below cruel eyes; six foot two, colouring dark, age twenty-nine. An illiterate child could tell that this wasn't Bruce.

'Don't you think you ought to chance your own passport?' I asked anxiously, when I hurried back to the car to tell him the Fokker had landed.

'No. I know Zeller. The first thing he would have done was put a stop on my documents with every Central American government which would listen, and we know that Mozon has been listening to whatever the Yanquis want, since his life depends on what they give him.' Bruce stood carefully,

247

the various guns we had collected left hidden in the car. 'The last gamble, my dear, and those Seguridad papers he was carrying ought to help. Try not to look so worried.'

The passengers for the Kingston flight were jumbled into an ill-natured queue in front of a kiosk filled with officials. Green and gold stripes and lanyards, crossed machetes on their collars. I thought of Espinoza, and tried to calculate how many weeks it was since I'd come through here before, but couldn't concentrate long enough to find an answer.

I stood to one side of Bruce, hoping to shield him from chance jostling, trying to scourge my mind into believing that we would pass that barrier. Less than twenty-four hours had passed since I had killed Zeller and then Rodrigo, and only minutes ago I had still been thinking how strain was more tolerable than time to think.

But not this kind of strain.

Someone bumped into me so hard that I staggered and had to clutch an elderly man to prevent myself from cannoning into Bruce. 'I'm sorry, I'm sorry,' I said distractedly, panic seizing my lungs.

'A pleasure, señora,' he answered, staring.

A vast negress shoved past sobbing, and embraced a row of shy and beautiful children passing the barrier off the incoming flight; I heard Bruce grunt from the impact and felt cold sweat on my back.

Those Seguridad clerks were taking several minutes for each passenger; I stared at them and at the guards fingering weapons just behind, and hated them for existing.

After a moment Bruce moved and came to the other side of me, good hand holding my arm. 'I remember a story told me by a professor in Peru. You've heard of Francesco Pizarro?'

I nodded, wondering whether he was delirious already.

'The conqueror of the Inca Empire. Well, he was once rebuked by a Jesuit father for not even attempting to treat the native population with humanity, and he replied. "Father, I have not come here for such reasons. I came here to take their gold." '

I licked my lips, groping for a reply which might bring him back to his senses. Only two people between us and the guarded barrier now. 'I never liked the sound of the Conquistadores much.'

'No, but it was at least an honest answer. The rest of us usually prefer to kid ourselves about why we are hated in this part of the world.' He released my arm, and smiled. 'Wait for me on the other side of the barrier.'

I found myself facing a lump-faced clerk behind a counter, two guards standing at his back. Bruce had stepped aside so the old man was between us, too late for me to risk attracting attention by refusing to go through the barrier while he still waited. I stared at aggressive-looking guards and the clerk slapping contemptuously through my passport, trying to think about the centuries of injustice which made Comayaguan officials what they were. Bruce had not wanted me to face them while so obviously filled with hate and fear that instinct alone must tell them there was something wrong.

'You have no renewal stamp, señorita.' The clerk pointed at my date of entry. 'After two months the police must renew your permit to come here.'

I had no idea how long over the two months I was. 'I went to the Seguridad at Quihuli, where I have been staying, but they refused to renew the permit. They said conditions were too disturbed for a foreigner to stay. That's why I am flying out today.'

He looked up and gave me a long unfriendly stare from eyes like curdled egg. 'They should have given you a temporary extension to enable you to travel.'

I smiled, physically using muscle to curve lips which felt like cardboard. 'Lieutenant Espinoza of the Seguridad gave me a lift down as far as San Bernardo. I did not know I needed an extension just to reach the airport, and I suppose he forgot.'

One of the guards said something about me and the lieutenant, and the other snickered. All three of them were staring at me now, enjoying watching me squirm. Don't hate, I thought. My God, Pizarro surely has a lot to answer for if the mess down here began with him.

The clerk snapped my passport down on the counter top. 'The law is made to be obeyed, señorita.'

'I'm sorry, I just didn't know that particular law,' I said as reasonably as I could. I didn't know either how I could stop them from seeing me tremble, or hearing the falseness in my voice. Both of the guards were watching me with open lust, but one was young enough to smile even while his eyes undressed me. It helped to make him seem human, and I put out my hand for the passport, repeating, 'I'm sorry, señor. I didn't know, but the Seguridad in Quihuli made it quite clear I wouldn't be allowed back anyway.'

Which at least was true, I thought, hysterical amusement as instantly and dangerously close as fright had been a moment before.

He hesitated, then shrugged and stamped it. 'I hope you enjoyed your stay in the land of the Mozonero Revolution, señorita.'

I was through.

The old man took nearly ten minutes to pass, arguing plaintively about tax clearances.

Then Bruce was next.

Calderon's linen suit was short in the leg and loose over the hips on him, but the jacket was what showed and it looked well cut and respectable. It was Bruce's face though which ought to make anyone wonder and then start asking questions. Ashen, swollen-lipped, almost fleshless. I swallowed painfully; he looked as if he might collapse at any moment.

And suddenly I realized why he had not waited for a better time to talk to me about writing Rodrigo's story. He wasn't sure himself whether he could pass that barrier.

Believed perhaps that he would not pass it, and so chose the best time he could to show me how I might endure without him.

He said something to the clerk and the man laughed, his

bureaucratic surliness taken by surprise. He put out his hand. 'Your passport, señor.'

Bruce took it from his pocket, held it, then put it back and fumbled one-handed for something else. 'I want your stamp on this as well, *por favor*. I am travelling on a joint mission for your Seguridad as you will see, so I intend to claim the cost of my ticket, you understand.'

The clerk stared at Zeller's Seguridad pass, which was clipped to an official recommendation and the Quihuli identification I had taken off his body. 'I cannot stamp this, señor.'

'Why not? I simply want evidence of my flight today when the expenses form comes through. Or perhaps you would prefer to stamp the ticket stub?'

The clerk agreed that he would very much prefer it, caught as he was between Bruce's confident manner and his own fear of defacing such high-powered papers. 'A ticket stub, certainly, Señor Zeller. That is Air Jamaica's property and not my concern at all.' He stamped it with a flourish. 'I see you have injured your mouth, señor.'

'I'm much obliged to you.' Bruce folded the papers away and tossed Zeller's passport on the counter. 'Life is a good deal tougher on other faces than mine in Altiplano Province at the moment, although come the spring I am sure your Mozonero Revolution will scrape up the last of the resistance there. What time does tomorrow's flight back to Comayagua leave from Kingston, do you know?'

The clerk shrugged. 'Perhaps eight o'clock, perhaps ten. They are not efficient, you understand.'

I watched the clerk's hands, the blood chilling in my heart. His fingers flipping through those passport pages, the turn of his head as he glanced down, as he must not glance down for more than seconds of unseeing routine; his face as he discussed the iniquities of Air Jamaica. Zeller's photograph was plain for anyone to see, the uncompromising black square of it leaping across space to where I stood.

The younger guard said something and they all, including Bruce, joined in a heated discussion, while that

251

passport still lay open between them; no one in the queue ventured to complain about such unnecessary delay. Bruce drew attention to them in the end. 'Soon I shan't dare to fly back here tomorrow as I am ordered to, when some of these people will still be waiting if I take up much more of your time!' He nodded to the guards. 'I shall see you again then, if you are on duty.'

The clerk stamped Zeller's passport and stood up to hand it back. 'A good flight, señor.'

The Jamaican pilot had kept his engines running as he had done when I landed, his crew laughing as grit whipped over the Comayaguan ground staff.

I stumbled on the steep steps leading up to the aircraft, and turned in panic in case Bruce fell. But while any fragment of his strength remained, he would force his remaining senses into serving him efficiently. 'It's too late for you to have second thoughts about staying,' he said, smiling at me as I turned, and we entered the aircraft together. Sat and strapped ourselves in while the strong Comayaguan wind continued to blow through the open fuselage door, bearing the smells of Progreso with it.

Please shut that door, I thought, unable to believe this really was the end of it all, and more than half-expecting a jeep full of Seguridad to come tearing across the tarmac. For the love of God, roll those steps away, and shut it.

The door closed with a thump and the stewardess went through her patter, but the pilot wasn't waiting for such niceties. The Fokker started taxiing immediately, and Bruce's hand closed over mine as we left the ground. Neither of us spoke.

The rest of our lives remained for all that must be said, for love and for remorseless memory; now it was enough to watch the bright spring green of the Comayaguan plain give way to jungle, the glint of the Caribbean lift over the horizon as we climbed.